...RSEMEN AND TH...ARAVAN OF THE APOCALYPSE

Sean Daly

Copyright © 2021 Sean Daly
All rights reserved.

---

hey little person, handwriting is terrible, though that's not particuarly interesting or relevent, enjoy this book. tell me what you think,

love,
sean

*Bonnie, thanks for all the help you have given me.
This truly never would have happened if it were not for you,*

*Also, thanks to Adam for bugging me to write for years,
sorry it took so long.*

Chapter 1

Approximately three billion miles from a beaten Mini Cooper floating in the depths of space,
were four men in a powder blue, equally beaten Volkswagen Campervan. The temperamental vehicle was parked perilously close to a cliff edge, at the sandy waters Caravan Park in Llanfwrog on the west coast of Anglesey, Wales. The Caravan was built like a tank, with none of a tanks personal and welcoming interiors and finishing's. It was so sturdy that if the cliff edge eroded from under it, it still would refuse to move as it felt it had to have some principles.

Far beyond the Caravan, Wales, and Earth, in the vacuum and blackness was the still slowly rotating Mini Cooper. Its window wipers were frozen, as was the little scented tree with the phrase *Be Happy* on it. Other than its location, the only other oddity of this celestial and rather out-of-place machine was the roof that had been torn off on the back right seat. In the Caravan, one of its occupants passively pondered where he had parked last night.

In somewhat of a hungover haze, he remembered that it was somewhere near an asteroid, but only that the asteroid in question happened to have an asteroid-like aesthetic. Amongst the many drinks last night, this seemed like an apt description bordering on the point of over-elaborative. The Mini drifted as if it could for eternity and was haloed by the intense brilliant light of a star. As it continued to drift it was shadowed by a gas giant hanging like beauty incarnate…or at the very least that is what the owner liked to believe. He felt strongly that that would have been the eulogy that the car would have wanted. In reality, it perhaps would prefer to be saved from the menace of progressive space rust and some extremely lost and confused horseshoe crabs who, unbeknownst to them, were previously destined to be the car owner's lunch. The owner was at heart a somewhat lazy individual prone to procrastination, and it somehow felt better to concoct a poetic end for the vehicle rather than exert any energy in locating it. In his defence, it was a Sunday morning and the snooker had just started. Unbeknownst to the owner, the car happened to be by an asteroid of no distinctive visual qualities whatsoever. In fact, it was so nondistinctive that even the least imaginative of vandals of unknown origin, inexplicably fluent in English, had spray-painted the word *asteroid* lazily across its dimension invoking apathy boredom and obscure stunted anti creativity.

So perhaps this Mini Cooper with its scented tree *was* destined to float unendingly through the titanic nothingness. Ebbing into indifference and void that incalculable forms call home. Floating with the blinkers still on, unbeknownst to his owner, the hastily bought birthday gifts for his friend would most likely remain forever in the glove compartment. It would remain nothing more than a curiosity to any bored child that broke into an observatory. Later that evening, some hooligans spray-painted *automobiles* on its torn roof.

God was very real. He could see himself in the mirror, in the reflection of a spoon or as a distorted shadow on a dark shop window front and to him that was enough. He could play with his Rubix cube and even move the little drinking bird toy on his cluttered desk. In his eyes, it was a non-question. He even had a son that he was moderately indifferent about. Non-things did not have sons. He wondered long and hard about the paradoxical notion of what nothing has.

I should know that, he thought touching the side of his mouth with his tongue.

Today was a bad day and he was trying to do anything to get his mind off it. He sorted out his box of floppy discs anally and with great concentration. He peeled an orange he had no intention of eating. He sat by the phone patiently and with great concentration. But it was already too late even if it did ring, the damage had been done. At this point, God had simply had enough. He reasoned that the universe was a cruel place and no longer wanted to be associated with it. It can be said he was a being of great patience, but downright rude and inconsiderate behaviour he detested. That last second that had just ticked on his Halloween skeleton cuckoo clock was the last straw, the last second he would abide their behaviour. He started to collect his things, muttering profanities under his breathe. A kazoo from his short-lived career as an improv comedian found its place in the left front pocket of his cargo shorts. The original series of *Battlestar Galactica*, His lucky red cufflinks and Also, of course, the Sirius star system, to which he had an affinity, were stored in his duffel bag .

"Stupid idiotic place. Pointlessness! All of it..." God kicked his wicker paper basket and placed his head in his hands. "Bendy straws get more appreciation than me! A can of corned beef washes onto a shore and the isolated natives' worship that. What kind of world I ask! I send a burning bush; they worship pillars of marmalade!" That last example made little sense to him but he was too angry to address it.

So grumbling and feeling very sorry for himself God scrawled his divine plan of everything on the back of a coaster and left it on his desk titled 'the divine wager with a half empty felt tip pen. He left the world to the whims of Chaos, Pan and Din before he, rather clumsily, popped out of existence leaving nothing behind but a coriander scented wisp of smoke. Some might say this was a somewhat hasty and impulsive affair, but God's feeling of detachment had festered for some time. It was impulsive, but perhaps the Universe could redeem itself. It *could* change and live up to his expectations, a manifestation of his dreams and hopes.. Unfortunately, it could not be said, for when he had been in the Universe, he had been alone, and no-one had remembered it was his birthday. Leaving the universe was the easy part. The difficult part was what was on the other side? So, pondering that gate he had ascended into an even higher reality outside of existence and time where a costume party was being held. A young thought-form and his pan-dimensional life partner Fred threw some beads over God's head.

"It's my birthday!" he shouted above the noise.

"What?" said Fred in a non-linear algorithm.

"I said it's my birthday! I'm thirteen point eight billion years old!"

"Oh forget that!" said Fred through a singularity.

"The stripper is here!" came a yell.

The stripper started to strip layers of perception, shredding dimensions until she became a point of convergence for sporadic waves of arousal. From seemingly nowhere, but specifically somewhere that was possibly not there, a drink appeared in God's hands and a single tear ran down his cheek. He had found his Shangri La.

Chapter 2

As Sunday mornings had the habit of doing in Anglesey in late autumn, the wind whipped everything it could as if it had somehow been slighted. The rain danced a horrid and thunderous tune on the roof of an unmoveable monolith that was the campervan. With some glee, the sun was hiding. It was at this point that the four men in the Caravan sensed that the Universe was more empty than usual, lacking in core and essence, greyer and muted. It was very subtle, and the cause was not immediately apparent. It was guessed by the occupants of the Caravan that it was merely the hedonism of the night before. Or maybe it was that they were, in fact, in Llanfwrog on the west coast of Anglesey, Wales in autumn.

Over a game of travel scrabble, one of the occupants noticed a disturbing lack of reality, nestled in a tear in space that the clouds were avoiding. Looking out of the window he wondered if that was the true cause of the subdued atmosphere. He was about to get worried but one of them remembered they had some duct tape. They were still a little drunk from the night before, so no-one bothered to ponder how stupid the remark, the idea and, ergo, the person was that dispensed this wisdom.

"Just got a text message mate," muttered a huge bulk of fat that was once, long ago in the annals of time muscle but was now just ever expanding fat. He donned a huge hat with horns curling upwards, made from thick brown torn cowhide. He had a short sword sheathed on his right side and a dagger to his left. He looked like a guy that had eaten his fair share of meat raw, and possibly meat that was still living during the eating process. He looked like baths were a bi-monthly ritual, enjoyed and endured. He appeared as though he had spent many decades never quite reaching sobriety. Then there was his great red beard, so great in fact, that under it lived another beard. His hands were dry and scarred, hairy and podgy. Hands that had seen the world and over time knocked a lot of sense out of it. His feet stunk under huge fur boots, a menacing spike on either end. Stained from millennia of rampant carnage. His fur coat oddly enough did not fit this motif. It was not downtrodden like the rest of his attire; in fact, it was not indistinguishable between stains or blood. Or bits of food. Or any other lumps that could have easily been from the remains of an elephant to a live fish that had had a series of unfortunate events. Most beings that ran into this man would begin to have a bad day. His social skills were not exactly honed and carrying your girlfriend over his shoulder and punching you in the face is usually a hello. It was well looked after because it had cost him a hundred and ten pounds and he was immensely proud of that. It was the only time he had ever purchased something, most of his belongings were either pillaged, acquired, or persuasively handed over to him. His sword also did a bit of persuading. It was a legitimate practice in his eyes as the transactions were usually polite, but in the face of a seven-foot monolith armed to the teeth, with very few teeth, and a necklace with lots of teeth, you tend to be polite.

"Wait, this is from yesterday, it says; 'Wait…waited, waited for all. I waited for all the all day and you guys; you guys did…didn't…turn…up. Hold on I gots it. I waited all day and you guys didn't turn up. Where were you, it's…it's my birthday. I'm really er? Pissed…I'm pissed! Where were you, it's my birthday, I'm pissed."

A sickly pasty guy opposite this monolith sighed. He looked like he probably spent some time working for the church, but probably hadn't in a kind of limp and soggy way.

"This is painful. Whose idea was it to teach him how to read? It's been five years and he's almost figured out how to use that phone. I need a drink…" He rose from a futon, his skinny bony figure lankily meandering towards the coffee. "I hate Sundays. It's been said ad infinitum." The ancient yellow kettle painfully tried its hardest to boil looking as if it wanted to apologize. As usual, the coffee, like the sun was also hiding.

"I hate this relic; maybe we should think of a new abode. Like, I don't know, a flat rock that we can sit on. One with less moss than the others or less moss from this caravan. Maybe we can fashion banana leaves as a roof. Find some stones for a zen garden. We could make it work." He said looking around the Caravan with a sarcastic scowl.

"So it reads, 'I waited all day and you guys didn't turn up. It's my birthday, I'm pissed. The Four Horsemen of the apo-apoc….I can't pronounce this word," he said glumly.

"Why should you? It's only your job. It's an apocalypse, Mr War. Eugggghh, my cup is broken, and it's dirty. What do we have that stains a cup green?" Famine lost hope for his existence, a morning ritual followed by slow poisoning. He lit a cigarette.

"The four horsemen of the apocalypse are nowhere to be seen when my world ended. I have forwarded…for…no that was right. Forwarded Famine's money. I can't deal with this, I'm leaving, and…

and I'm not coming back?" Wars eyes lifted slowly.

"You guys he's not coming back…"

There was an uncomfortable silence.

"You know what I hate about Sundays?" Said Famine whilst examining his broken cup. "Everything. The Anglesey Daly post, the snooker on this eleven-inch black and white cinder block, let alone the weekly search for the car. Where is it this time Pestilence?" Famine finally found the coffee and briefly thought of smiling, but thought who does the coffee think he is?

"Leave me alone, guys I don't feel too good, I think I'm ill." Pestilence lay in the corner; there was an aura of grey sickliness lurking around him.

"That one never gets old," remarked Famine. Pestilence's face was blotchy, freckled, and pitted. His red hair on the other hand was thick and rich, giving him the look of an unappetizing carrot.

"I believe I thought 'the brilliant light of a star shadowed by a gas giant hanging brilliantly haloed it.' Or something to that effect." Pestilence, with great care composed himself and reached for the board.

"Am I the only one playing scrabble? Because for the first time I have an X and I can actually use it." Pestilence looked expectantly toward Death.

Death did not look remarkable. If you told an art student from Pratt university located in the Brooklyn area of New York city to depict him, you would get remarkably close to how death looked. Unless that is, said student was making a statement about patriarchy and depicted him as an ashtray filled with beans. He was, essentially, a skeleton in an extravagant hoodie, but it was the things you could not see that you noticed about him. It was things like the glow in his eye sockets that compounded aeons by aeons. It was an inevitability to all, soul-shattering to others yet peaceful to a few. He was cold precision, an unfathomable intellect. There was a sense of waiting and knowing, silence and penetration. All of this was conveyed, rooted into you. It was the feeling that he could be behind you when he was in front of you. It was like he knew you. He was Death. The end. He was Abaddon, the angel of the abyss…but he was also difficult and good-mannered. His head, or more so a skull, or even more correctly a shaded figure under a dusted robe, tilted slightly upwards as he started to reminisce on the day he met Sarah Mingley.

"He's doing that thing again," said Pestilence.

"What do you think was in that sandwich?" asked Famine, clutching his stomach, realizing he may be in some trouble. "Do you think it was crab? I have trouble with crab." Death's world receded into his head as he started to recollect.

He recalled the campsite was a three-mile walk to the nearest pub, two miles east of Beach Gribin. The landscape was flat, dotted with fields and cows. Not many holidaymakers bared the brunt of the coastal winds in Llanfwrog on the west coast of Anglesey, Wales in late autumn. But the ones that did were mostly parents on a stretched budget trying to convince their children of how fun it was. They would point out the water hose, hours of fun there. They could look at the dog in a cage, not pet it but look. There was bird watching which consisted of several tens of thousands of pigeons. Sometimes a cow would appear just to be different from the other cows.

Death was twenty three miles east of Llanfwrog in the small idyllic village of Llangefni. In the conventional sense, he could not feel the cold, but it registered, as did the sunbeams that almost reached the ground in a valiant effort that can only be applauded.

"What have you done to me!" Kneeling and arched over in a pose a gymnast would envy and clutching his chest, The Englishman wondered if these were to be his last moments. He writhed in pain as the figure stood still as ice. He was giving more thought to the weather than to the man in his last moments.

"We all have our time Brian Aldiss. Now, I promise, this will not hurt a bit…" Death stated like a phlebotomist. He raised his astral scythe and struck him. Like every living being before him, the soul of Brian Aldiss disappeared entirely out of this dimension in a wisp of smoke. It always surprised Death that the smell of reaped souls tended to have its own individual scent. In Brian's case, it was tangerine with just a hint of lemon.

"Excuse me, who are you?" Said a girl from the other side of the hedge. Death slowly, but with great noticeable effort, started pushing Brian's corpse with his foot toward the hedge and out of sight. He stood as still as a deer caught in the headlights of a 1959 Rover P4 90. This sometimes had the habit of happening. He awkwardly turned and moved his head into a clumsy position, trying not to convey guilt.

"Why I... I'm the er, tooth fairy." Death was unaccustomed to deceit, but luckily no facial tics could ever have given him away.

"You don't *look* like the tooth fairy," the little girl remarked, hands on hips. If on a whim he wished to, Death could be seen, but why his dimensional adjacent form could sometimes be perceived by children was an oddity to him.

"I'm... on a diet," he said feebly.

"O-*kay*, if you *are* the tooth fairy, do you want to join my tea party?" Death did not know how to deal with children, or people for that matter. It is just that most people he met usually scream and shout, bargain and cheat, cry and break down. It was difficult to make friends if everyone you met you had to kill. Occasionally, the curiosity that was mankind instilled a rare desire for Death to socialize, but it had never gone down well like one interaction he had had in another memory. It was two summers ago whilst witnessing the end of an elderly priest's life he hesitated before swinging his scythe.

"The weather is pleasant," he started clumsily.

"The Grim Reaper! Here to take me from this mortal coil!" The priest uttered dramatically. Again, Death hesitated.

"The Wright Brothers, they were pioneers..."

The priest fell to his knees.

"Into God's hands I lay my soul!"

Death gave it one last shot.

"Is there any place near that cooks good quail?"

The priest trembled at the sight of the scythe inches from his head.

"Nothing ventured," said Death with a swing.

Death shook the memory away as he found himself back with the child.

"Well..." started Death, hesitantly. He realized he had been lingering awkwardly in thought whilst the small child at his feet looked up eagerly. It was out of character for Death to be hesitant about anything, but a child requesting his presence made him distinctly uneasy. However, Death knew he needed to grow socially. That, and he was in the mood for some tea. It would be a nice change from the florescent green of whatever it was that Famine tended to hand him before having another go with the kettle. The child sensed his unease, which was an amazing feat given how, from her perspective, he was but a shadow under a hood.

"*Please?*" she insisted. Death looked around slowly taking in his environment. To his utter disdain, he realized the tea was imaginary, but at this point, he had already sat down. He was surrounded by toy bears, a stick in a hat, a tiny Action Jackson action action figure that the kid next door had lost just that morning, and a Danbury Mint porcelain doll that Death absolutely adored. The seat was tiny and the intricate flower decorations, to Death, was nauseating.

Chapter 3

Marsha peered through her pound-land discount blinds to see her daughter playing tea with her friends. Suffering from pedophobia, the irrational and rampant fear of dolls she had, on several occasions, tried hiding and disposing of the wretched thing. The last she saw of it was when it was enthusiastically sellotaped to the ceiling in the loft. She had no idea how her daughter repeated the act of retrieving that Danbury Mint porcelain doll.

"Hey, Marsha!"

Marsha felt a shock go through her body as her husband demanded her attention. Marsha hated that her husband's verbal utterances were seventy percent of the time conveyed with a yell. She had just spilt an off-brand, *I Can't Believe It's Not A Banana Milkshake* on her wireless keyboard. Almost instantly the 'F' button refused to work.

"Marsha, who is Sarah sitting with now?" The husband was squinting at the stick in a hat. It was the newest of the group and, to Sarah's credit, it showed both a great imagination and a lack of it too. The husband adjusted his glasses, completely incapable of seeing Death. Out of loneliness due to being benched at his bowling game last Tuesday, he muttered something, not caring whether he was being listened to.

"In the garden, last week, she said it was the ghost of Charles Colson."

Marsha had been briefly confused, but reasoned other feelings were more important and stopped that nonsense. Though funnily, that thought had also left her confused.

"Charles Colson?" She said with an imagined eagerness. She could have stayed quiet; she knew he would have elaborated, but this way she gets points for listening.

"That's what I thought, couldn't get the damn name out of my head. She said 'You know the Watergate Seven?' Well, I looked into it, and turns out he was a counsel for Nixon. Now how on Earth does a little girl get that kind of information? It's not normal, Marsha. She is supposed to be playing with, I don't know, bikes and things and talking about elephants and stuff. Granted, my knowledge of a child's reality doesn't quite work, but my point stands. She said she got that creepy doll from Charles Colson."

A shudder ran down Marsha's back.

"Don't believe a word she says honey, she stole next doors Action Jackson action figure and told me there was tea for me. I looked in the cup and nothing. She's a thief and a liar."

Her husband had a frantic look on his face. He ran to the window and sure enough, next to the stick in the hat, was the Action Jackson action figure.

"No way! Does she have the Action Jackson action figure? That thing is so cool! It has three catchphrases, a song, and a tiny M4/M4A1 carbine gun! Are we not so lucky to live in this world, Marsha?"

"Yes," said Marsha, deflated. "We all love government-sanctioned death."

Her husband was almost out of the door licking his lips, eyeing the Action Jackson action figure.

"No!" Marsha barked. "Dishes, dear!"

Chapter 4

An ethos Death found he had adopted was that in awkward unfamiliar situations, do as the host does. It is not an all-encompassing philosophy and tended to lean askew. Death had once found he was alone with Pestilence, who was in the process of making a corn beef sandwich. Not accustomed to one-on-one time with Pestilence, and with nothing of significance to say, Death also made a corn beef sandwich. He mimicked every swipe of the butter, every sliced sliver of meat and so on. Eventually, Pestilence faltered whilst processing this situation. Out of awkwardness he enquired, "Do you eat?"

On this single ethos of taking his social cues from his environment, he had managed to drink his imaginary tea, wipe his mouth with a bib so his mommy and daddy would say 'well done,' talked about Charles Colson and the stick in the hat's bedtime chores, and learned not to speak to strangers. She said it was okay for her to talk to him because the tooth fairy was not a terrorist with a gun. It was so refreshing being out of the Caravan and talking to real people, he was enjoying himself. He had just reaped the soul of Brian Aldiss, and his corpse was just a few feet away festering and bloated but he gave himself a pass and decided not to think about work.

"So, Death started. "I think if Missy Grail liked Tim when you liked Tim, she should have said something rather than tell Cheryl you're a poo-poo head. Missy should get told off."

Sarah shook her head frantically.

"That's what I said! But it doesn't matter, my mom says if someone is mean on the outside, it's because they're sad on the inside, so I just feel sorry for her."

Death nodded.

"That's a very mature attitude, Sarah."

Sarah looked at her new friend, he looked so dark and sad, but she knew what would cheer him up. She reached for the Danbury Mint porcelain doll and handed it to him.

"For me?" said Death. Death was Omniscient. Every possible permutation and outcome of any possible situation was evident to him. What was, is, and will be. He was usually so tuned into his Omniscience that nothing surprised him. Nothing was novel, no experience unique. Even spontaneous emergent quantum phenomena were counted like everything else. It was for this reason that Death switched it off. He had to so that he could be bearable to live with. Famine and Pestilence would bet on the snooker and Death would blurt out the results. He knew the winners of channel five daytime television talent contests; he knew who had what cards, and why War was happy when he had been so short-changed in his mental faculties. His Omniscience gave precedence to boredom and solitude and without it, he could join in feet first. He could be offered a beautiful present and be moved deeply. Without his Omniscience, the only thing he could not get the hang of was chess. He always forgot how, in his words, the horsey moved.

"Thank you deeply, Sarah Mingley. I will cherish this for eternity. You are going to live a long and happy life. Also, Cheryl is a poo-poo head."

Chapter 5

"I have to say, I'm worried about Death. I mean, oh crap, I trod on something here. Think it was a snail. Ha!" said Famine with some gusto. "Maybe Death will appear now."

Pestilence gave him a good-natured smile.

"Screw off, that was funny. I mean yeah, we lose the Mini Cooper every week, and we sometimes find War in a random harlots' cave…although I do not know why every barely clothed Playboy maiden he finds seems to live in a cave. It is the 21st century. Even you, Pestilence, occasionally wander off on your never-ending quest to find the perfect toilet." Pestilence smiled. It had been a long quest.

"I think we are in Llanfwrog," remarked Pestilence lazily. "But we never lose Death. I mean, its Death. Every Iota of his being, every modicum is precise and predictable. Time is like a landscape in which he can see every possible action.. He wouldn't have trod on that snail."

Pestilence scratched his orange head.

"Death has been experimenting with turning his Omniscience off. I think when you threatened a certain cavity with that broom handle after he warned you that your colonic attempt will be unfruitful is when, for the sake of the friendship, you took priority over his Omniscience." There was some condescension there. Pestilence did not hide it, but his good-natured smile (though somewhat sickening to Famine) was enough for him not to make a retort.

"Oh, what fresh hell is this." Famine spat slightly more confrontationally than he intended.

In this small idyllic clean neighborhood they had stumbled into, Famine was immediately on his guard. Children were playing all manner of games. They were not vandalizing street signs or terrorizing the elderly. Neighbors with their jumpers around their necks were talking about the badminton game. A father was telling his son about some fishing trip. What was worse though, and this was really sickening, was a woman in a polka dot dress kissing her husband on the cheek as he put on a hat and got into his car, suitcase in hand.

"It's like this whole neighborhood is an experiment into the disturbed," remarked Famine. "It's like an advert trying to sell Aunt Bettys family farm bread."

"I like it!" declared War. Most of his utterances were unintended declarations. Both Pestilence and Famine stopped and stared at War. Famine had often wondered if there was more to him than one might suspect.

"I barely think this is your thing, Mr. War." An ice-cream van turned a corner. *Of course, an ice cream van,* thought Famine

"It's got its charms if theys is a nice place to rest one's axe and hammers, it's a place where family values stills run in your neighbors, their friends and their wives and daughters. Get meself a pet pig, kill that guy with the ponytail, I could make it work."

'Remember War, we are looking for Death.' Famine passively rubbed his hands together

"Right you are sir!" said War triumphantly. Famine sighed as Pestilence mumbled to himself. It was a strange mumble, it almost had an urgency to it. Against his better judgment Famine sighed again and looked expectantly to Pestilence.

"He's over there, with that girl, some bears, a stick with a hat, an Action Jackson action figure with removable guitar, and a creepy as hell doll he seems to be cradling."

"I said, what fresh hell is this too soon, it was far more apt for this situation."

Pestilence shrugged at Famine's annoyance

"Say it again then. Might not have as much impact, but at least it's out of your system. I know you, you'll be dwelling on this all day. It'll bug you and you'll take it out on the toaster. It's a miracle the thing works at all, and I like toast." Famine looked disdainfully at Pestilence and shrugged. Turning to Death he theatrically threw out his arms and proclaimed;

"What fresh hell is this?!"

He mouthed *thank you* and Pestilence gave his patented good-natured smile.

"No seriously, I could be wrong, but it looks like Death is having a tea party. Anyone think he is getting a little peculiar lately, a little off?" War shrugged. Pestilence merely went to say something but did not. Famine continued.

"I saw him reading a book the other day, it was called 'My First Chess Game' for ages 3 to 5."

Death spotted his friends looking at him quizzically. He met their gaze and slowly bought his tiny ceramic teacup to his jaw.

"Death…what in God's name are you doing? And don't say what I think you're going to say," asked Pestilence.

"I'm having a tea party," said Death, bringing the cup slowly to his jaw again with an audible sip. It was what Famine thought he would say.

"Yeah but…why?" Famine detested life's inclination to present oddities hidden as the norm.

The little girl heard the word Death and looked to him with a forlorn face beginning to manifest. Death decided to mitigate the situation.

"I'm not Death. I'm the tooth fairy."

Pestilence was about to help Famine bring Death home and hopefully never talk about this disturbing scene again, but he spotted an old outhouse and decided to investigate.

"How rude of me…" started Death. "This is Sarah Mingley. She invited me to this tea party and this," he lifted the doll, "is Bethany."

Famine approached Sarah.

"Hello Sarah, I'm the whatchamacallit, the Easter Bunny or something ok? I look like this because, because I…I've been sick. Very sick. Had this lump I was worried about, well I will not bore you with the details, suffice to say, be careful about your diet. The crab may look fresh but let it sit for two days in a VW campervan in a tray above the heating unit…"

Sarah looked blankly at Famine.

"Anyway, as I was saying. I have also been dealing with an inner ear infection since the plague, which is why I look like this. I suppose what I'm trying to say is…"

Famine looked down at Sarah expectantly; he suspected she believed the narrative.

"Me and the, erm, Tooth Fairy here we have to go and, oh I don't know, get some teeth. Yeah that's plausible enough. And give people chocolate. Do you mind if I take him with me now? Only we are late, and there's this thing, and my Nan is under a cupboard and her hair is on fire. Ok? Nice to meet you, say goodbye Death."

"Goodbye Sarah. Thank you for Bethany. The tea was sublime."

Sarah waved enthusiastically.

"I have had such a pleasant afternoon," said Death. "I should spend more time with my Omniscience off. Who was keeping an eye on War? You know he cannot be left alone. Look, he's going away with that barely clad maiden over his shoulder and Pestilence seems to have disappeared altogether."

Death and Famine looked around.

"I'm in here, just be a minute," said a muffled voice followed by a flush.

"I want to go home," said Death optimistically.

"Me too my friend, me too. Oh, we found the car by the way."

Pestilence saw his friends some way up the road. As he followed, he noticed a grown man steal an Action Jackson action figure from a little girl.

"Wait up guys!" He looked back at the outhouse wistfully.

"Five out of ten I would say."

"Sorry," said Death, finally back in the room and out of his recollection.

"So, we didn't meet up with the big guy last night?" His intonation gave away his discomfort in saying the phrase 'the big guy.' The goal was flawless integration; the result was dead air in the room. He really was trying to adopt slang and youth-oriented jargon, but it only felt flat and forced. It especially affected Famine who would cringe every time Death tried to slip this sort of thing into a conversation. "I am sure I saw him somewhere. Didn't we get him a Rubix cube with twelve sides, with the stickers of supermodels along with the slinky that goes upstairs, and the yo-yo with the invisible string? They're all classics." Pestilence shook his head.

"I think it was mayo and crab. There, my word is *opulence*."

"The coffee turned yellow. Is this kettle from another dimension?" Famine flicked the kettle with a well-groomed fingernail.

Famine took a sip of his 'Super Happy Mega Morning Coffee' from Japan. It was made with coffee beans genetically engineered to sober a whale and it all came back to him. The drinks, the girls, the dancing bar patron playing the flute in the shadows...Pestilence did have mayo and crab, he did remember! The car was by an asteroid, and half hour ago War woke him up and pointed out of the window to a rip in space, where he told him where to find the duct tape. They missed their friend's birthday party, the presents were in the glove compartment. In that dim light, with the influence of plentiful flowing Affligen Blond Belgian Beers, Evelyn may have been a man. The rip in space. It hit him;

it wasn't just being in Llanfwrog on the west coast of Anglesey, Wales. Famines eyes widened.

"I think I know. Guys?" he pointed to the sky. "What do you suppose that is?"

Chapter 6

It is said that anything can happen anywhere for no reason. That the mastery of our agency equates to merely an illusion governed by the whims of chance and the accidental and incidental. For Brian Aldiss that could not be truer. He could have sworn he had died. He was sure of it. He *was* dead. But how could that be when the woman behind the cashier was handing him cigarettes at this exact moment? At this exact moment handing him his change? There! It just happened! She smiled at him! Dead people do not get smiled at. How did he even get to the shop?

Over the next few hours Brian was in a haze. He would poke people in the back to see if they registered his existence. When he still wasn't sure of his corporeal form, he started asking the passing public if they could tie his shoes he had unlaced. Was he in Anglesea? Like a passing dream, a light that shone on his memory began to dim. He could not quite grasp it as it fluttered away. He felt as though, in a fit of PTSD, he had truly and categorically, without a shadow of doubt, lost his tenuous grasp on his sanity and everything that defined him.

Redemption! The answer!

Brian's inner monologue ceased its incessant chatter as he had stumbled across a giant grey bleak monstrosity masquerading as a building. There was a silver plaque pretending the building was more affluent than it was. It read:

Floor 1 - All You Can Eat Dessert Food. Try Our Cactus.

Floor 2 - Open Offices To Let (with a rag of parchment sellotaped to the side of it that read 'Wednesdays, a seminar on how to be your proctologist')

Floor 3- Doctor Price Of Psychiatry P.H.D - Walk-Ins Welcome

"Well that's a touch of serendipity," thought Brian aloud. He stumbled into the building, tripping on the small and impossible to notice step, hitting his head on the *mind your head* sign. Part of its lettering appeared worn down from years of people who were seeking either desert delicacies seminars, or questionable psychiatrists hitting their heads on said sign.

Brian assessed his surroundings suspiciously not trusting any aspect of it. An inexplicably large canvas on the wall advertised Opuntia cactus enjoyed by a truck driver called Dale with the caption 'I don't mind the taste!' Next to that was a picture of who Brian assumed was

Doctor Price. Brian had to squint his eyes with great concentration to make out the statement '2 months sober.' One door in the lobby had a guard that Brian felt was completely perplexing. Seminars, dessert foods and psychiatrists didn't usually require armed staff.

Brian gingerly approached a generic table to his left and addressed a bespectacled short man with a handlebar moustache, sporting a very noticeable hairpiece. Not quite sure how he knew, Brian realized it was on backwards. Pinned to the mans shirt was a button with a smiley face that read 'I'm new, help me learn.'

"Doctor Price walk in?" Brian questioned. The gravity of his situation hit him. After the certainty of his own demise, he needed the wise counsel of a trained professional. Or at least a possibly alcohol-dependent psychiatrist. A psychiatrist that shares a building with edible horned desert vipers…

"Elevator is broken. Due to national security issues I need you to sign a waiver that you did not notice the guard at the door or any scream-like noises emanating from within. Also the steps to your right will lead you to Doctor Price. You pay on exit depending upon the time spent. Here is a leaflet. Fill out the form with your basic information and tell him Mitch said that was my hole punch. I bought it from home, and I have a receipt." Brian nodded, signed the waiver, pocketed the leaflet, and scanned the form.

Have you now or ever been convinced you were a council to Nixon? Brian read. He confidently ticked no. *Do you know the answer to the next question without referring to it?* Again, bewildered Brian ticked no. *Did you not tick yes or no straight away and instead proceeded to this question to see what it is that you either knew or didn't know?* Brian ticked no. *A mathematical problem is a problem that is amenable to being represented, analysed, and possibly solved, with the methods of mathematics. The result of the mathematical problem solved is demonstrated and examined formally. Were you previously aware of this description?* Brian gave up and proceeded up the stairs. He felt somewhat numb and despondent. Floor 1 had an overwhelming scent of peaches. Floor 2 had a disturbing Earthy scent and Floor 3 assaulted his olfactory senses with mothballs. No one else was in what he assumed to be the waiting room; the water dispenser was the giveaway, along with a 'do you have gout' advert pinned to a board on the wall.

A confident rap of the door conflicting with his state of pure apprehension was enough for Doctor Price to open to Brian. A non-imposing relatively cliché looking Doctor Price presented Brian with a blood-red Chesterfield chair.

"Barbary fig cactus?" said Doctor Price, presenting Brian with a small bowl.

"No? Ok. Cannot get enough of these... San Pedro cactus is strange. Psychedelic due to the mescaline. Not legal here of course but still, good memories. So, I am Doctor Price. We usually charge £49.99 an hour for private consultations. Mitch has sent me up your basic information. We used to do advanced information, but people complained as they were quite intimate. Plus, it took 4 hours and there was some homework. So, Brian Aldiss. How can I heal you today?"

"That information I provided, it made little to no sense."
The doctor grinned.

"How far through it did you get? Did you complete the quiz on therapod evolution and its relationship with modern ratites?"

"No, the math bit I think..." The doctor was slightly disappointed. He had put a lot of work into that information pack.

"So good afternoon Mr. Aldiss."

"Hello, Doctor Price. Brian Aldiss. As established. Your receptionist Mitch mentioned a hole punch?" Brian had no idea why he was going through this avenue of conversation. Perhaps it was as simple as not wanting to recount his trauma, half wondering if he had made a giant mistake walking into this building.

"When you see him, tell Mitch he can have his hole punch when he has finished painting my shed! I am sorry, I don't need to burden you, very unprofessional. Please tell me why you have decided to seek out some help. Were you referred to us by a GP? Hear about us through friends or family? Or perhaps from our article in the magazine *Air Blimps Aficionado*? I haven't had much luck with clientele seeking help from that article. I had a blimp salesman here once though, he was very persuasive." Brian looked blankly and the doctor looked a little defeated.

"Uhm, it came with a hat?" The Doctor carried on.
More silence.

"Has er, has a little blimp logo? You know? To wear in the house in the cold..." the Doctor, receiving no visual or audible feedback, decided to move on.

"Any who! This is a safe space if you are into that, here that is, not down there. Well, you know, you signed the waiver. Would you like some tea?" The Doctor himself went for a second bowl of cactus.

"No I'm fine, should I just talk? I feel I should talk, if you are finished that is."

The very psychiatrist looking Doctor Price nodded.

"I have a recurring problem, a strange problem. The kind of problem that I now realize if you are talking to a psychiatrist about, you may find yourself under watch for 72 hours. But I need to talk to someone. Who better than a Doctor? By happenstance, I stumbled across this establishment. Sort of synchronistic given what happened to me."

"What is it you believe happened to you, Brian?" The Doctor swiveled in a circle on his chair wondering about home time and when he can play with his friends.

"It was..." Brian took a deep breath and composed himself.

"Well, it was Death. An apparition. A material specter of some kind. He was there, he was standing over me and I was dead. I felt this extreme discomfort as I sort of popped out of the universe drenched in the scent of tangerines with a hint of lemon! I was overcome with non-existence. By my calculation, I have lost about a weekend. The last clear thing I remember is I was at the shop buying cigarettes..."

The Doctor interjected.

"Brian, choose to hear my words. Missing time is a not an uncommon phenomenon. It is usually associated with alien abduction. The victims see all kinds of things from apparitions to lost loved ones. I would not rule out aliens. Carry on. I'm interested. This is good stuff."

Brian was beginning to doubt the notion that this was wise counsel

"You seem like a strange psychiatrist. Though, I have no frame of reference."

"I'm a psychiatrist above a glorified cactus shop in a tiny dusty office, with a fifty-year-old chesterfield chair accepting anyone from the street. What did you expect? Have you seen the size of this window?" Was doctor Price's retort. Brian continued completely disregarding the Doctor's admission of incompetency

"On the way here, I verbally abused a dog, gave an old lady the wrong directions to the bingo hall and I kicked a pigeon. Or at least that is what the police officer told me. I do not know why I'm doing these things. It's the recurring problem of missing time. It's happened before, a few times. I see Death looming over me. Sometimes he tries to awkwardly start a conversation, but it always ends in the same way. He swings his scythe and then *emptiness*. Some days later I return, sometimes great distances from where I was with no memory of the interim." The doctor had a big smile on his face.

"That is fascinating," he started. "So you seem to be at the start of this journey and it begins with a scene of you in a psychiatrist's office? Isn't that a little cliché? Somewhat lazy? Forgive me, I'm thinking aloud, but I want to know more. Please continue"

"Okay, so where to start. I'm not what you would call a lucky man when it comes to you know... that stuff?" The doctor looked blankly like a pigeon being told to use a microwave.

"The psychical thing with you know, women. I'm hopeless with women. I always have been but lately, they approach me smiling! This one girl knew my name and thanked me for the lobster. How do you explain that?"

The doctor nodded.

"I couldn't begin to guess. Perhaps some strange synchronicity? Random chance? A visual hallucination? Maybe in this missing time, your mind was superseded by a more dominant or even placid self that seemingly has a life of its own, and that you did have lobster. Any auditory hallucinations?"

You were dead Brian, something whispered. Brian located a small saguaro cactus that may have said those words. Right on cue, as if the universe were mocking him. Brian gulped.

"You don't happen to have a tape recorder that is adding to our conversation located somewhere around that cactus, do you? Or perhaps an exceedingly small man hiding behind it? Can you perhaps throw your voice? Maybe a pet parrot that got bored of sitting on a stick, you know, the smart ones that sing show tunes that may be bored and decided to join our discourse?"

"No," said the Doctor authoritatively.

"So, is that a maybe on the auditory thing?"

Nothing has changed, you will die again...

"No, I won't!"

"No you won't what?" said the Doctor softly through his half-moon glasses and elbow patches. Brian had no defence. *That did not happen,* he thought.

Yes Brian, yes it kind of did...and stuff...

"Shut up," said Brian. *Why is this happening to me?*

"I didn't say anything," said the Doctor. Brian tried to recover his facade of sanity only he knew of no words to help him with this. There was an uncomfortable silence whilst a very strange expression started to form on Brian Aldiss's face. It contorted like he wished to convey something, and then again as if he didn't agree with whatever it was that he was thinking, and yet again as if he was content with the silence. It was easy at this point for him to cut his losses.

I have got to get out of here.

Out of embarrassment, fear, anxiety, the myriad of cacti, this Doctors shiny bald head and dusty office, or the fact his legs had made the decision already without him, he let himself out whilst mumbling apologies and thanks. He accidentally trapped his foot in a waste paper bin and fell to the ground, but then harnessed the strength to jump back up. He mumbled thanks and apologies.

"Mr. Aldiss, if you can sit back down, please, I don't think we're finished here," Brian mumbled thanks and apologies once more and sat down.

"If you can dislodge your foot from the basket, please."

Brian mumbled thanks and apologies. He was pathologically polite, but it never registered as it was always mumbled and barely audible. He tried to dislodge it, every second was severe psychological pain. He attacked the basket with all he had.

"Ahem, it's stuck! I cannot apologize more, I really can't. Hold on maybe if I…"

With a final push he was free.

"I think I know what is wrong with you Mr. Aldiss. You are incapable of showing aggression. Now, I'm not saying aggression is a good thing, but some situations require it in small amounts. It is like self-serving actions. Sometimes they are required. You are incapable of experiencing the rich spectrum of emotion that the Buddha gives us, negativity is repressed and, in every situation, you apologize even when you are not at fault. People can use you because of this and that can be very damaging. I encourage you to start learning how to say no. I want you to scream. I have got to know you over the last few minutes, and I don't pretend to know you, but I am trained to pick up on things others might not register. After all, that is my name on that diploma!"

Brian looked up at the plaque. *The Regents of the Arden*

University have conferred on Steven Landon the degree, Doctor of Philosophy.

"You seem like a perfectly pleasant if somewhat extremely troubled young man. My behavior modification methods *may* work. I want you to stop saying sorry. Start an argument for no reason, try your best to have anonymous sex with women or men if that is your thing. Hell, maybe both. Go crazy! Not literally, of course, bad choice of words. Try challenging an authority's sexuality. That could be fun," the Doctor chuckled. Brian felt perhaps Doctor Price was not taking this session too seriously.

"I want you to stop saying sorry."

"Yeah sorry about that. Oh, sorry, I didn't mean to. Yeah, I have a problem."

"Quite. You see I believe that these lost moments, this other self so far apart to who you are, is the part of you that wants to come out, that you must build a bridge between these opposing forces. I can just throw drugs at you, but I believe that rather than just rejecting and medicating this side of you, if you exhibit its behaviour then perhaps nature will take the course and these blackouts will stop happening. Say no, start an argument for no reason, scream as loud as you can in public, talk to people, get to know them carnally, start a fight, question an authority figures sexuality," reiterated the Doctor. Brian sat in his comfortable safe reliable state of mental disarray.

"So, I wasn't dead? Because I really felt dead. I felt this emptiness, hate and self-loathing. Insignificant in an unforgiving universe, the tiniest cog for the most inconsequential part of an even more pointless computer, whose probable purpose probably only amounts to figure out why the cog that is me is moving at all. I mean, is that normal?"

"Yes, we all feel like that. What do you do for work Mr. Aldiss? Are you in a relationship? What friends do you have? Do you have a social life?"

The walls felt like they were closing in on Brian.

"Can you open a window perhaps?"

The Doctor got up. The window was a foot and six inches wide. The lever to open it resembled a toothpick that someone had thinned down with an army knife.

"Wow watch that wind blow. Isn't it amazing?" Brian mumbled under his breath, feeling a wave of disassociation and apathy.

"Better?" The Doctor said while he maneuvered himself back into his chair. He seemed to be paying more attention to a bundle of papers on his desk than Brian. He waved his hand and Brian interpreted this as to carry on with the previous question.

"I used to work in an office. Had my own cubicle. Basic data entry. It involved entering data from various sources into the company computer system for processing and management. I had a slightly broken fluorescent light above me. It was three years before I had the strength to complain. Every 32 seconds it blinks 3 times. Every 49 seconds it shut off for 4 seconds. The bin for the entire floor is next to my desk. Whenever I think someone is about to talk to me, they discarded half-eaten egg sandwiches into the receptacle. The thing with egg is it tends to ferment. I tried to empty the bin myself once but was told I did not have the necessary qualifications. I received death threats from the waste disposal unit. Half of the time I didn't know what I was doing and why I was doing what I didn't know I was doing. My boss was a narcissistic control freak, but I suppose he tried his best."

"There, Brian, there. Do not make excuses. If you want to vent, where else but here?" For the first time that day Brian smiled. That is, until he carried on his venting.

"Sometimes I went for a cigarette and just didn't want to go back in. I stood there for hours and no-one said anything. I lost that job a month or so ago."

"Due to the blackouts?" inquired Doctor Price.

"No. It was payday. Everybody got a package but me. I had to find my boss to sort it out. Only he didn't know who I was. I had worked there for six years. I saw him every day. I even showed him my passport. My files call me Mr Aldibbs, so there was trouble straight off. Eventually, after I reminded him of the time I saved his daughter from drowning and she sued me for sexual harassment at the company picnic, he started to have a slight recollection that he knew me from somewhere. It took two hours and fifty-three files of work I'd done over the last three months to prove I worked there at which point my boss asked who I was and what I was doing in Mister Aldibbs cubicle. I tried to tell him that it was me, I was Mister Aldibbs. He said no, Mister Albibbs had a beard, played golf and died last week. Eventually I apologized for pretending to be Mister Aldibbs and was escorted out of the building. I haven't been back since."

The Doctor laughed out loud.

"Sorry I did not mean to laugh. It's all just so tragic." He nodded and grunted a sound of merriment under his breath. Brian heard him mumble egg sandwich as the Doctor was still fixated on his papers. He felt he was making progress, but he had been in this room too long. He even wondered with some rarefied jest if it was light outside. The window had no chance of helping him. The light was probably still trying to find the tiny crack of a window in the wall. But progress was progress and he had yet to find the will to face what was outside. The phone rang as Doctor Price lazily picked it up.

"Yellow submarine? Oh, Mitch, hope you are well. Doing a lot of hole punching here, how did I live without it? No! You paint MY shed! Look, forget it for now ok? What do you want, and do not say the hole puncher. Really? Daniel Egan? When was his appointment? He is in the waiting room now? Okay. Well, I'm able to see Brian another time if he feels it necessary. Egan's appointment is profoundly serious. Send him on up."

"Everything ok Doctor Price?"

"You have been here for what, 3 or 4 minutes? I cannot in all good conscience charge you for your time. I cannot, I stress cannot miss this next appointment. The very fate of the world is at stake so I shall wrap this up. Ok, look., it is quite clear that one of a few things is true. You met Death, in corporeal form, and you are yo-yoing between here and the great beyond. You are either having bouts of amnesia and are possibly hallucinating as a result, or you are developing a serious case of psychosis. Now I do have the right to detain you and recommend a seventy-two-hour evaluation where we may start you on a regiment of antipsychotics. However, I cannot physically detain you and you can walk out of this building now never to be heard of from me again. Ha, the only way I can detain you is by enlisting the help of the downstairs security guard but he's making sure they don't come out." Doctor Price doubled back. "Forget I said that..."

Chapter 7

In Llanfwrog on the west coast of Anglesey, Wales, a small frog that was perched on a fallen branch a few inches from the water was having an existential crisis. It wondered if there was more than this, more than the instinctual drive to mutter its utterances in any other way than a ribbit. He began a thought. *I ribbit, therefore I am!* It was a profound crystalline epiphany as if sent from some ineffable Muse. He found himself seeking knowledge and wisdom And started to ask himself questions like what were those lights above him when the shiny round thing went to bed in the sleepy time?

Hidden in the reeds was a water vole. It had no existential crisis to overcome, it had no wants, needs or desires it felt were lacking. He was a simple creature with a simple goal. Giving no thought to the sun or the stars it saw, with some glee, a frog. Behind that water vole was a cat whose only thought was how dashing he looked in his reflection in the water. Not far from that branch Famine was trying to make sense of his situation.

"Ok well I am sort of maybe a little bit, don't want to push it but *maybe* I'm somewhat certain that is a hole in the universe," said Famine as the ball on the rope attached to a pole stuck in the ground came his way. He didn't bother to hit it back to Pestilence.

"Famine, I spent ten minutes setting this up, if you are not going to play, don't. I'd ask War but have you seen the size of those hands? This was twelve-pound fifty from the 'Bits and Pieces and Odds and Ends and This and That' shop. Pestilence sat down in the grass.

"That is unquestionably unequivocally definitely something I would with certainty probably categorize and describe as possibly a hole in the universe."

It was early morning and Death lounged in an all-weather rattan sun lounger. He was struggling with an admission he knew he would soon have to make. Something his colleagues, no wait, *friends* were unaware of but how could he tell them? Look how happy they all are! Pestilence was enjoying the sun coughing black stuff into his hand with his head sunken. Famine was uttering certainties at the sky and War was enjoying a semi-drunken half comatose state face down in an ants nest. Death was keeping an eye on events. He knew what the tear, with its lack of reality nestled into it, was and had some good sense to know what it meant. God had left the universe; he could smell the ethereal residue from here.

The general populace had no such perception that anything was amiss besides a slight apathy permeating their realities. It wasn't a severe reaction for the populace, they may have just been a little less enthused when they went up the ladder rather than down the shoots. But to the Horsemen, the silver slit encased in the light made of play dough nestled into a purple spiral spotted with golden lights was present, beautiful and alarming.

Famine did something akin to composing himself, it was little more than a deep breath that failed to adjust his outlook. He did, however, decide to delegate.

"Death, I can surmise, given your awkward stance and trying to look inconspicuous by whistling that crap tune nonchalantly, that you may know something about this spatial anomaly."

"Whatever could you mean good sir? With my mind awash with profundities and constructs I dared not ponder upon said spatial disturbance whose arrival, like you, baffles me. Look! A lost cow! Lets all turn our attention to that!" Death pretended to cough into his hands. The cow being addressed turned its head to be polite. A hooded figure was pointing at it. It shrugged its cow shoulders and went to investigate the grass across the fence that seemed greener.

"Death, you always speak in that irritating fashion when you are lying. Look, that up there? That is not normal. I know we are immortal representations of the human condition, destined to end the world, walking the borders of reality itself which to some, given, is not normal...I regret this tangent. Death, tell me what it is or so help me God I'll take the Bethany doll and introduce it to War."

"Nice weather we are having," said Death trying to stall. "It's been raining sideways for the whole morning, that's why we have been playing scrabble. I'm sure I saw the wind pick up a shed..."

Famine held the Bethany doll and opened a 1946 Percy Spencer experimental microwave. Famines eyes were on fire. Death conceded. He thought he pulled off his deception with the arrival of the cow. How the weather ploy failed was a complete mystery. Fearing for Bethany's safety he presented what he knew.

"It's God. He has left the Earth. He has left the universe, the multiverse, the omniverse, there is no atom or particle in the many planes of existence still governed by him. God is gone, there is no longer a God, this is a Godless universe."

Pestilence interrupted.

"So if someone got slightly startled and said 'My God,' it would have to be figurative and not literal?"

Death nodded.

"God has departed. We are not entirely left to the whims of din and chaos. God, in a contingency plan for unforeseen circumstances, automated many existences functions and utility through his 1976 Apple 1. It comes with an impressive array of floppy discs. Essentially, my friends, the end is nigh. From what I can conclude he is now on a plane of existence transcending even himself, but where that may be and how to get there even I cannot perceive."

Pestilence was the first to speak. He raised his hand and was acknowledged by Death.

"Thank you. Is it possible that we completely neglected God last night? In the throes of hedonism, crabs and the many bottles of wine that we got from Dionysus, who annoyingly always refers to himself as the Greek God of wine?"

Famine interrupted.

"I hate that guy, like that makes him special. 'I'm the God of wine, drink from my bounty,' like no one asked. Can you be a God of less importance? Your divinity amounts to what is happening to War right now, dreaming of sweet nothings whilst comatose, congratulations, live forever bathed in your mediocrity, they give anyone divinity right now. It's embarrassing. We'll see a God of haircuts soon at this point."

"To be fair I think I faintly recall War drinking that yellow whiskey from that blind Viking guy Hod. There is still some left by your cup." *That's why it was stained yellow,* thought Famine triumphantly.

"Ok," continued Pestilence. To piece together what had happened they needed to work together. To set the mood he donned a deerstalker hat and a long-stemmed cherrywood pipe.

"So, I think the plan was to pick up God, we were going to the ethereal bar in the ineffable plane, it was going to be a surprise party. This morning War got a text message saying God is leaving," pondered Pestilence. A memory flashed back in Famines mind.

"We drove there in the mini cooper with the roof ripped off so we could fit in War. We parked it by an asteroid so we wouldn't lose it. I think by this time we may have been slightly inebriated." Pestilence smiled in thought.

"My conclusion, the text war got earlier about God leaving, he didn't mean his job or his world but the entire Omniverse. I thought he was just going to Africa for a few months to find himself and yet it appears, indeed, the end is nigh. It's all rather elementary." Pestilence laid down the tobacco-free pipe that he bought into existence to make a boring point palatable. Death began to speak ominously.

"The protocol was always to be commanded by God. At his will, we ride forward. We are the ones that the Lord has sent to patrol the Earth. From time immemorial in the depths of existence, we govern this realm. Atop the white, red, black, and pale steeds. That at his will we are brought forward. Famine will strip the land and salt the Earth. At Pestilences volition plague will ravage and fester the Earth. War shall exercise a righteous grip on the souls of men. And then Death, the final word. By the word those of purity shall ascend." Famine and Pestilence were captivated. Death raised his left hand and waved it.

"We have not been commanded now, have we? Instead, the one true constant has left us in his wake. This is an apocalypse but not one that should ever have occurred. This is a grey area and I am not sure how to proceed."

"So it's a slow and crap apocalypse? I'll put the kettle on," said Famine in a rare instance of empathy. As he opened the caravan door a crab made a daring escape.

"The infestation is back!" hollered Famine from inside the caravan. Famine had no idea where they were coming from. With great hesitation Famine nervously flipped the switch for the kettle who, in a fit of paranoia, tended to electrocute anyone who dared interrupt its existence. On cue, a jolt shot through Famine's extremities. Smoke rose from his head. He tried again with the kettle and was once more granted a jolt that shot his slippers off.

"Why is every little thing against me! I hate this place, and I hate you, you stupid ancient yellow bastard!" Famine, seeing red, yanked the lead of the kettle which panicked and gave him another jolt. The pain only made him surer of his conviction that the kettle needed to die. Pestilence saw Famine marching out of the caravan with great intent, marching toward the edge of the cliff, kettle in hand. Adrenaline rushed through Pestilence as he sprinted toward the kettle and its abductee. Pestilence tackled Famine to the ground, the kettle rolling toward the cliff where it hesitantly stopped, balancing perfectly and precariously on the edge.

"It has to die!" screamed Famine in Pestilences armpit.

"I'll get you, you yellow bastard! Every fucking day for weeks in this hell hole!"

"Famine calm down! It's just a kettle!" Famine was close to tears.

"It has to die!" As the kettle perched perfectly between life and death, Famine and Pestilence observed the tiniest feather floating from the sky. It landed on the kettle. Immediately the life of the kettle came to its undignified end, shattering on the rocks below.

"Well, there goes our tea. Can I just say? Please stay away from the toaster." War burped himself awake. He swatted away the ants and threw his bulk into the caravan. He went toward the missing kettle confused.

"Yes War, Famine has decided we don't need tea in our lives. There is some yellow stuff in that cup." War shrugged and drank it down mightily.

"Why don't you use sir Deaths whachamacallit, little kettle fella, he keeps it in that there Ted Baker textured satchel."

A golden light shone on the satchel serenaded by a chorus of angelics. It was strange, they had never even registered it until War had acknowledged its existence that very moment.

"War, how did you come to know there is a kettle in here?"

"Well, I know lots of things. Not just a perfect Adonis of a man me, the refined mind is this." Pestilence looked at Famines face and engaged in damage control.

"Let him have that Famine."

"So, I'm in the big tent thing what's attached to the van roasting me a pig an I hears a boiling kettle only it sounds like it's boiling. I post my head by the window and as you are asleep, he's making tea with fancy silver things if you can imagine. He then packs it neatly into the satchel!" War was proud of his retelling of events, he always assumed he was underestimated but in times like this, he was sure of it.

"So for weeks, we have been using a decrepit ancient yellow abomination of a kettle who electrocutes anyone that looks at it, that constantly makes tea as cold as the day is long, and all this time Death has had a secret working silver kettle that he uses at night while we are asleep? I'm flabbergasted. The nerve! You know what? I was thinking twice about opening this satchel, violation of privacy and all that but if that bastard is keeping secrets like this from us, I'm opening it. I am! This is what is happening now."

Bathed in the golden light Famine gingerly unzipped the satchel, savoring every moment. Inside the bag was the most beautiful thing that any of them had ever seen. It was a Breville IKT197 silver kettle that retails at £29.99. It even had a warranty sticker still on it. You could make out the embossed *Breville* logo.

"Son of a bitch, he has been holding out on us. I thought he was incapable of deception. He's always pathologically honest. Look at this beauty! You are not going to electrocute me now, are you?"

"Unless..." started Pestilence.

"Unless it was never the kettle in the first place but faulty wiring in the van?" Famine had not considered this.

"I was having a moment Pestilence, forever with your infernal logic." Famine lifted the kettle with great care as if he were cradling a newborn. Filled with water and the plug deftly inserted, the kettle ramped to life, eager to serve. Famine turned expectantly to Pestilence with a smile plastered across his face. There it was, four cups of delicious Anglesea's finest tea substitute.

Chapter 8

Death laid back in his all-weather rattan sun lounger, looking towards the tent attached to the caravan as his friends arrived with tea. The sunken feeling emanated from Death whenever he was presented with the tea born in that van. War approached first. He patted Death on the shoulder.

"Sorry old skipper," he said, before laying back down in the ant's nest.

"Here you go Death, a nice warm cup of tea." Death looked at the tea. Something was awry. It had steam coming from it for a start, and the tea had diffused in the heat. Occom's razor suggested they had found his kettle.

"You have been holding out on us Death. Any other little things you forgot to mention? Perhaps a stash of good pillows hiding somewhere whilst we suffer with a sack of hay?" Death had no defense, it was just he enjoyed having something that was just his.

"I have nothing to say that will undo this trespass, I vehemently apologize. If you are willing to overlook the obvious treachery, I also have a secret toaster. You are welcome to use it anytime."

"Agreed," said Famine and Pestilence in unison knowing a good deal when it came.

"I have a confession to make," said War somewhat soberly.

"With the possible, possibility, I gots it, of the end times, You knows how it was my job to hire the caravan from the guy at the stables; we gave him zircon crystal fragments and left the horses so we could holiday here? Well, me beard be damned I can't remember who I gots it from or where he is. Could be here in Wales could be anywhere really."

"You tried your best War, don't beat yourself up over this, it may have been our fault really for trusting you with a relatively untaxing task. Besides its ok, Death is Omniscient, he can just tell us, can't you?" said Pestilence.

"About that Pestilence, I was inebriated and had my Omniscience off. In fact, since this morning I've been having trouble with it, I think I am being affected by the spatial anomaly. I guess that my Omniscience is somehow tied to God. Without him it's getting difficult to count the atoms in this cup. 8.36×10 to the power of 24. I think I'm off a few molecules. I have an idea, I need to find Brian Aldiss. I have a feeling only he can help us now.

Chapter 9

"Crap I'm late! Well I have done 4361 steps, not bad, may hit 10,000 today. Da da dee dee dee dum, where is my phone? I lost my phone my phone my phone... dee dum. There it is..." Seth Dales was in an exceptional mood. Today was the day he was to be promoted to store supervisor at the Celtic Corner Sports Centre in Castle Street Anglesea, a short walk from Beaumaris seafront. He took in the sea air, looked at the cloudless sky, today was going to be a good day.

Seth slightly strutted toward the weathered grey sea wind-battered shop front door with "Celtic centre" proudly printed on a piece of driftwood. He noticed something to his left. Someone had painted *wall* on the side of the building. He did not fret, part of being a supervisor was dealing with these occurrences. He only wished the vandals had a better imagination.

"Sorry, I'm a little late boss, got into it with a seagull." His superior grinned and pointed at a tent.

"This is your problem now. He is obviously crazy and I don't want to deal with it. He seems to pay for everything he uses. I have had students from the Royal Welsh College of Music and Drama asking me if it's street theatre. I'm going to lunch. Good luck."

Brian sat in his tent. He had walked in, paid for it, and then erected the Vango Soul 200 tent right there under the nail clippers. He wasn't loitering, he had designated this space as his sanctuary. He had entered this shop and simply didn't want to leave. At first, he stood in a corner for a longer than anybody would feel comfortable, reading the many leaflets on a stand. He then meandered toward the Costa coffee machine. The owner was paying him little attention. That's when he saw the camping equipment. He was in denial about how long this situation was feasible but for now, all his needs were met. There was a bathroom, the Costa Coffee machine, he even spotted a few cans of 'Heat This Meat' in the back. He looked out of the window. *I just can't do it,* he thought. He really couldn't. He could no longer face it. This was his home now, between the Filson tin cloth packer fishing hats and whey protein powders. Outside those automatic doors, splattered with newspapers flying in the wind due to a less than vigilant paper salesmen, and a strong easterly breeze was a world he could no longer associate with. The outside world was nothing more than an assault on his senses. But most of all, Death could not get him here.

Seth cautiously approached the tent. A wire ran from an outlet on the right-hand side of the door selling fishing tackles and athletic cups and fed into the tent. He could smell something akin to oxtail soup.

"Hello? Sir? My name is Mr. Dales. I am not equipped to deal with this situation. Sir?" There was a rustle in the tent and a glow as if something inside was getting hot. He heard a toaster ping.

"Ok look, I'm getting freaked out here. I lack the necessary experience to understand this situation." The tent zipper slowly began to open and Seth saw a hand emerge with a wad of cash. The wrist flicked to release it.

"That should see me through the month landlord!" said a voice from the tent. Seth began to understand why his boss delegated this situation. Should he phone the police? What was the rule? This was an unexampled circumstance.

"I'm afraid I cannot take that money, sir, you have to leave the premises. Is there someone I can call? A family member or a friend?"

"I invoke adverse possession, squatters rights!" said a muffled voice. Seth patted his person intently for 12 seconds and again found his phone. He opened the yippy search engine.

"Squatters rights only apply if you have occupied the land continuously for twelve years." There was a short silence.

"How do you know I haven't been here for twelve years? Maybe you just never noticed me," the muffled voice continued from the tent.

"You are in an imposing one-man tent in the middle of a small shop using a toaster and eating soup, you are not hard to miss sir. Now I really must ask you to leave." Again, there was a short silence.

"I invoke maritime law!" Seth's head sunk.

"I'm not even checking that. This is ridiculous if you're not going to leave of your own volition, I have no choice but to make you come out!" Seth grabbed the zipper and opened it. From the other side Brian pulled the zip back down. Again, Seth had another go at the zipper awash with the scent of oxtail soup. Brian zipped it back up. This went on for some time and Seth began to feel irate. In Brian's head, the psychiatrist advice came back to him. *Challenge an authorities sexuality.* This was difficult for him as he bore no ill will to any sexual identification.

"You only want me out of this tent to ravage me." Brian immediately felt bad, that remark was very much out of character and again he questioned the legitimacy of his one-time doctors' advice. *Start a fight for no reason.*

"I want to start a fight on you for no reason!" Brian shouted, encased in his tent.

"I'm sacrificing the tent!" shouted Seth through his name badge. Seth looked intently for a sharp object and settled on a Gerber Bear Grylls army knife. Seth went full throttle at the tent door. He yanked Brian by the ruff of his neck out of the Vango Soul 200 tent. The fondue set knocked onto the tile floor. In front of Seth was a disheveled man in his mid-thirties in a tattered suit, his short hair pushed to the side and he had the beginnings of some facial hair atop a strong chin. He smelled slightly of tangerines and a single bent cigarette poked its head out of his chest pocket. It was at this point that the manager sauntered in to grab his hat. He turned to his right. His soon to be supervisor, if he was not very much mistaken seemed to be grabbing a man by the neck brandishing an exceptionally large knife that made all the other knives feel inadequate.

"Seth! What in holy Hades are you doing to that poor man? Let him go this instant! What is wrong with you!" The manager did not recognize the emotion that he was experiencing. He had nothing to compare it too.

"Maritime law! Maritime law doesn't apply!"

"You have seemed to have gotten pathologically insane in the space of five minutes, what could he possibly have done?" asked the manager.

"Sir, he kept zipping the tent up every time I zipped it down..."

"So you thought to retaliate to that transgression of a zip being tied, yielding a blade was appropriate? That is not a proportional response! And you knackered his tent!" Seth loosened his grip letting go of Brian and dropped the knife on the floor.

"Seth, I'm sorry but you're fired, this is beyond the pale. Collect your things. Never in all my years..."

"But, but... he wants to fight me! Said it himself, this was self-defense! I'm not the bad guy here! You cannot just say no to the world and hide in a tent in a shop, I've never encountered anything so ridiculous! He is crazy! Ok the knife looks bad..." He looked guiltily at the blade next to his nondescript shoe. How he had gone to be so angry in such a short period was perplexing. He had never acted this way. An emotionally healthy person might try to learn from this experience, knowing that inwardly there were some anger issues that needed to be addressed, and that working on himself to be a better person should be of the utmost importance. However, Seth's response to being fired was filled with bitter rhetoric; it contained oddly specific things about his bosses wife's promiscuity and language to make a pirate blush. He had given the best six months of his life, and that one summer internship when he was 15 to this job. He knew that the costa coffee machine was his idea. He knew that he was the brains of the operation and they would all rue the day they crossed Seth Dales, especially the tent-dwelling freak whose reckoning will be swift and ruthless.

He was wrong, this was not a good day. However, he reasoned maybe it was not something external that defined a good day that he was the one with the power to make that happen. It was a choice. He could fixate on the negative, replay in his mind what he should have said, or he could cross the door threshold into a new life, a life of his choosing. If he chose the outlook of positivity, then that is what he will experience. *Maybe this IS a wake-up call* thought Seth. *Maybe this did need to happen, maybe I'll finally write that screenplay, pick up my guitar*. There he was, on the threshold of a new day, a new life. The sun shone and he embraced the sea air. One step to freedom.

What Seth Dales was not aware of was that as he was deep in this new strange positive outlook on that threshold, a puddle of fondue was inching ever closer to him. *The girl at the chemist, what was her name? Sarah! What harm could befall me in finally asking her out?* thought Seth. The puddle was now at his nondescript shoes. *I could patch things up with my Dad, I can go finish my degree in applied mathematics*! Seth found a smile coming across his face. Filled with optimism he took that step. Slipping on the fondue he lost his balance. His last word excitedly left its master.

"Bugger!" falling backwards Seth impaled his head on a piece of the tent pole. His ending was instant.

"JESUS FUCKING CHRIST!" shouted the manager who Brian assumed had a name. The manager reached out with his left hand blindly tapping the counter behind him looking for a phone. He grabbed an angular object and looked at it, only to find an Action Jackson action figure. He muttered under his breath, passed the figure to Brian, and again blindly fumbled for a phone. He thought he had it, looked at it and saw it was a ketchup bottle. He could not keep his eyes off the horror presented to him. He grabbed for the phone again. No that was an old banana he never planned on consuming. Fourth time lucky, his hand clutched the receiver.

However bad it was for the manager, it was worse for Brian, for now at Seth's body stood Death. It had found him. Death pointed dimensionally adjacent to the manager.

"Excuse me, Brian Aldiss, perhaps this is not the best of times, but we need to speak."

The manager in panicked tones was recounting Seth's untimely demise to the emergency services dispatcher over the phone while Brian legged it out of his sanctuary, the Action Jackson action figure held tightly in his grip. He jumped in his car that he had finally found earlier that day.

"It's an apparition, it is not real, it can't touch me, it can't interact with me, it's a figment of my imagination, a stress-induced construct... nothing more." He wondered about his death, the ever-present polite grim reaper. about how he would die. Perhaps behind the wheel and this very car. The local kids would say-

"Remember that dude that died in that car?" and the friend would say-

"No." And then the first kid would say-

"Actually did I make that up?" and that would be how he would be remembered. Brian did everything to free his mind from Seth and Death as an ambulance now sat outside the Celtic Corner Sports Shop. A hearse would have been more appropriate. Perhaps a structural engineer to assess the damage to the tent. A local dog to help with the fondue. He blamed himself, it was just his pathological leaning. Still, he tried to occupy himself. He checked the fuel gauge. It was full, it always was. He checked the key. That was present. The lighter was there. The radio was on low volume. He could make out some country music from a classical radio station.

He checked his mirror and manoeuvred it to face behind him. *That was strange* he thought. *I don't remember having a coat back there*. The dimensions were not right; there was something off about it, something sort of three-dimensional. It was evident that he had lost his faculties, all of them. Mind, mentality, sense of clarity, reason. It was like the talking cactus from earlier, it was lack of sleep, it was stress… it was moving. But that didn't mean anything. *It still wasn't real* he kept telling himself.

A bony finger from a sleeve reached to the back of his head and still, he tried to rationalize it. *It's a friend playing a prank* he thought, it didn't matter that he didn't have any friends because that would just be picking on people that didn't have friends.

"You're not real! You're an apparition, you can't touch me, you can't interact with me you're a construct!" A bony finger poked the back of his head and it hurt.

"This sort of thing happens all the time!" At this moment in time, the term denial could not be more apt. Brian had a manic smile as he waited to pull out. The bony finger became a bony hand and reached for his cigarettes. This was ok for Brian if a fleshless hand fancied a cigarette who was he to argue? And yes, there goes his lighter too, the one that didn't work, the one he just bought this morning against his will.

"I left a game of scrabble to be here, and I was winning." Brian did not like that voice. The deep monotone verbalization sank into his bones. He demanded of himself to confront this intruder, to demand an explanation. Perhaps threaten to alert the authorities or at least at the very bare minimum to turn around, but he knew none of that would ever happen. The cactus was one thing, he could exist in this world knowing that occasionally sentience may embody office décor but to be fair the cactus only barely spoke. This situation involved a hand devoid of flesh stealing his cigarettes and speaking about scrabble.

"I had the word Quantize. 76 points. Of course, that included the 50 point bonus for using all my letters." He could just leave; he could just get out of his car and walk away. Or jog, maybe even sprint...

He would have to buy some more cigarettes and maybe a new car but that small inconvenience was certainly favorable to the stress-induced talking hallucination. Against his better judgment, he first decided to face his tormentor indirectly via the rearview mirror. It was indeed a worn black hooded cloak with smoke protruding from it.

The back seat of this car was anally cleaned, and Death's sinuses were attacked by the scented tree. It was a black Ford Merkur, a sturdy sensible car. The cigarette was short-lived and he stubbed the thing in an ashtray.

"My ethos in awkward situations is to do as the host does. In this circumstance, it is smoking a cigarette. I must confess perhaps in this case that ethos is not all-encompassing for I feel this particular vice is not one that agrees with me. Perhaps I am doing it wrong?" Death sighed at the nubbed cigarette. In the length of a plank (time quanta) he processed every instance in history in which a cigarette was smoked; he seemed to have imitated it quite correctly. Perhaps, he thought, if he tried again, he would like it. It was now he looked up to see Brian sprinting past an ambulance.

Chapter 10

"I told you I will not have it!" *How did it come to this?* Satan thought with black blood pumping through his veins. If he could, he'd swap this moment with being sober at Oktoberfest with sausages in his pants, being set upon by hungry Germans.

"But dad! I can't always live in your footsteps, I don't want to do what you do, I don't have to believe what you believe!"

"Do you know what you are asking? Do you know how utterly inappropriate this is? Do you not understand everything that we are? Do you know what this will do to us? I said no and I mean it, get those silly ideas out of your oddly shaped head immediately! I will hear no more about this!"

"They are NOT stupid ideas; it makes sense! It calls out to me! I know this is who I must be, and you can't stop me!" There were many things he despised about his son. He was an oddly proportioned gangly young man with soft unoffending effeminate features, an awkward stance, and an overbite. He was inexplicitly estranged from the reality that he had constructed for him, to condition him for Evil. Such a controlling grasp was what he perceived to be an admirable trait. But those constructs had a way of escaping his son. He went out of his way to purge influences he deemed undesirable. He did not stop at hope, nor happiness, family or love. He would mould groins for his Action Men as to deter from the dolls otherwise asexual nature. Generously endowing the figures had an unforeseen adverse effect. Proportionally, his son felt inadequate His maleness was somewhat crippled and this may have led to the baton lessons.

He hated his son's weak chin and the fact he listened to jazz which was just noise that had gotten bored. He hated his open-minded nature which he thought was plain stupid and frankly, dangerous. He hated that his son brought out a desire in him to make a list in his head of all the things he despised about the mistaken little crotch goblin every time he opened his mouth with his friend Thomas. Thomas was a great interpretive dancer - he should have seen him in the summer when he blew all the other boys away... the boys.

The only reason he had tolerated his son's existence, albeit on a razor's edge for this long was the lone distant hope that his manufactured environment would protect his son from certain evils. Like the baton teacher who, he told his son, had happened to meet his end in a totally and utterly unavoidable accident. It seemed the baton had head-butted a hammer several times before throwing himself into some feral bullets. The library statement was that this was a totally and utterly unavoidable accident and after that press release, an anonymous grant was given to the library, which has since thrived with custom and had never been happier.

"Oh yes, I can!" He had to remind himself what he was talking about, the inverted rant left empty air in the room. With his ears feeling numb and no medical training to speak of, he surmised he had just had a stroke. There was something about footsteps. He had completely lost his train of thought.

"Jeeves! Have him killed! And bring me his shoes!"

"You can't just have me killed you fucking psychopath! This job has done a number on you hasn't it dad?" Satan had an annoying habit of smiling when being insulted. It was hard to try and fathom his intents wants or desires. It was almost impossible to discern how he was feeling, because he sported a very similar array of expressions for almost all occasions. This was not one of those circumstances and instead, he sported an expression that said *I didn't order salt*! It was not his intent, but he gave it no thought as he was vehemently beyond anger.

"I mean it; pass me that trident I'll do it myself! Get here, you weird freaky oddball! Stay still you spotted pheasant!" He was at this point chasing him around a Bordeaux dark oak mahogany table. That was pretty much his only objective and intention. After seven laps his legs started to give way. It was proving a little more difficult than he would have thought, however this was an impulse affair and positively tedious, eventually monotonous and ultimately fruitless with a side consequence of certainty about the stroke.

"Do you know as to whom it is you are talking to? I am Satan! The desolate! The barren! Behemoth, I am the serpent! The sour fruit! Your mother's sister calls me Santa but she's verbally dyslexic." The last comment he felt did not truly express the volcano inside, so he took some peptic medicine.

"Yeah, and it's typical, it has to be. I had a war with God! Look at me I can't grow, I'm a two-dimensional character, all I know is malevolence. I'm a sadistic bastard!"

"Yes, son but Christianity!? I'll have you know when I was in the garden with Adam…" A strange pride at that name made him look intently at one spot in a corner of the room. Reminiscing of times past. Between an empty spider's nest and some uninspired graffiti, it was as if that spot was the focal point of all that defined him, all his successes.

A man ran screaming through the room.
"He's messed up man! He's messed up! He's bleeding; he's in a bad way man!" Shouted a beatnik wearing straight-leg cigarette pants, a black turtle-neck sweater, loafers a beret and a pair of dark oversized glasses. He stroked his beard manically.
"Get him some medical attention! For the love of God! Get the man some cheesy pasta!"
"That was not normal… even here. Is the society of improv back? I thought they lost the war to the custodians." Said Satan temporally making allowances for the trespasses of his son to observe the surreal presentation.
"Yeah… it was a little… not normal." Said his son as well in a state of displacement.
"A little inconsiderate… you know this being hell and screaming for the love of God, for the love of God in front of me; Satan."
"Dad I think it was just for the love of God, he said it once."
"Well, still. This is a big place. Billions of damned souls and he runs past me… Jeeves? Who was that man?" Jeeves was a butler, his father was a butler and his father before that, also his father and his father was a French existentialist, that spent his life pretending to be a koala to make some strange statement about the price of beans. Then everyone agreed he wasn't quite right and the butler gene must have skipped a generation, but the French existentialist koala man's father was a butler, and his father before that. His sons were butlers, they never played with Action Jackson action figures, they played with butler dolls and would follow their friend's Action Jackson action men with tiny plates of sandwiches and tea. Being a butler was all he had ever known, but he was smarter than most people he had ever known, and due to the butler code of knowing one's place, his only outlet of character depth was a slight dry cynicism.
"That sir, is the incarnation of your anxiety. Remember that curry you found in the fridge of your first apartment in the sixth circle of hell? Opposite the MOT garage, the curry that was florescent electric blue and

demanded you killed it? that it could not bare to live? that every second was agony? Well upon consumption of said curry for a week in your delirious state your symptoms manifested a reality unto themselves. Your psychosis and paranoia incarnate are in therapy and together have convinced themselves that they are not in hell. We have hunted down your ego and had it shot, courtesy of the Douglas Adam's fan club."

"Well, whatever it is it's a nuisance, have it killed! But over there in the pit, this is new carpet."

"Yes, you tempter of elderly gentlemen." It took a second for everything to converge to its original heated atmosphere.

"When." Started Satan calmly "I was in the garden with Adam..."

"Oh blow the trumpet of Gabriel for the inevitable walk along repetition boulevard; let us all bask in this story for the millionth time! God deemed mankind a liability when it came to free will and you saved them. Yeah, we know, but was that for them or was it just so you can stick another thorn in God's paw!?"

"That's it, get here you little bastard!" Again, he refrained from killing the boy in the distant hope that he would fulfil his destiny at the throne of perdition though on many occasions he had come remarkably close, the trouble being he could never get close enough. His son had been blessed with spindly legs, and no-one in their right mind would interfere with this family affair, which meant everyone did because no-one in hell was really in their right minds to start with, and if they had been when they came to hell they certainly weren't now. His son had recently hired a golem to guard his door at night knowing his father was afraid and adverse to golems. The inhabitants of hell awed and ahhed when seeing Satan's son running like a whippet, with the heavy bumbling Satan destroying half of hell trying to catch him. It showed a rare set of family values.

"Classic!" His son shouted over his shoulder as he ran quite literally for his life. "Contradict me and I react with violence. Get away from me you horned beast! What the fuck do you think you're doing? This isn't normal, tell him Jeeves! This is exactly what the therapist is on about! You never listen to me!" Satan had backed his son into a corner and advanced. Yes, today was the day he killed him; he was sure of it.

"Oh, is that what this is? Daddy doesn't listen to me, so I'll fuck him over with Jesus? is this just a way to get a thorn in my paw? God is a megalomaniac! He's genocidal, homophobic and a racist child!

Probably... he never showed it, or said it, or even implied it, but I always suspected! He is the worst character in history! The whore of contradiction. When something good happens to a human it's God's grace, his *divine* will, his mysterious ways. It's not mysterious, it's non-existent, he doesn't earn that. His propaganda demands that they believe that! All this whilst he does fuck all. To further spit in my eye when his stupid creation known as the Universe inevitably founders then it is my doing? To me it seems he doesn't help, intervene or guide, but takes credit when by chance good happens. When it goes wrong, which is all to do with him by the way, then who spits in my eye? He does! What do I have to be guilty of? The tower of Babel fell because of him. What loving divine unerring being will kill them all with a flood, and then have the arrogance of saving those who please him? Unerring I ask, creating knowing it'll disappoint! I was there for man and stood in the face of his cruelty!"

    It was at this point that his son tried to part himself from an old habit of theology and shouting and through his therapy he tried another option, love. He wanted to establish an 'of the moment intervention' with his true intentions clouded, it was either genuine concern for his father's growth or genuine concern for his skin. Maybe a little of both.

    "Dad, you shout from the rooftops, justifying your transgressions, taking pride in what you tried to do in the name of good, and then shout from those same rooftops rhetoric of your evil and impending wrath. With one hand you are drawing us close and with the other pushing us away. The therapist says you have a lot of issues with God and that you must find closure. You have so many issues because of your unhealthy destructive relationship with God that couldn't progress, all because you were crippled with jealousy. You did things in the so-called name of good, but you did it to undermine him. You convinced yourself that when the action was taken against you for such said acts, it was victimisation. You have created a whole identity out of this, ignoring what is in your head. I don't think you are this murdering irate son of a bitch at all."

    For a second he thought it may have worked and for a second Satan said 'well...' and looked around weighing things up. As that brief spec of empathy fleeting and distant appeared, a column of divine light shone out of his head. Satan was after all once an angel, and a divine knowing, sometimes against his will, released in the unfettered stream of consciousness and Godly wisdom, released with the sound of church bells and chimes. It was, upon the first witness, an unnerving sight to see Satan understand everything, his face contorted to express that knowledge. He composed himself quickly and shook away the light.

"Ok see that guy over there?"

"Yeah, that's Michael, the blind pianist."

"See this trident?"

"…yeah."

"See him dead on the floor now?"

"My point is Dad, I think you have to admit some hard truths. I think that you have been less than honest with yourself for far too long. I mean you're always threatening to kill me and by rights you fucked me up in ways mom wouldn't imagine but with God, I see past that. The therapist has made me see that. Humans live their lives in a spiritual limbo. A state of wanting. Even the most devout can only live on faith. There is no measurable certainty, something that can be quantified with evidence and reason. It is a state of confidence and nothing more. Yet still, they pray. I know God exists, solipsism aside, his presence in me is like Shangri-la."

"Wait for the therapist! Jeeves have her hung drawn and quartered!" Jeeves elegantly left the room. Satan would have accepted this as a phase until his son pulled out a cross, holding it warmly with a smile on his face. Satan started to steam in its presence, he was now plainly alight.

"Do you mind?!" his son tucked the cross away.

"Meet with God dad, seriously." With that his son left from the corner, very slowly and deliberately, meekly and cautiously, and once at a safe distance he turned it into a run. Satan, the ruler of hell, the fallen angel, had to watch his spawn run away like a little girl. Satan sat down on the dead pianist and with his right hand grasped his trident. He took a deep breath.

"How can I see past the whole 'damnation' thing, we haven't spoken since Job." He muttered. Jeeves came into view.

"Your son sir, he wanted me to…" Jeeves seemed to struggle with this last part

"…lay it *down* to you." Jeeves had a way, through good breeding, to never impose himself, nor stay in anyone's presence for even the slightest amount too long. This was because when people's feelings and emotions come out, he found himself becoming too emotionally attached. It was just a product of his loyalty. He was in hell because as an embodiment of the phrase, the butler did it.

"If you must Jeeves." Satan lifted his trident from the limp body, the blood black and white.

"He said he has a 'group' and pardon me, sir, this is not my opinion and hardly my business and these are his words. He wishes me to inform you that Hell is a changing place. Brimstone and fire have been replaced by work offices, unions and cigarette breaks. Rather than eternal torment we have funny e-mails with dancing postmen. We have changed, so has he (God I believe), you should realise that and help yourself. Bye dad."

"And what do you think Jeeves?"

Jeeves cleared his throat

"It is not my place to think sir."

"And that is how they all should be. That's why I like you Jeeves. He shall live! For now…"

"Yes, your er, odiousness."

So meeting with God. That little shit might be on to something, how can I turn this to my advantage? What plan can I concoct? I mean I have avoided him out of principle. It's not like hey one day you're there with three winged bitches for every hugely endowed beast of a man. Or Appletini's that'll knock you out for a week. And then sent to a dog eat dog, man eats man and Fred the four-headed creature from the seventh ring that'll eat anything other than Doug the uneatable and be ok with it. I suppose it has left me a little bitter, I just, I didn't deserve that, I didn't. He over-reacted, he always did. Ten thousand years I've been here twiddling my thumbs, there is only so much you can do with a trident."

"Sir I mean your er, filicidal-ness."

"I don't know what that means."

"Neither do I, sir, it's just hard after ten thousand years to come up with new synonyms. Ways of reflecting oh what's the point, I have three heads."

"I mean at first it was unbearable, I waited on his call, waited for him to take me back and I gave up hope. When he finally tried to get in touch, well I was bitter, twisted, hurt even. He still calls from time to time. Did you know that I got a postcard from Liamfwrog in Wales the other day? I was invited by Death to celebrate God's 13.8 billion year party. A strange entity that Death. You know he's older than me? Some say he may be older than God. No one knows. Gives me a tingle down my spine.

Never been comfortable around that guy. It is decided! I shall speak to a professional. Bring me the therapist!"

"Your slightly erroneous, you just had her killed."

"Well, what do we have?"

"A slightly baffled P.E teacher…"

"See, that's what I mean! It is this place! This hell. Oh, this would not usually bother me but bringing up God! I suppose I play a practical use, but I feel bad you know? I mean I have tribes of weird people with bones hanging off them, crocodile teeth, never done a thing wrong except but not believing in God. But that's a sin punishable by certain damnation in the pits of hell, and given these people never heard of God, at least one that doesn't resemble a goat with wings and a bad haircut, here they are! If it wasn't for the pinball machine I'm sure they'd be quite an uprising."

"Your agnostic towards the mentally impaired. I am informed that after a bit of paperwork, such matters are being resolved through your son and the HR department in concert, with the grand pillars judicial system of the high plane. Rectifying such mistakes is the goal of both departments. Hell, really is a changing place."

"Do you know I had a guy here last week that used a condom in his only ever sexual experience, died of a heart attack and came here? I mean that has never happened, the explanation was that he honestly believed he deserved to be here, and so here he came. What sort of God I ask?"

"Did you not kill him with that silver trident with the red trimming?"

"Well yes… there was something about him, a rebellious dangerous, over-throwing look to him."

"He was eighty-four, blind and resembled Gandhi," said Jeeves somewhat overstepping his place.

"Yes, he did a little didn't he. So, concerning God. I can try and out-do him! Act like a big shot, make out that this whole Hell thing is working out for me, the BEST thing that ever happened to me, and then spread rumours behind his back, break him down from the foundations. No, it'll never work. Maybe dayside. How do you kill God exactly?"

"Er, your defender of Scientology, Doctor Who is starting."

"Then cancel my appointments."

"I'm sure Judas can wait an hour."

"And get me some curly fries on the double Jeeves!"

"Curly sir?"

"Have you ever known me to eat it any other way Jeeves?"

"Well your spoutiness, there was that phase when you insisted on the blood of virgins sprinkled over a light layer of cheese but I think that was mostly to impress the siren of Mesopotamia. Or a result of those mushrooms we found in your son's sock draw."

"Oh yes. I mean, how dare you question me! And I do not care if I asked you that question, not the *how dare you* to question me, that was quite an important nay integral to the point! I say curly and I mean curly! You are slipping Jeeves, I can see it in your eyes! I will not have it! Now, leave me!"

"Yes, your surveyor and thief of forgotten socks. Meeting with God tomorrow?"

"Jeeves that's brilliant! I'll see you'll get a promotion of sorts with that sharp mind! Something in agriculture. I've always thought of you making a good scarecrow. I'll meet with God!"

"Yes of course you appreciator of daytime channel five television."

"You see I'm not a bad guy, I mean yes the whole Satan thing and yes I'm a murderer, ate my fair share of enemies but I've never even killed a spider in the bath. You know what scratch that, I never wanted to be a bad guy. Well, I like that I am a bad guy, I wouldn't have it any other way. There was a time when I never set out to be a bad guy. Well, overthrowing God being my prime directive taking most of my time… I suppose er, I never should have been a bad guy. It was them, they made me this way. I was too radical, too insightful, they couldn't handle me. No, I was on fire."

"You're on fire now."

"What?!"

"Nothing Lucifer."

"It's just he pisses me off! He's the kind of guy that will write every sentence with an exclamation mark like he's so fucking happy!"

"We talked about the language, you said you were going to work on that," said the P.E teacher meeting Satan for the first time and enjoying the role play. It was either this or the mandated hula hoop hour.

"He's smug. You see I wanted to shift the whole *evil* façade. I'm allowing drastic changes and seeing them as fundamental; Jeeves says

I'm behind the times, out of touch, losing the battle, but he's wrong! The tyranny has been toned down and I think that's progress."

"It's a good start, the Jeeves thing is a lie isn't it? He didn't say that did he..."

"It's all files and computers nowadays in place of autocracy. But this is what I wanted to talk to you about. I thought, you know, the family angle, have myself a son, fresh blood, take Hell to new places. Now the little bastard wants to be Christian. Why find good in God? Why not in himself, in me, change together?"

"So we talked extensively about God and how he has affected you, but do you plan on doing something about it? Your son has come to me."

"You know what the last thing God said to me was? He said that all things were counted."

"Er Lucifer? My question?"

"What does that even mean? I like that whistle by the way. Is that the Waltons Key of C brass penny whistle? You're right, I shouldn't hide in the pit, twiddling my proverbial thumbs while he hogs all the glory atop his Hidskjalf throne, he stole that from Odin by the way! Whiling away his days drinking frozen strawberry daiquiri's and smoking Upmann half corona Cuban cigars. With a breeze through his damn stain glass windows and not a corpse in sight, good for some aye Eustace?' The PE teacher was called Mark. 'The respect and admiration, I had that once. I deserve to have that again! But look at me, I don't even have the respect of my son. The whole damnation thing, I just don't know how to get over it. I need closure, it's as simple as that, meet the guy tomorrow. Great work Eustace. Have a promotion! Something in accounting. And give me that whistle."

Chapter 11

"I can't sit here forever," muttered a distressed Famine sitting in the Gwesty Holland hotel pub with War and Pestilence. To Pestilence's left a short man in a Falls Worth Harris tweed Baker Boy cap ran to the men's room to violently empty every morsel of nourishment that he had consumed in the last 36 hours. To Famines right, a guy wearing the same hat ordered a triple cheeseburger. Behind War, a small child kicked the wall.

"Some mead in your finest goat horn," demanded War of the barkeep, smashing his clenched fist upon the table. The bartender looked to his left. Carlsberg glasses. He looked in front of him under the bar. His screenplay. It was about a humble bartender making it big in Hollywood by managing to sell a screenplay. To his right were the goblets and goat horns. He tried to find any logical reason as to why these obscure receptacles had materialized and came up with squat. He was not even sure he knew what mead was but right there on tap was Kinsale mead with a little logo of a drunk wolf. The bartender, who, like a lot of people, had a pair of hands and used them to carefully ferry the drink to the seven-foot human-shaped monolith. He suddenly had an urge to finally tell his postmen that the deliveries go in the porch, not near it, not by it, not in the bush, but *inside* the porch. He even left a note once but still the parcel was in the bush

"Shouldn't she have come by now? Could we not have met in a less public forum? War is getting some strange looks and I think we're affecting these people."

"It's gots its charms!" War mightily declared happily, knowing most things have charm.

"So, Death left abruptly, mentioned a Brian Aldiss and buggered off, leaving us to have to pay for the Daly Anglesea post from that enterprising 12-year-old from two tents over. Our one got crab faeces on it, and I hadn't finished the crossword puzzle." Famine looked around the pub. He scoured it for anything worth noting and came up short.

"You know? I kind of like Llanfwrog on the west coast of Anglesey Wales," started Pestilence. Famine felt a shiver down his spine and into his tail bone.

"No, I mean it! I know, Famine, that you have described this place as a fetid cesspool of human flotsam and jetsam. But look, this is nice.

War has his horn of mead. I'm enjoying this purple concoction. How can you be down with a good pint of Guinness? There is a bowl of Bombay mix, a couple of fruit machines and I have to say, this aged leather seat is comfort incarnate, it truly is." The silence that ensued disagreed with everything he had just said.

"Not a scantily clad lady in sight..." sighed War. It was then that Pestilence was overcome with joy as he spotted the lavatory which he had to investigate, leaving Famine with War.

"War can I ask? You are happy, right?" War wiped the mead from his beard, grunted and smiled

"Yeah, Ime's happy! Always have been since I was a nipper!"

Famine had a pit in his stomach.

"What is that like? I mean happiness, joy in all things? How are you not downtrodden by the drudgery and suffering? How did you live with our old kettle?"

"Well, I guess mead helps. Look outside you see rain. I see the Gods washing us new and clean. A guy is rude to you, yous mutter under your breath *guy is rude to me* and I has meself a new hat! And whatever else of interest he has, that's how I gots this pocket watch. I guess it's the old outlook thing. But its something inside, its honour, its adventure, its pleasures!"

This outlook fascinated Famine.

"You see I'm the opposite, rain is there to rid you of any morsel of hope you managed to muster in your waking moments. When someone is rude to me, well, that's my idea of normal. Only freaks smile and wish you good morning while waving, people on buses avoid sitting next to those people. I don't know, the closest I got to true happiness in the last month was when we found Death's secret kettle. Can I ask you another question?"

War allowed this with a wave of his hand.

"How did you get into this line of work?"

"Same as you, I should imagine. So God is in all things, right? He also is all things. We are likes expressions, a part of a big thing. An aspect if you choose. I was formed in thought and asked what I was. I screamed, "I AM WAR!" Next thing I know a hooded fella asked me what colour horse I want. As for the kettle, nice way to wake yourself up in the morning."

Pestilence returned, producing a small pad of paper and a stubby pencil. jotting down his findings.

"6.2 I should imagine all things considered," he said.

"How did it go?" asked War.

"Paper was single ply, quite course so not great, but it's got one of those toilet guys, gave me some paprika aftershave that assaulted my senses." Pestilence put away his pad and nursed his purple concoction.

Static began to form on an empty chair at their table. For a second a woman manifested, only to fizzle out of existence. War looked confused, but then the pub menu left him confused. Static buzzed once more. This time she was here a little longer, and even spoke

"Testing, testing..." She fizzled before going up in a wisp of smoke.

"Give her a second." said Famine. The static formed once more into an attractive red-headed woman who looked to be in her late 20's. Her eyes were wide apart, and bangs covered her forehead. She donned a horse-bit print silk-twill shirt and skinny jeans with a pair of Buddhist prayer shoes. She wore a painite gem on a thin silver chain. Noticing it, she tucked it away.

"Hey, guys! Famine, looking well-fed? Pestilence, a real healthy pink to those cheeks and War?" War excitedly paid attention. She would always give him gifts, he was not sure why. She pulled out a kitten from a bag. It was half the size of his hands. Famine suspected that kitten was not long for this world. He gently looked at the tag on the collar that read *Mitsy*. War was in love.

"Muse, it's great to see you here. We haven't spoken since, well hmmm...I'm trying to think. If only someone can give me some inspiration!" Muse smiled at Famine who had been besotted by her for millennia.

"A drink? Drink? Drink to quench your thirst, liquid for sustenance. Look, I'm getting all silly!" Famine swayed his arms limply back and forth.

"Wine? I'll get your wine...wine is good-mannered! That's normal. I know normal." Famine approached the barkeep who immediately craved some Bombay mix.

"Your best wine sir!" The barkeep picked up a hard backed book labelled *wines and you, a bond for all time* and perused it intently.

"Our best wine is a 1787 chateau Lafite..."

"Sounds good, ring her up!"

"That will be a £156,450."

Having only £12.56 to his name, Famine ran over to War.

"Can I borrow that acquired pocket watch from you War? Won't be a moment, Muse!" He ran back to the bar pulling a hamstring. The barkeep did not look too pleased. The Bombay mix in the bowl was gone.

"Look at the pretty watch, er..." he glanced at the name badge that simply read *Landlord*.

"Er, Landlord."

"What of it?" was the gruff response.

"What of it? Look at its fine construction. It's a Tissot brand whatever that is... not just any metal that. What would you say that's worth, aye?"

"Not £156,450 mate... Now do you want a drink or what?"

Famine hoped it did not have to come to this. He started to sway the pocket watch in front of the Landlords eyes.

"As you can see Landlord, using my powers of hypnotism, I have your entire consciousnesses in my grasp, its malleable form molded by my whim. You will pour me a glass of the 1768 chateau Lafite on the house, and you will be compelled to give me twenty pounds."

The landlord looked at Famine like he was an idiot. To accentuate his lack of being hypnotized, he made a point to look deeply into his watch and again met Famine's gaze.

"Ok then Landlord, house red it is." It was always worth a shot. He did not fully understand, War was always so easily hypnotized but Famine guessed that was due to fewer faculties to subdue. He reasoned more lessons with Death were in order.

"Ok, that will be £12.55, sir." That left him, by his calculation, one English penny. He walked back to the table.

"Not getting yourself a drink?" asked Muse to Famine. Famine looked forlorn, one penny in his hand.

"I'll get this round bunch of lightweights!" shouted War scaring a local cat. On his trousers was a sizable pouch with a drawstring. He emptied some of its contents into his enormous grip. Famine saw at least a dozen gold coins within his grasp, and that was just a small portion of what must have been in the pouch.

"War, the currency, the abundant currency!" War looked perplexed.

"Part of my treasure, everyone must have treasure. Can't pillage and battle pirates without getting a bit of treasure. Don't you have treasure?" His request was completely sincere.

"I have a penny to my name! That's not just an idiom, I have a penny, look at it!" He presented the penny. "Look how sad and pathetic it is!" He must not have been coming across well to Muse.

"I know we spend most of our time adjacent to this reality but, while I'm here, I'm poor and have nothing except that secret fiver in the pizza box that's been atop that shelf for weeks, and even the crabs got to that."

War looked glumly to his friend.

"Would you like some treasure? I've gots lots of it all over this planet. From Alaska to Peru! You know hows the caravan left wheel is sunken whens we drive?

"I always suspected, without being rude, that that was just because of you..."

"Me and the quarter tonne bounty of gold silver gems and artefacts!"

"Why did you never mention that to us?"

"You never asked, just assumed yous all had some treasure... here, take this pouch. Buy more than a pig with that!"

Famine held the beautiful gold in his hands. GOLD in HIS hands..."

Muse spoke up when she felt she had a chance to join the conversation. First, though, she took a sip of the house wine

"Free gold, can I get in on that?"

War shrugged happy to share. He reached for a pocket inside his fur coat and produced a handful of assorted coins. Pestilence coughed waiting for his turn, but War was oblivious to the subtle intention.

"So, the reason you texted, something urgent?" Muse asked, admiring a phoenix etched into a coin. Pestilence began to think there was no treasure for him.

"First, how are the eight sisters? How is life, what's er... new?" bumbled Famine.

"The sisters are fine; they all have triplets. Christmas time is a bitch, to buy the presents I must start saving in March. Life is good, spreading inspiration, that whole deal. Well, I would have to say it's the hole in the sky that has us all completely baffled. No one has seen God, we think he's locked himself in the office. My bar is doing fantastic though! Lots of interesting characters from across the Omniverse. Dionysus is a regular."

"Ah, the ethereal bar in the ineffable plane. Also, we hate that guy," smiled Famine. Muse looked around the bar. She focused on the landlord who just that second had an idea of how to reduce his mortgage.

"So where is Death? Always fascinated with that guy. You know he's older than me right? I think some say he's older than God."

"Yeah, I think I've heard that a few times, only second-hand like. Death is a bit sparse with any details pertaining to his beginnings. All we know was that two dragons may have been involved. Now though, Death is a bit evasive with his whereabouts. That is part of the reason we wanted to tap you. You see, Death has a connection to God, an affinity. They are like two sides of a coin. They are entangled, what affects one affects the other. *He* knew what that lack of reality in that tear in space was the second he observed it. It's God himself. God has left the universe, the multiverse, the Omniverse, or so Death says. Without God's integration into this plain, the Omniscience Death possesses has become somewhat limp and ineffective."

Muse contemplated this.

"So why tap me? Surely this is an archangel matter? I'm just a Muse, as important as kismet. I'm not sure what I can accomplish."

"First of all, I have spent time with Seraphim, the caretakers of God's throne. They are a deplorable class of snakes, always biting on each other heels. God's absence would be an opportunity for them. One will try to take the throne and I guarantee civil war will ensue. We needed someone we can trust to try and find some answers. We have known each other since time immemorial, and I have complete faith in you. We need to get an idea of where God is. As the owner of the ethereal bar, you have access to an Omniverse worth of travelers from all planes and dimensions. If anyone is to find out any morsel of information, it's you. I remember you telling me that on occasion you have had the custom of three gentlemen in Brioni Vanquish 11 suits and Flavio black flat brim Moda fedoras. That you could not read them like they were something unknown. Outside of your influence. If anyone like that passes your way come to this plane and tell us. But otherwise, keep this under your hat. From what I remember your bar has an ancient dust-covered portal to God's complex, does it not?"

"It hasn't been used in centuries but yes, we have a direct route. I keep it in the cupboard with my pop vinyl collection. Just got Kurt Cobain. Long lonely nights, fathers credit card and next day delivery, a dangerous combination. OK, I'll do it. Anything to help. I'm sure someone knows something. I wonder if the barkeep will accept ancient treasure?" Muse sauntered off to the bar.

"You're besotted!" Pestilence grinned through his thick ginger hair. Famine threw a coy smile, retracted it immediately and muttered.

"You don't know what you're talking about. Why didn't she say something? Doesn't matter if she did, I don't care, I'm a rock! An island I tell you!"

"Was on this island once," said War. Pestilence and Famine looked expectantly at War, after a few seconds it was evident that that was the entire anecdote.

"You're infatuated! You are, I have not seen you smile this much, well... ever! I think she likes you too you know."

"And what is that based on exactly Pestilence?" Famine looked behind him to the bar and a smile of longing attacked his face. Pestilence just laughed into his dwindling purple concoction. Muse came back with two fingers of Johnny Walker whiskey.

"So I guess the forthcoming riders of the apocalypse have found themselves out of the water. No God? Does that mean no End times? I will hate it when it comes, I have a fantastic loft apartment in Birmingham. You should come to visit someday," said Muse, softly holding Famine's hand. For the first time in millennia, blood made it to Famines face giving it a red complexion.

"I mean, I'll have to check my schedule but could pencil that in! Yellow pencil, a pencil with lead..." Famine flustered. "We use pencils to write things down..." he sang. He swiftly cleared his throat

"I mean, talking to Death, he said were in a grey area at the moment, not being commanded by God, we are not sure if we have autonomy or agency in the matter."

"Maybe you need an executive decision, but who am I to interfere? So War, how have you been my love?" Muse pushed her hair to one side.

"If this ends time are to be then that they be. All good things must come to an end is what I am told, but why does it have to come to that I ask? Spending these last few weeks in..." War stopped, looked around and saw an Anglesea daily newspaper.

"… in Llanfwrog Anglesey Wales," he said with great exertion.

War chimed in.

"I have gots to meet lots of these humans. Yes, there is the troubles but there are the goods too, and it just stops? Seems a little unfair, unwarranted. Isn't that right Mitsy! I also gots a new fur coat. I paid one hundred and ten pounds for it!"

"War, you are unappreciated in your time, one day we will all wake up to find, in your way, you are wiser than us all. You do make a good point though. Doctrine dictates after the ascension and the annihilation of time, Death, War, Famine and Pestilence incur their wrath. Well I'm preaching to the choir. But I will miss this place, something will rise from its ashes. But what these people have achieved? Only 12 thousand years ago they created agriculture, in a short century or two they went from blimps to jet engines. Their ingenuity and creativity, their exploration, in the world and within, their tenacity and boundless potential even shocks me, and I'm Muse. Well, I think that's me done. When you remember where you lost your keys, and that random spark of light hits you and they're they are under the cat, think of me. Pestilence?"

Pestilence looked up and the Muse flicked a golden coin to him.

"War, take care of Mitsy and Famine? Honestly, make time to see the Birmingham loft apartment. Thanks for the wine and I will do my best to eke out some information for you. All sorts cross my path. Adios amigos." Muse turned into static and disappeared, then reappeared again for a moment, before the static dissipated in a caramel scented wisp.

"Ok Famine, did you not see that? The hand on your hand, the invitation, *twice*, to visit her loft apartment. I'm telling you she's interested, and don't think I didn't see those rosy cheeks. As Pestilence, I have complete authority over the physiological responses associated with emotion and desire... how the body reacts. And you, my cynical contemptuous emotionless husk, have a chance to be happy for once. You are smitten!"

"Take that back or I'll eat an eel pie in front of you. As far as physiological responses go, I know you'll immediately, upon my consumption of said eel pie, run into the nearest outhouse to vacate your entire life's worth of cheap whiskey and egg sandwiches. She's just a friend. I mean yes, she's beautiful, with a litany of great attributes and yes I can still smell the caramel, and ok, every time we meet I go weak at the knees, but I *do* love her!!"

The slip of the tongue made Famine bow his head. Pestilence let out a guttural laugh.

"Ok so I'm madly in love with her, what do you want from me!"

"I just want you to be happy," said Pestilence somewhat condescendingly.

"Barkeep! Another goat horn of mead!" banged War on the table. A minute later the Landlord walked over and passed, with both hands, a goat horn of mead for War. In a disassociated state he also gave Famine a glass of 1787 chateau Lafite and handed him twenty pounds.

Chapter 12

Brian Aldiss could run no longer. He had no idea where he was. He looked to a street sign that read *Red Wharf Bay*. That could have been anywhere. He was hungry and fatigued in his tattered suit. To his left was a pub, *The Tavern On The Bay*. If ever he needed a drink, it was now.

"And stay out!" shouted a man that was far more handsome than he needed to be with a complexion that can be blamed on Charlotte Tilbury hydration skincare.

"You haven't heard the last of Pete Sweeney! A curse on all your houses, a curse on your fat mom! Have a good life with the curses I bring upon you! Curses I tell you until the day is long!"

The drunken postman lazily leaning to his left argued with his balance, the balance won, and the postman lay face-first on a fire hydrant.

"I lost my hat!" he whimpered.

The handsome man shifted to the side for Brian's custom. He looked at the tattered suit, back at the postman and lamented his vocation. He had dreams of an upmarket high-class establishment, the kind of place where sophisticated artists and poets would drink coffee and discuss Immanuel Kant and Rene Descartes. A place of atmosphere. With a sad whistle, he returned to his pub and his broken dreams. Brian found himself alone at the bar. Three elderly gentlemen were playing a game of cards Brian did not recognize.

"A three, a six, a queen and 5 on the role of the dice! That's Metza!" declared a small ancient man in a deep Eastern European accent, his coat was 2 sizes too big, and he looked as if he had lived in pubs the majority of his life.

"Not Metza, I have a 7 of clubs, and..." he shook a magic 8 ball.

"It is decidedly so, now what's Metza?" The other two old men groaned as the victor pushed all the foreign currency toward him. A rock-ola bubbler vinyl jukebox was playing some generic country-rock song and there was a great view to the beach. Brian was greeted by the proprietor, a man behind him cleaning the gravy that the postman had thrown.

"Welcome to the Tavern On The Bay sir, what will it be? All these bottles of craft welsh pales are half price on account of a ruthless gravy assault."

"What do you have if, say, Death is after you?" The proprietor scratched his neck.

"Erm...a pint of bitter? I mean, I don't understand the request." The proprietor pointed to the bitter tap and Brian nodded.

"It's not an expression, I mean in a sense Death is after all of us but for most people, he's polite enough not to manifest and try to start well-mannered conversations. For most people, it's 'what is that pain in the chest, can't quite reach the heart medication, head goes thud on the carpet,' but for me, it's more like seeing him standing over me, as real as my mother's red blotchy face. It's, I mean, I have no words..."

"So Death is after you? I never met the chap myself, have a long life ahead of me. The only thing that's worrying is this knee, personally, when we were young, we had the left knee and the right knee. At my age, it's the good knee and the bad knee. Look!" The proprietor threw his leg on the bar and lifted his trouser leg. The knee was at a ninety-degree angle to where it should have been.

"You're a strange man," said Brian.

"You are the one haunted by specters."

He had a point. The proprietor took his leg off the bar.

"Haunted by Death. What is he like? Generic looking? The cliché bony finger and skull under the hood? Like anyone at the Pratt university located in the Brooklyn area of New York City's art department would depict? Is he here now?"

Brian looked around while an old man shouted "Metza!" with some poker chips in his hands. A couple in a back booth was in the process of eating each other's faces passionately. An owl perched on a branch outside and blinked mindlessly. But it appeared at this moment that a shadow over his shoulder was absent.

"At the moment no, but it's only a matter of time. Whose cigarettes? er... a landlord?" Brian did not recognize the brand.

"It's Jafari."

"Brian, former data entry specialist, current evader of the grim reaper." Brian laughed at how ridiculous he was coming across but that was quickly replaced by a deep pit of paranoia and fear at the magnitude of his predicament, and genuine concern for his safety wellbeing and socks. They were nice socks, the kind of socks that are never accidently placed on the feet with the heel accidently on the upside.

"Nice to meet you, Brian. In all honesty, that pack of cigarettes has been here longer than I have. I vape myself, using a voodoo drag two platinum, with a Valyrian tank coupled with watermelon chill element e juice. You're welcome to them if that's your vice."

Brian smiled without being coerced.

"Have no idea what game they are playing, I think the one that looks like a monk almost had Metza but didn't have the right domino, but they keep to themselves, no trouble. Its usual postmen, toll booth attendants and substitute pe teachers, those are the ones you must watch. What do you do if you don't mind a still young-looking guy in the right light asking?"

"I'm insignificant really, should be of literally to no interest. Kept my head down my entire life, just trying to take it for what it is. Recently got fired of sorts. No idea where I am. Think I left my phone in my car a few miles back as I ran literally for my life. I should be of no interest, I can't stress that enough. I have no discernible qualities to speak off, nothing that makes me stand out, always existed in the background I guess, life is what happens for other people. I've come to accept that that is not for me. Life, that is. It's not like I'm depressed as such, it's more I have become comfortable with life being an underwhelming stunted ordeal. I just don't deal with people very well. I play the tuba, make my own jerky and collect action figures. I left a perfectly good 1996 rare Action Jackson action figure in the car. So why would I be haunted by the pale horseman? Why am I allowed a peek behind the curtain to the mythological inner workings of reality where constructs like Death are personified? I am an atheist, in its entirety, it is a rejection of a claim, that is all. Does God exist? I see no evidence. Produce evidence and your claim will supersede my previous set of ideas. The universe should be naturalistic and quantifiable. Measurable and underlined with math and science, logic and reason. SHOULD be... but if I have witnessed an incarnation of biological senescence, a literal embodiment of Death, and it is not a product of me or my inner delusions then that calls into question everything I have come to believe about the processes that govern this universe. Death is an angel, by proxy that implies a God. The theological becomes reality."

"Think you lost me there. You look hungry, here is a Vegemite sandwich." Jafari handed over a bap that Brian never noticed. He was intrigued with this tattered man. It was not as if he believed him, his story was fantastical. But none the less he wondered how far down the rabbit hole this story would go.

"If I met Death, I think I would have a few questions like, is fishing allowed in the River Styx? Do you think black is the best colour for your robe, ever thought of a light chartreuse green? You know, skin is quite fashionable... What do you mean I owe you twenty quid for the boat ride? Only been in it for three minutes. Why is the boat lazily listing to the left?"

Brian smiled.

"See? A smile! It's not all bad my new friend."

The postman walked back into the pub with a fake moustache he had made from random brown leaves and some sellotape.

"Barkeep? Pint of Somersby cider! Long day at my work where I work, just got off a triple shift I have! The first time this week I've managed to go into a bar, definitely have not graced one in a while like saying this place five minutes ago..." He readjusted his moustache.

"Listen your gravy slinging bastard, if you don't leave my new friend is going to set Death on you and your curses. Want that? Want a reaper on you?" The postman gasped in horror.

"Please! Not the angel of the night!" The postman ran like a whippet knee first into the fire hydrant. A P.E teacher saw an irate Jafari and thought better of whetting his whistle in his establishment. While no one was looking, he took a sodden wallet from the postman's pocket.

"That'll buy a baguette!" He said with a sociopath's grin. Halfway up the road, he was pickpocketed by a toll booth attendant.

Brian had an empty drink in front of him and Jafari poured a Braxzz brand porter into a glass

"On the house, looks like you deserve a small win, even if it's just a beer on the house. The house wears it like a hat."

There was a brief silence between the two.

"So, you said Death is polite? When did you last see him?

"There was an incident in a sports shop, a fondue-based incident that led to an unfortunate set of circumstances. It was then that Death said he needed to talk. After that, he was in my car helping himself to my cigarettes. Then I ran."

"See if I were you, I'd be so intrigued. I would have to know what he wants. What irks him, what his favorite cheese is. I reckon next time he manifests, talk to him and hear him out."

Brian shrugged nonchalantly

"He's killed me before, a few times. I just keep coming back here."

"Oh, in that case, yeah, I mean, if he's trying to kill you, he may not end up being your best friend. Bargain with him, cheat, play chess or Metza. Metza is so confusing though, neither of you would have any idea of who is winning. When that monk guy produced the Pokémon card is when I got really confused. So, you have been dead before and returned to human form, right? Wow, did you meet God? Or like, an angel of some sort?" Jafari enthusiastically questioned.

"Pretty much death, amnesia and consciousness."

Jafari looked at Brian's tattered suit.

"What are you? Mid-thirties? My son has a similar build to you, same age I should imagine. I think I still have a few of his suits. He currently lives with his life partner Terry. More into stuff with lace and bows these days. Let's see if I can find you something."

"Wait..." stuttered Brian. "Why are you being so nice to me? I mean, you listened to a fantastical claim with no judgment, you gave me cigarettes, drink on the house, now you are offering me a suit? This is a rare phenomenon I've only ever read about. This is altruism! The barman that listens to your troubles is usually just a worn trope in bad movies. I can't take a suit; it doesn't feel right."

"I don't know, you just seem amicable, I guess. I'm grabbing that suit for you, ok? I won't be a few minutes." Jafari wandered past a man still cleaning gravy and opened a back door that Brian assumed led upstairs, or if he had to bet, maybe downstairs. Brian walked over to an empty booth and sat down with his porter.

"I almost had Metza once, didn't have the right chess piece though. After all that time trying to get the monopoly shoe too," a voice rasped.

Brian became as white as an albino ghost wearing white Halloween makeup. His legs turned to jelly and decided they would delegate all functions to a gasp instead. Two bony hands held the daily Anglesea newspaper covering his face. He turned the page with a hum.

"The Sirius star system is missing apparently. Astronomers are baffled. Ah! Someone seems to be selling a Wedgwood wanderlust apple blossom tea set." Death lay down the newspaper on the table and looked deeply at Brian.

"Now, can we talk like adults, or do you want to run away again, because I don't have the time or inclination to play cat and mouse with you, Mr. Aldiss."

"You're Death aren't you! Look, I know I don't have much to live for! I know I have wasted my life! My last closest intimate experience was blocking my neighbor from going down the stairs and talking to her about Febreze, but it's still a life dammit and one I WANT to live! Just please, don't reap me!"

Death sighed understandably. He realized from Brian's perspective this whole ordeal may be jarring, nay, terrifying. It wasn't a slight on Death. Brian's paranoid temperament was just an apt reaction to the circumstance.

"Let's sit outside Brian, smells like the gravy in here."

Brian's legs were still on strike.

"How about you go outside, and I stay here and live for another forty years? But do drop in and we'll have dinner. Nice to meet you, I guess you need to be going."

"I'm not here to reap you, Mr. Aldiss. For now, I guarantee your safety. Outside, please."

Brian picked up the foreign cigarettes and his porter. With great trouble, he walked after the hooded figure. *I'm following Death...* The moment was surreal. Death didn't take steps but rather glided as if he was secretly wearing inline skates. The mental image of Death on skates was almost enough for him to laugh his way out of this situation. He again thought about running in the opposite direction. He could do it right now, however, it was clear that he could not hide from Death.

The beer garden was pleasant. A handful of customers sat in the sun having interesting conversations, laughing and enjoying life. A spike of envy and inadequacy pierced Brian's gut.

"The term beer garden was taken from the German "Biergarten" defined as an open air space that provides beer and food. It has Bavarian roots where breweries would plant gardens above cellars to keep their lagers cool." Death looked up to the building.

"A Georgian style building. Popular in the 18th century. Look at the symmetrical composition and formal classical details." Death sat down, markedly taller than Brian. Brian accepted his position enough to try his foreign cigarettes.

"Those things will kill you," Death remarked ironically. He picked up one of the cigarettes and ran it under his small and oblong nasal bone. He courteously put it back in the packet.

"So Brian. We have met before, a few times, do you have a

recollection of this, bar the sports center and your vehicle?"

Brian took a sip of his porter visibly shaking.

"So I am safe? You are not going to send my soul to a distant abyss? To the chasm of nothingness?" Brian pleaded his case.

"For now, I guarantee your safety," reiterated Death.

"Do you recall any interaction with me?"

"The last time you reaped me I was waiting for a bus, a small girl was having a tea party to my right behind a hedge. You told me that it wouldn't hurt, not a bit. Everything went tight and a blast of orange light hit me. I smelt tangerines with a hint of lemon and then, nothing. I cannot tell you how much time had passed, it may have been minutes, it may have been hours, even centuries for all I know. After a while, I come back having lost a few days while my body is on autopilot doing all sorts of things."

"That explains something. Over the last few weeks, I have sporadically been reaping you, but days later you come back on my radar. If the essence takes time to find its receptacle, it isn't recognized by me. At first, your return was an aberration but as it turned into a pattern, I realized perhaps just sending you to the beyond was not a pertinent choice. Your return is indicative of something else. If I had my Omniscience, this would not be a problem. I think I have figured it out now though, and if I am right, I can correct this situation."

"By correction do you mean permanently ridding me of my existence? You said I was safe!"

"For now, I can guarantee your safety," Death replied solemnly.

"You keep saying that, but to clarify the evasive language, am I not longed for this world?"

Death counted the ants in the beer garden. Two hundred and forty-six. Three injured, one dead from Brians entrance into the garden. Death wondered how he could differentiate the plight of Brians desperate grasp on his mortality and the death of this random ant. He wasn't fluent in ant, as it was taught to him by a hornet who picked up the language whilst on holiday at the rim of a man's sugary alcoholic mixture. Lacking the antennae to get the prose precise, he resorted to stridulation, the chirping sounds. He only really knew how to say;

"The pleasant day we are having, can you give me directions to the nearest termite mound?"

One of the ants threw some pheromones on the ground to convey the message of;

"Shit Clive is down!"

Death looked up to pay attention to Brian.

"If you treasure life so much you will assist me, the longer you are in my service the longer your life will be. Alternatively, I can separate your essence now and your fate will be my namesake."

Brian had but one simple metaphysical question.

"Are you real? Look, not too long ago I was in a commune with a somewhat post-verbal cacti. I reject that as reality and you are an extension of that, so I call into question the validity of your existence!"

It was at this point that Jafari peered through the window. He spotted Brian talking to himself and, all things considered, Jafari was not irked by this given Brian's pathology. He breathed condensation on the window and made a smiley face, the suit in the left hand.

"Brian my new friend, I have the suit, nothing fancy, just a men's Avelino charcoal pinstripe three-piece suit. You look as white as an arctic hare!" A smile crept on Jafari's face.

"He's here, isn't he? Death? Death is with us! What seat is he in?" Brian nodded to his left.

"Have you determined if he's real yet? Ask him something about me! We have just met, you know nothing about me so if I can confirm certain details that he describes, then you'll know he's legit!" The logic was flawless.

"Death will you participate?"

From Jafari's perspective, Brian was addressing an empty chair.

"I do not engage in parlor tricks but if this means you trust I am who I claim to be, then so be it, but time is really against us." Death thought whilst pondering the tare in space with the lack of reality nestled within it.

Jafari produced a pad of paper and a pencil he used to take down orders that tended to involve fourteen steps to make coffee.

"Ok, so you don't think I'm just agreeing with you when you give me details about my life, I'll write down an answer to a question and you tell me the answer. We'll then see if they match. Makes sense?" Brian nodded.

"What is my full name."

Death gave Brian the answer

"Jafari Keita."

Jafari stepped back a little and showed Brian his name on a page in his hello kitty notepad.

"Correct! And I have such an unusual name, hard to guess I imagine. That's spooky. Ok, what are my wife and child's name." Death again provided Brian with the answer.

"Wife of thirty-three years is Janet Evans. One son by the name of Ekon."

Jafari became very suspicious.

"Oh I get it, it's a wind-up, the whole thing is a wind-up, isn't it!? Who put you up to this was it, Steve? You had me going there. No way a stranger could know that. Talking to Death. It's brilliant, the whole bit, I bet you even wore that suit as part of the ploy. Get old Jafari to believe in specters!"

Death gave Brian a few more details.

"Every third Saturday of the month you have secret ballroom classes. You knew your son stole your wife's earrings because you overheard him on the phone telling his mate Terry about it and you never told that to anyone. In five seconds someone will shout Metza and you are about to sneeze."

"This is ridiculous."

"I'm as surprised as you are," said Brian.

"Metza!" came bellowing from the bar. Jafari sneezed.

"My Omniscience is spotty, yet I still seem to have a localized knowing," stated Death.

"Mvunaji Mbaya!! Mvunaji Mbaya!!" Jafari lay down the suit on the chair and carefully stepped back.

"You are in commune with Mbaya! Or you are a Mchawi?"

Brian looked to death.

"He's saying I'm Death and wondering if you are a wizard. It's Swahili."

"I am no wizard Jafari, this is as jarring for me as it is for you, you have confirmed his existence for me. All I want to do is run and hide but I'm afraid that action will lead to death, so I'm essentially abducted right now."

"You speak my language?"

"No. Oh and thanks for the Vegemite sandwich," said Brian with the bap in his hand.

"Well, I am never going to get this chance again, to communicate with Mbaya. What of me? I'm fifty-nine, when will I die? How will it happen? Has my son got a long life ahead of him? What of God? I have believed all my life but at times I wonder if the belief is a fool's errand and then I hate myself for questioning my beliefs. At times I wonder if I could ever truly know."

"I don't have time for this..." said Death with some urgency. Brian looked at a distressed Jafari and again to Death with a look as if to elicit sympathy on Jafari's behalf. Death began a small speech and relayed it to Brian.

"Death says that it will be detrimental to your mental health for him to disseminate such information regarding you or any of your relatives' mortality. As for God, at this moment in time, it is not something he can discuss but belief is not unwarranted, it is encouraged. He did however say not to go to the new Ghost Fighters movie."

"Why? Do I avoid a bad fate by avoiding the movie? Like, if I have seen it something terrible will happen?" Jafari was gripping hard on the backrest of a chair.

"No, apparently it's just a shit movie."

"Well, that was underwhelming. You'd expect more, right? Well, I seem to be ingrained deeply and wholly with something akin to dread so on that note does Death drink? Can he drink? I'll seek out something for you two. Brian," Jafari nodded and faced the chair to the left. "Death," he nodded to an empty chair and retreated.

Brian stubbed out his cigarette becoming more comfortable with this emergent status quo.

"Given my existence proven true, I need to see a man about a horse. My associate..." Death did not want to say War.

"Hired a caravan from an equestrian. We had little money, but he was interested in our horses. It was mentioned that they were particularly virile prize steeds and ready for breeding. So, we traded the horses with the caravan for a few weeks. Unbeknownst to him, there will be no viable offspring as these said horses are immortal representations of myself and my associates. The associate in question has, well, misplaced the card with the equestrian's details and I have somewhat lost my ability to, well, locate this gentleman."

"Well, how can I help?"

"There is only one explanation as to why your reanimation occurs and it's tied up with the equestrian. I cannot find him without you. I'm going to influence you now; this won't hurt a bit."

Death poked an astral finger through Brian's skull who became cross-eyed smoke rising from his head. An expression that read *only lightly toasted please* was plastered upon his face. Brian lost all fine motor skills and dribbled from the left side of his mouth.

Brian was inside his own mind. There was a great hall. To his right, fifteen-foot-high pigeon boxes spanned the side of the hall, and there was an information point on a plaque that simply read *Brian's compartmentalization*. To its right there was a reference book. He picked a page at random. It read *Fears, A through F compartment 12R*. He scanned the vast pigeonholes and twelve-foot up a third of the way through the compartment 12R. To his left was a gallery. The pictures were of key moments of his life. His now-estranged father, mother, sister, brother, dog, alongside himself were at a water park feeding blue knuckle hermit crabs. He
remembered that day. The crab bit him. Another picture was of him graduating high school with a girlfriend who died, but who he also saw two weeks later at a vinyl shop. The pictures went on in this fashion in a neat little row, all behind Q line chrome ball top-roped partitions in red velvet. The floor was of a light staggered wood, the ceiling a great height away as if the floor was annoying it and it had to run off, feigning a cough but assuring it that once it had passed, they'll go for brunch.

In front of him were two glass doors leading to a spiral staircase. From a human-shaped lack of matter, a small bespectacled man in a tweed suit with elbow patches, a pipe and half-moon glasses appeared.

"I am the curator of this Museum, the halls of Brian Aldiss. Not an appreciated man in his time, of little accomplishment, a keen mind just out of his grasp. A man of so little importance and grace that he would be laid to rest unremembered and forgotten. No heroic deeds to speak off, no real conquests if you fathom my insinuation. A sad wasted life, an unlived and undeserved life, a life bereft of anything kindred to happiness, love or joy. The sort of life that even a jellyfish would think was uneventful. The kind of child a father called buddy as at even the age of twelve he never bothered to learn his name." The man smiled.

"Hi Brian, I'm Doctor Miles. Big fan. Really. The stories I tell about you! But something strange has happened to stop the monotony I see. You've met Death! He is old you know, some say he's older than

God. Look he's over there in the pigeon holes. Where is my head, I'm so sorry, would you like a cup of tea?"

"Okay I have finally lost my tenuous grasp on reality, it just exaggerates in magnitudes, from cacti to Death to this!" Brian looked at the wall with a schematic of the building. *The Lost Room* caught his attention. Noticing it, the Doctor laughed.

"That is a room of everything you have ever lost, from yo-yos to your virginity. We just have a small trophy with 'Virginity' on a silver plaque but don't worry, sanity is not in there yet." Brian continued to look at the schematic 'Achievements.' Again the Doctor laughed.

"Have not been there in years, it's where I keep my antique liquor bottle collection. Come on over, Mrs. Belch will make us some English tea."

There appeared an old lady in an apron, her hair in a net and soft eyes sunken in a thousand wrinkles.

"How do you take it, love?"

"Anyway, I can find it!" said the Doctor. They both giggled and she poured the tea knowing exactly how he liked it.

"This must be Brian! Welcome to your unconscious! Death, careful on that ladder you'll break your neck!"

Death gave a thumbs up.

"So that's where this is? I am in my unconscious?"

"Death just needed to find a wobbler."

Brian was confused.

"Oh, I'm sorry Brian, in unconscious jargon a wobbler is a device that links a person with an object, a kind of entanglement. If you were near an object at one time you can be inextricably linked, if you find one you find the other. Now, if I know our Brian it will be PG tips and a Maryland cookie. Oh, Doctor, the class from the local school are due at the museum, the class is teaching a course called; *How it can all go wrong, a study of Brian*. Brian bowed his head, depressed, angry, anxious, annoyed and a few other new emotions that compounded the first lot.

"Got it!" shouted Death climbing down the ladders.

"Sorry you didn't get to finish the tea, take the cookie though, will still be good in your realm," said the old lady. The Doctor shook his hand.

"Pleasure."

"You know a bit about pleasure!" smiled the old lady with 50 years of tea stains on her teeth. The Doctor laid some Eric Nording

tobacco in his pipe, lit it and took a deep breath.
"A bit? Don't undersell me!"
Death patted Brian on the shoulder.
"On our way Brian. Definitely something between those two."
"This won't hurt a bit." Death pierced Brian's head with an astral bone finger.

Brian was back in the chair of the pub garden. He looked at the table. There was a fresh porter and a note that read.

Couldn't wake you from an open-eyed comatose state, here is a drink on the house. Hope you're not dead
– Jafari

To his left Death looked down at a yellowtail shiraz white wine. He took a long sip. Brian found a Maryland cookie in his pocket. It was a small win, but a win, nonetheless.

"I'm getting used to you Death. I mean, I'm still paranoid every second. Do you have to carry around that scythe? Is that seven-foot razor-sharp silver twinkling in the light a weapon? It's not good for my pathology. Just a reminder that I'm sitting with an embodied singular intent. Death."

"I am more than a singular intent Brian. I am not an autonomous reactionary being. I like bird watching, a nice cup of tea and I am impartial to this wine. The scythe was never intended to be a weapon, it was an agricultural tool used for cutting long grass and corn. Do you like it? I'm particularly fond of the purple trimming. It's made from sandalwood. Also, I used a sharpie pen to add this lightning bolt. You have had a hard life haven't you, Brian? You have deserved better, but sometimes good happens to the undeserving and the righteous go unheeded. The world is far from perfect. If you are among the luckiest, perhaps you'll leave this place a little better than you found it. But for most of us, we just need to cherish those brief interludes of happiness, sparsely interspersed with the monotony and grey."

Brian found this to be sage counsel.

"But I can relate Brian. It's difficult being me. Since the inception of creation, I have held a zenith position with the prime mover. I have memories of a time before, these brief fleeting moments. I have witnessed the origination of life from abiogenesis in the fetid soup of proteins and amino acids. I have watched it grow and change, evolve and adapt, this beautiful tapestry forming before me. But I was always outside of it, a shadow in its light. Of the boundless abundance of life flung across space and time it is your species that fascinates me, captivates me. You have so much potential, and I am burdened with the knowledge that someday it will end by my hand and will. I have never had a friend." Death again took a sip of his wine. Brian sympathized with him.

"I am sorry, I perceived you as a phantasm. A coldly calculated inevitability. I didn't realize you were a being that, well, felt. Death, I am at your disposal, what do you need me to do?" Death gave two thumbs up.

"Now I have the wobbler-" in Death's hand was a fifth-dimensional cube, too complex for Brian to see it in its entirety, "- I can see a man about a horse." Death finished his wine and stood up. He trod on an ant and apologized as best he could. It was the one that was in the middle of helping Clive. Seeing Death ready to depart, Brian downed his porter. Going through the doors back into the pub, Brian stopped at Jafari.

"Thank you for everything, and for acknowledging me."

"You gave me my faith back, thank you, Brian! Here, some jerky for the road." Brian's left hand held the suit, with his right he pocketed the jerky. Death addressed Brian as he passed the three elderly gentlemen, and gave him a tip;

"Say hit me. Roll the dice, it will be a six and then you can avoid the shoot and get the ladder."

Brian approached the table.

"Hit me," he said tapping a deck of cards. It was seven. He picked the dice and rolled a six and climbed the ladder to the hundred.

"METZA!" cheered the three old men. They pushed a handful of foreign notes Brian's way. Exiting they stepped over the drunken postman and there was Brian's car.

"I drove here, thanks for not running away again."

Brian was smiling.

"I'll drive," said Death whilst Brian ate his Maryland cookie.

Chapter 13

"This is amazing! I have never seen anything so beautiful!" Famine was on his knees, tears down his face, a trembling of his lips.

"Sure, is a sight to behold," grumbled War.

"I still don't know what was wrong with the old one," remarked Pestilence. Famine lit a cigar in triumph.

"I thought you were going to cut down?" Pestilence groaned exhaustively.

"I am. I have seven patches on my arm and five on my neck for good measure."

"They don't work very well, you should vape. As a cessation method, it's unparalleled."

Famine weighed this up.

"Smoking shouldn't come with instructions and, to answer your earlier question about the old one, it was a rotten tattered unreliable broken-down crab infested near-death piece of complete trash unfit for a peasant. But this! This is camping in style! This is living the dream!"

In front of them was a coachmen chaparral 373MBRB bunkhouse fifth wheel RV.

"Camping shouldn't be about accommodation. It should be about beaches, even in late autumn. Chip shops with those great crispy bits soaked in vinegar at the bottom of the cone. Portaloos and showers that are as cold as that Greek guy Boreas's nipples. There are seventy thousand people in Anglesea all with a story to tell. We can talk to actual people."

"It has two bathrooms, so you won't have to go in after War anymore."

There was a slight inflexion at the end and Pestilence smiled.

"Well, I suppose I can give it a chance." Pestilence patted the dark green exterior. Famine had thrown his cigar perfectly into an ashtray without looking, a skill he had been perfecting for centuries.

"Can fit ten men in this, or maybe four Wars. Not a crab in sight."

They entered the pristine wooden interior.

"Something is wrong..." muttered Pestilence under his breath

"What now Pestilence?" Pestilence shrugged.

"It doesn't have a smell. I'm not picking up turpentine, brake fluid,

WD40, no leftover takeaway, whatever War had eaten the previous day- nothing, it's kind of freaking me out."

"Forget the smell, this is a castle! 3 bedrooms, two bathrooms, a tri-fold out sofa, theatre seating, kitchen and living area, a dinette for four, dual pane windows, four door fridge freezer, AC units... yep, she'll do alright, she'll do just fine."

"Well, I guess I'll have to christen the facilities," said Pestilence wandering into one of the two bathrooms. War tried to whistle. He had never quite managed it, every time a drop of saliva forming on his lower lip. Pestilence filled the silence by whistling himself. He patted his knees to add drums. It was to the tune of *The Sound of Silence.*

"Hello darkness my old friend, I've come to talk to you again..."

They both trailed off and Pestilence made fart noises for no particular reason. War picked up a stick and passively poked the ground. A small badger appeared from a hole with a displeased expression

"Sorry," said War throwing away the stick. Famine pulled out his yo-yo. He was learning the cradle trick. War took out a flask from the innards of his coat and drank a good portion of it, at last count he had on him three flasks of varied gin and brandy's, a goat horn with a cap containing roman posca wine and a thimble of his greatest creation. He called it *Horseman*. A brew that in one small measure could topple an elephant. A thimble a day is all he needed to maintain his near sober state. War passed the flask to Famine who took a small sip to be polite.

"Weather is turning War, last of the sun for a few months I should expect. Haven't seen a rainbow in a while. Do we still have those?"

"I know! Knock knock."

Famine bowed his head.

"Who's there?"

"A little old lady!"

"A little old lady who?"

"Wow! I didn't know you could yodel?"

"Well done War, great joke, let's leave them for a while now aye?"

"Until how long?"

"Until one of us is dead."

Famine paid attention back to his Yo-Yo. They both heard a flush. Pestilence departed the van, a positive mood shedding itself into reality. From his side pocket he grabbed his pen and pad.

"You guys up to much?" asked Pestilence.

"Just passing the time," replied Famine.

"How are the findings?"

"A solid eight. On the upper echelon of toilets, I would say. Nice, complimentary Febreze, dove soup, hard to beat. The seat seems to have a warming technology to it, space to stretch my legs, no splash back on the flush, sound of flush doesn't persist too long. This could work." Pestilence mused, hand on chin. He exited the vehicle and they walked to the back.

"Look at the back!" Famine exclaimed excitedly. "It has a bike rack, storage is ample! Again War, how can we thank you?" War cocked his head to one side.

"Only treasure."

Pestilence laughed.

"Who would have thought the dealership would accept ancient Mesopotamian gold coins?" Famine patted War on his vast back. War was enjoying his moment in the sun.

"The way I see it like, it's more about the journey to the treasure than the actual treasure, that's the fun bit. Without the treasure, you're just causing trouble."

Pestilence was looking through the window to the kitchen.

"Famine you have to see this!" Famine ran in a gangling fashion.

"Pestilence, is that the casa Bugatti ViaRoma kettle next to the Duelit NewGen four slice toaster? This puts Death's setup to shame. We have to test it out!"

"I ams just going for a nap in this castle," said War, hearing it described as a castle. He went into the middle entrance. To the left a kitchenette, to his right a generous bathroom, in front of him a glorious bedroom with small tables and desk lights on either side. War stopped with a sense of trepidation. The sheets were white. Not yellow, brown or green with a slight moss problem, but white. Even being on the high side of seven-foot there was ample room. His feet didn't stick out two feet beyond the bed's frame. He noticed a switch with AC written on it. Well, that could mean anything he thought. Arctic camels? He needed help.

"Guys? What does AC mean? Only there be a switch thing. I don't want to reset the computer."

Pestilence placed a hand on War's shoulder with a smile.

"Never change my friend."

"It's air conditioning War, no computer involved. Well, I'm sure the inner mechanics may be a computer of sorts but that's just me being pedantic. If you switch it on War, you will have cold air blowing to keep you cool."

War went back to the bedroom and looked again at the switch.

"Air con-conditioning..."

He reasoned it was already too cold being late autumn. He saw another switch that confused him. TV. Well, that could mean anything, he thought

"Ok, we need bread, do we have bread?" Pestilence shrugged.

"We can scavenge anything we need from the old caravan."

Famine shuddered at the thought

"That wafer-thin super budget imitation 'you won't notice the difference' mock bread we got from those cobblers that for some reason was also an apothecary haberdashery and a rare bird shop? It was the turtle I didn't trust, you looked at it and it just froze."

"It was good enough for you before. You know, since we came into money you have changed. You've become a snob."

"I've always hated that bread, I mentioned it every morning for weeks!" said Famine slightly louder than was necessary. His head vein considered throbbing.

"Ok let's raid the carcass of my four-wheeled antagonists, the bastard of a thousand annoyances. If it had a human name, it would be Diabolos or Abigor."

"Ok Famine, just remember we are loaning this caravan still. I know that look, you want to sacrifice it to the Gods. Burn down the whole thing in a ritualistic cleansing of the soul. We are just here to see what we can scavenge, and we are going to walk away.

Stepping into the small caravan the carpet squelched under their feet as they noticed a small exposed pipe gently dripping water. Something scurried across the floor and under the small one door fridge.

"So, fridge, what wonders do you hide?"

Famine found four AA batteries, a bottle of WD40, and what once long ago in the annals of history may have been some haddock. There was some genetically engineered long-life milk, a single egg and a Nokia 3210. It was not even worth expending the energy of opening the door. He picked up the Nokia 3210 and on its back in black marker was *WRA*.

"Found War's phone in the fridge, a nice change from the

microwave. How did you ever put up with this place Pestilence?"

"Don't know, hadn't given it much thought. If I was a fan of crab, I'd be okay since on occasion one would commit ritualistic suicide by jumping into a pan of hot water used for your tea in those rare mornings that you didn't feel the need to be electrocuted. You know, I've been working on my manifestation. Look at this."

Pestilence laid out his hand and a small rabbit with a persistent cough appeared and then fizzled out of existence almost immediately.

"Ah, almost had it there. Made a three-legged frog for 3 minutes before he left, he rued his creation, called me a sadist and buggered off."

"Muse taught me transportation, last time I used that we were all in the car and the next thing we knew the entire vehicle is floating 3 billion miles away in deep space next to an asteroid that was generically asteroid looking." Famine let out a burp.

"Yeah I'm going to have fond memories of this caravan my old friend. Despite all odds with everything against it, it persisted, dragged on through the drudgery, whipped by that westerly sea air, kept together by rust and duct tape. It has to be applauded." Pestilence wistfully smiled.

"I found the bread. Its best days I'm afraid are behind it. The teabags are ok and I don't mind taking a chance on that genetically engineered milk if you don't mind. As long as it's not purple like last time." Pestilence came across a journal that belong to Death. He opened a page at random and read 'the horsey moves in an L shape.' He threw it in a bin bag to be saved. He had also collected fifty-three issues of new scientist dated from 1995 to 2012. He picked one up semi mindlessly. It read 'issue 2007, 16th December 1995, hot rocks that changed the world.' He was bored just reading the title. He found a voodoo doll that looked very much like him with a pin in his stomach. A note was duct-taped to the feet saying 'Take that Pestilence you bastard, that was my last yoghurt.' Pestilence smiled. It was a good yoghurt, but it was Famines fault for initially stealing his pillowcase. Death's previously secret kettle hiding satchel weighed a ton as he moved it out of the camper van to the side. He would have to enlist War to move his treasure, with a frame like War's it would be like holding a butterfly that was slimming down for swimsuit season next year.

"Find anything worth saving?" asked Pestilence of Famine.

"Of the fifty tins of fruit, beans, spam, chopped tomatoes, Heinz tomato soup and tuna the only thing barely in date is haggis in a can. We have a fajita kit but no meat or trimmings, essentially, it's crap bread and powder. Some whey proteins?"

Pestilence shrugged guiltily

"Trying to add mass, I'm six foot and nine stone. You can play my ribs like a xylophone."

"We have a defective Action Jackson action figure that says are you, horny baby. Yeah, appropriate gift for a kid. Plates bowls, cutlery spoons, spatulas. Nick knacks, odds and ends, bits and bobs, this and that, these and those. That leather jacket that does not suit you that you bought after that sci-fi action flick, its accompanying sunglasses. A spare key with a G on it hiding in the glovebox. 200 Lambert and butler cigarettes. War's vast collection of alcohol, some home-brewed, some that would make you blind and some that would straight up to end your life and one small Capri-sun squeezy bottle with straw. Twenty one copies of the Anglesea Daly newspapers. Several crab bits, I think they have gone cannibalistic. A framed photo of us 5 years ago in the Isle of White. That is when they had to rescue War after he got lost for 6 hours in the corn maze and after a while, he just broke his way in one direction right through the hedges. We couldn't pay the fine, so we worked at the ice cream shop for three days as compensation. What else? Some ketchup in the mop bucket, Death's spare scythe, a fan that has one setting, that being broken. Er, travel scrabble, chess set, book named *'My first chess game.'* Monopoly, the game of life, a book called *'How to get her through hypnosis.'* A bonsai tree and I think that's about it."

"We also have Muse's address and phone number on this Lilly scented napkin." Famine managed to hide his joy with a yo-yo."

"What you are doing with that?" inquired Pestilence.

"Dunno, just bored. Invented in Greece in 500 BC. So where are we going to get bread?" Pestilence channeled an epiphany.

"The enterprising kid two tents over!" Famine clicked his finger in comradely "Speak this in hunger for bread, not in thirst for revenge!"

"As you say Famine," quoting *Shakespeare for no good reason*, he thought. They departed the old caravan with several bags of eclectic belongings ready to move into the new VR. They were tucked away from the rest of the campsite by a row of alder and rowan trees. A small path breaching the middle of the trees led to the rest of the site. Famine and Pestilence emerged. Famine looked down at his clothes. He was wearing a t-shirt on top of a long-sleeved shirt. It was stained and had not been washed in a week. The fabric at the bottom of his trousers by his heel had come away, a hole forming on the bottom of his left sandal.

"It's not even early afternoon yet, fancy taking some gold to a clothes shop Pestilence?"

He nodded but stayed silent, focusing on the upcoming bartering. They spotted what looked to be a 12-year-old wearing woolly hat and knee-high trousers, dirt on his face and somewhat reminiscent of an orphan chimney sweep. He stood in front of a homemade bench of driftwood and loose nails. There was a crudely painted sign reading *'Harry's Hut'* attached to a pole in the ground.

"We could just go to seven-eleven? This kid looks like a hustler, look, he's flicking a coin up and down and catching it, a toothpick in his mouth. If he says morning guv'na, we know we're in trouble." They approached the bench.

"Look here, child! We want some bread and none of your crap!" Pestilence pushed Famine aside

"Let me, ok? So, Harry-"

"Who says my names Harry? Don't know where you get that information..."

"Is your name Harry? Only the sign-" Pestilence was interrupted.

"Maybe I am maybe I'm not, what's it to you guv'na?"

Famine had his head in his hands.

"Look, you little shit," Pestilence interjected, "whoever you are we need bread." He looked at the stock. "And some bacon, maybe some of those sausages. Oh the black pudding looks nice, a butchers dozen of eggs and this small lollipop I assume is complimentary?"

"Wellbeing as I like your face, right, I might at the right price be able to part with some of my top-quality merchandise?"

"Might? You are a shop!" Shouted Famine.

"Now now, who said I'm a shop?" The kid gave a wry grin.

"Well, the stall, the sign and said merchandise. It's all pretty generic if an under imagined shop..." Famine had an idea.

"Do you have a license for this shop? Do you pay taxes? Do you meet all the requirements set out by HMRC to run such a business? Because I'll happily report you to them, where I'm sure their anti-money laundering divisions will take a closer inspection of your, ahem, merchandise," Famine smiled menacingly at the child.

"Look guv'na how about the bread, the bacon, the sausages, the black pudding, the eggs..."

"And the lollipop!" Pestilence insisted.

"And the lollipop. Twenty bobs, can't say fairer than that!" The kid spat on his palm and thrust it forward.

"Twenty quid? Are they special sausages? Did the pig have an advanced degree?"

"Well, you pay for convenience now don't you guv'na! The way I see it, in ten minutes you can be eating sausage sandwiches. Can't be bad, can it!?"

Famine looked at Pestilence who shrugged and dug out an Inca silver coin.

"Now what am I supposed to do with that mickey mouse coin! Do I look like a coin collector? Now I should charge you a pony, but as I said, I like your face so a score it is."

Other than ancient treasure, Famine was still down to his last penny. Pestilence opened up his Greenbury vintage wallet and parted with a twenty-pound note. They grabbed a bag that the kid charged five pence for. Pestilence grabbed his lollipop.

"I hated that kid back there!" Spat Famine as they passed through the alder and rowan trees. Behind the new RV, sat precariously on the cliff edge, was the old caravan.

"Can I not just light it a bit on fire Pestilence, like a small controlled itty bitty barely noticeable fire?" Famine laughed to himself.

"No, but we better get that treasure out of there, I don't like the way it's leaning to the right in that fashion. Neither of us has any discernible musculature to speak off. That whey protein I think is a conspiracy, three weeks I've been on it and I've lost half a stone. We need War."

They both dreaded the implications of this statement. Waking up War was to gamble with your life. They walked to the awning attached to the left side of the RV. The foldout table and chairs were present and accounted for, nothing was hiding and the air smelled like fresh peaches.

"War?" whispered Famine when he entered the RV. War seemed to be nowhere in the immediate vicinity. Pestilence checked the bedroom directly opposite the middle entrance. Lost to the world in a deep slumber and cradling a scantily clad maiden, War dribbled sweet nothings onto his pillow.

"And that is how I lost my pig..." he spoke in his sleep.

"I'll give him five more minutes," said Famine.

"You are not doing it for him, you are doing it for yourself! Last time you tried to wake him from the grasp of Hypnos he projectile vomited on your new shoes, falling right on top of you. What was it, three hours until I came to your aid? Squashed under that monolith? I can barely think of an ordeal that would equal that, honestly the thought of it keeps me up at night."

"Ok yes, I'm scared ok? Remember in the Isle of White when he slept walked and destroyed half the campsite? After seeing what he did to that squirrel, I'll never be the same again. Sort of thing that sticks with you for life... Where did the barely clothed harlot come from as well? War has to teach me that, don't know how he does it."

"Well if you had eyes for anyone other than Muse..." Pestilence left the insinuation hanging in the air.

"It has been a while hasn't it Famine. Remember Antheia and Asteria back in Greece? The hot tub of asp milk?" They both relaxed in contemplation.

"I know what will wake War. We just need to cook sausages. The smoke will enter his nostrils and he'll levitate out of the bed. The smoke will become a beckoning finger and lead him to said sausages!"

"You can be a very strange person Famine." Pestilence threw his haul from Harry's hut onto the side table. With great care, he opened the bread. There was a second layer of packaging and, upon opening that to he saw the third layer.

"I think the bread is broken."

"How in Gods name can bread be broken?" said Famine. He grabbed a knife and slit the top to get to the bread.

"You are not supposed to do it like that! You take the sticker with the sell-by date carefully off, take the bread you need out and then reseal the opening with the sticker, Now what you have done means that next time we use this bread the top 3 pieces exposed to the air will become hard and inedible. I suppose we can use some cellophane."

"Alright this is it, the first good piece of toast in weeks. The inaugural pieces of toast," slipping the bread into the toaster setting it to two and a half out of five. He clicked the close button with a satisfying click.

"Pestilence I have always wondered, what does one to five mean? Is it a standard gradient across all toasters, or is it like a three on this and a two on Death's toaster? I think it will take a few days to find the perfect gradient."

Pestilence gingerly smelt the milk, which seemed fine, and turned on the kettle. A barely clothed maiden made her way out of Wars bedroom. She blushed and mumbled excuse me, leaving with her flip flops in hand. Famine chucked the sausages on and threw a few eggs in there for good measure.

"That singular egg from the old abode. Would be a shame to waste it maybe?" Famine shook his head.

"No way I'm going near that egg. I'm not even sure what animal it came from."

The intoxicating sausage bouquet penetrated all the nooks and crannies of the RV. A great rumbling sound shook the suspension, followed by the sound like a bison losing its balance on a patch of black ice. There were a few more assorted thuds and War appeared at his door triumphantly.

"Sausages!" he bellowed. Watching War eat was an ordeal. He did not so much chew his food as he did inhale it. On occasion, he would choke and Famine refused to let Pestilence help him, saying how else will he learn? That's when Death would intervene. The Cumberland sausages just tasted better when they were cooked with more expensive equipment.

Several minutes later after a full English breakfast, some of the best toast they had ever eaten and a fantastic cup of tea, they stepped outside to stretch their legs.

"War, we need you to remove your treasure from the old caravan. It's damp in there so watch your step. Remember to duck at the entrance. I suspect you may have a concussion after weeks with that doorway. I think you got the upper hand the way it's dented, the door barely closes properly now."

War slapped Famine jovially on the back who fell forward, his balance against him and fell face-first into the dirt.

"Oh sorry, there my old friend! Don't know my whostsit, own strength like." War helped him up.

"Thanks," said Famine half-heartedly. War took a step into the van and immediately battled the frame with the top of his head. He grunted to himself but the caravan was in more pain. He went to the back seat and with incredible ease and threw the quarter tonne bag over his shoulder.

"There we are, that should do it!" War put the bag by the RV. He patted the side of the caravan. There was a groaning sound followed by a crumbling sound that worried Pestilence. Famine noticed it too although War was oblivious, wondering where his sexual conquest had disappeared to. The cliff-side front wheel gave way and the whole caravan fell to fit the void left by the wheel. Again, another crumble sounded as two feet in front of Famine and Pestilence, a crack appeared in the sparse grass and mud.

"I have a bad feeling here Famine." Pestilence took a few steps back and Famine joined on cue. The ground underneath the caravan started to give way. Pestilence tensed up, gritting his teeth. The caravan was in a distressed blind panic but could do nothing to save itself. Twelve crabs let out a scream. A broken toaster looked up panic-stricken. Pestilence reached out an arm in vain. Famine was elated, he had never been so happy. War scratched his head. The crack in the mud in front of them widened.

"I guess the weight of the treasure was what kept it in place?" pondered War. "I would think a lack of weight would have had the opposite effect of not making the ground under it crumble." Remarked Pestilence.

The caravan could hold on no longer and, accompanied by two tons off Earth, it bounced off of the rocks and fell tail lights first into the water. Pestilence looked to Famine who had tears running down his face, a smile ear to ear.

"Out with the old, in with the new," smiled Famine.

"Well, who's going to break the news to the equestrian? He loved that thing."

"He gave us a lemon, there were plenty of vans to choose from, but they were all, every one of them, recovering from woodworm. We got the raw end of the deal with this and now the bastard of a thousand annoyances has finally departed this realm and this realm is better for it. I have no sympathy for it."

"Well Famine, I for one lament its death. I feel it served us well. War, a eulogy?" War looked blankly.

"Last words for the van War?"

"Oh right! Okay. We lived in you..." War looked around and guessed they wanted more. "And in a way, you lived in us? No, scratch that, you had a table. Sometimes I'd sit at the table and think, this is a nice table! With not a lot of space and having to sleep outside, I did not get to know you as a bed, but I'm sure you aptly accommodated."

Famine shrugged.

"As good as any send off I guess?" said Pestilence. War saluted the sea air.

"Well, it seems this chapter of our lives has come to its natural conclusion, not much else to say. I am so happy with my friends. You wish for something for so long, want it so badly, never knowing if you're going to find that release, and when it comes? You just don't know what to say. I have closure, its redemption is what it is. I just wish I could have savored the moment more. Watching that ground come away..."

"Famine, was this sign always here?" Famine looked to where Pestilence was pointing. It read;

'Do not park here: loose ground is a hazard.'

The sign leaned lazily backwards and very slowly tilted to the ground. It landed with a tiny force, barely affecting the grass underneath. Pestilence threw a single rose over the cliff edge.

"To the crabs, to the toaster, to the van," said Pestilence. War wandered into the awning and grabbed three plastic cups purchased from the odds and ends shop. Passing the cups to his friends he pulled out the capped goat horn of roman posca wine. He poured some generous measures and tucked the goat horn away on his vast person. War looked at his watch. It was two-thirty in the afternoon.

"And with that, who is up for some toast, tea and scrabble?"

"Only if I can have the shoe," said War.

"Wrong game War, scrabble is the one with the letters. Maybe it's cruel to have you join in."

"I gots a text from Death, you guys!" War said. It seemed he had been gone for hours.

"He says; *Got a great lead on where the horses are, with Brian Aldiss, I'll keep you posted, back soon.*"

Hearing the crash of the caravan, a young couple too tanned for the fidget climate came to investigate. Being somewhere where time stops, any new development was a chance to shake the monotony.

"He's a big lad," said the guy in a Moroccan robe looking at War.

"I wonder if everything is proportional."

"I was thinking that," said the girl in a size twelve Lascana beach dress.

"We heard a ruckus, like an explosion. Is everyone ok?"

"Everything is," replied Famine.

"It's just the best day of my life. Here, have a Germanic twenty-mark 1911 gold coin."

Chapter 14

Muse was sweeping the floor where the God of haircuts had been illegally squatting and running his business. She took down the framed poster of the top 1940's men's haircuts and he seemed to have bolted the chair to the floor in the night. A barber pole slowly rotated. He was disliked by most as he represented the devaluation of the term God and tended to throw his arms in the air and shout *'I can't work like this!'* at anyone who happened to interrupt him by merely announcing bingo. She held her hand over the bolts that unscrewed at her will. Once free she took the chair and looked around the bar. A blunt instrument would suffice, she thought, maybe something sharp. Looking at a large hammer that conveniently appeared, she noticed one side was blunt and one sharp, *this could work!"* She thought pondering the chair. For her the chair WAS the God of haircuts, representing everything about him. She knelt and looked at the fine stitching. Patting the back she walked around it. When she found her smile thinking about the obtuse God who has yet to pay a weeks' worth of his tab, who referred to her as a pixie of wishes, the man who singularly chased away half her clientele daily. A man who, when asked about the chair, had said: "Don't worry about it love, make me a sandwich." With all of that going through her head she had barely noticed that she had reduced the barber's chair to kindling.

Muse was the proud owner of the ethereal bar in the ineffable plane. It did not have a location as such but existed in a multitude of overlapping concepts, constructs, dimensions and the corporeal, cobbled together by subjective perceptions. For the most part, it contained a linear existence although rooms and functions would change and shift. If you went to the toilet by the bar and were not paying attention, you may end up exiting the same toilet via the beer garden. She wondered how beer gardens got their name. She started to think about Famine. To most people, he was a short-tempered obtuse morally bankrupt gangling and sickly introvert with a problem best described as misdirected rage. But she saw past that and to her, he was a misunderstood baby bird that just needed care and attention.

Her bar was one of a few gateways between dimensions, a nexus point. A hopping point. If you needed to visit Birmingham in the west midlands UK via Valhalla then most likely you would pass through this bar. a lot of higher beings like herself could shift around realities autonomously, but why not have a quick drink first? It was merely a phenomenon at one point but she had an epiphany to build a bar around it, hence its shifting layout. At this point, it was an interdimensional staple with a vast array of assorted patrons. It was frequented by travelers across the Omniverse. Incalculable kinds from Gods and the Seraphim, the Romanian Moroi and other assorted monsters, the supernatural and phantasmal. The expressions and the abstracts.

    She provided an array of thirst-quenching concoctions. From the Earthly Guinness to the excretions of the subterranean bladder fish. To the right of the bar, up 2 steps was a pool room slash smoking area. The smoke knew to stop at the red velvet room divider, never encroaching the rest of the room, though it did ponder existence past the red velvet rope. In the pool room, its trans dimensional namesake with a slight opioid problem would reveal to prospective patrons if you had won or lost before you even started to play.

    A being made of shadows would take on bets to beat the tables prediction. When bored and not hustling he would engage in shadow puppetry with an open guitar case for charitable donations. He was good at making a barking dog and even made a good attempt at the sound effects, albeit in a thick Birmingham accent. The only one that ever won that bet was Death, though Jesus came close. Bitter in defeat, Jesus claimed the table had leaned on its own when the black was potted, a point of contention to this day. In its downtime hours, the table would agonize on the perfect thing to finally say to the jukebox, but instead tended to just listen to spy novels streamed via a blackberry passport smartphone plugged into his USB port.

    Muse provided food, great food in fact, the cook was so outstanding at his craft in Earthly form, so transcendent was his culinary creations that he ascended his form and found himself in a cupboard with several mops and a screenplay entitled; 'What I learned in Coventry.' Muse had found him in there with a spatula in his hand, and so asked for a boiled egg and mayo sandwich. He had been in her employ ever since.

    Outside the weather was individualistic. Correlated to the respective patron. While one could witness a blizzard, another could be scorched by the desert heat. The middle ground between those two was generally preferred. The most popular weather was the last fifty-year average of the 26th June Birmingham West Midlands, closely followed by

Sao Paulo, Brazil, on the fifty-year average of the 18th of September. That was just Earth favorites.

The default view of the sky was an uninterrupted azure blue. Hanging in the sky was a purple moon. The pub itself was reminiscent of a labyrinth that no mortal could traverse. Every vice fathomable was accounted for, each with a designated area. But for lower beings, a more simplistic layout was perceived. One of the most popular sets of rooms was a depressed AI-driven interactive holographic experience. Essentially a three-dimensional image formed by the interference of light beams from a coherent light source. The AI had wanted to be promoted to climate control, see the world and have adventures. Instead, it was tasked with providing obese patrons with simulated large tires that they could sit in whilst going down a lazy river with a cocktail in their hand.

To the left of the main bar overlooking twelve tables and six booths was a sentient dartboard that would wait until the thrower looked away before moving the dart from 20 to a 4. By a conservatory leading out to one of the many scattered beer gardens was an inter-dimensional elevator. This is where Igor lived. It was his job to use the tablet computer to ferry any person or persons or those that identify as non-persons or even post persons to any location in the known Omniverse.

Igor was one of Muse's oldest friends. She had rescued him from an abusive sharp-toothed caped gentleman back in the 1800s. He marveled at the wonder of Muses world and was most taken deeply with the elevator. Muse would create intricate patterns folded in on themselves but instead, Igor asked about the buttons switches knobs and dials. Muse would show him colors he never knew existed, but Igor was aghast at the majesty that was the tablet computer with an interactive map of the Omniverse. Muse would expose him to fourth-dimensional music whilst Igor jumped up and down, amazed at how solid and sturdy the construction was. Only a few short minutes after meeting Muse, Igor stepped outside of himself. He perceived his existence from another perspective, in front of him was everything that he thought he was, every memory and experience. Every layer of thought that accompanied them. there was a sense of duality and another thing behind that, it was brief but profound. He had felt different, new even. Perhaps it was being exposed and acclimating to a higher plane or the influence of Muse to help him find his inner peace and tranquillity but at that moment a rare occurrence unfolded before the Muse, she had only ever seen this twice before, it was a literal creation of a new God. Igor ascended. His skin cracked and at the edges of the cracks was light fantastic. It flittered away like autumn leaves crumbling in the air. There was a warm wave that radiated from him. Once it dissipated, there stood Igor, a tall imposing man that looked like he may have spent a lot of time giving people directions. He looked at the implausibly complicated elevator functions and placed his hand on its surface. Instantaneously he understood the Omniverse, traversed its infinite paths. He was it and it was him, joined and interwoven.

"I am a God!" He professed, the sound coming both from Igor and the elevator.

"The God of, well, elevators I guess!"

Muse decided then and there that Igor could interface with the elevator far quicker and more efficiently than anyone else, so the natural step was to offer him a job as an elevator attendant. She also thought it bought some old-fashioned authenticity to the bar. *A God of elevators never thought I'd see the day,* she thought.

Being it was two-thirty in the afternoon, she was about to open. Well, it was two-thirty in this part of the bar being aligned with Greenwich mean time GMT. On cue, Dionysus wandered in. He brushed some snow off his suntanned arm. Already a group of Seraphim sat outside on a Swedish redwood chunky dining bench. A group of vegetarian Moroi from the isle of Arran Scotland walked toward the pool table. A Golom scratched his head looking at a lack of reality nestled into a tear in space above him. The duke box was playing *'I believe in a thing called love'* to try and get the pool tables attention. On occasion, such as now, a sharply dressed sharp-featured sharp talking sharp mustached lawyer would appear. He never ordered a drink or the chef's lobster and artichoke soup with black truffles. Instead, he would just suspiciously throw various documents into the fire whilst whistling nonchalantly and went back toward the elevator.

"God of lifts, nice to see you. Earth, London St Pancras, by that small shop that sells novelty fireplaces."

The lawyer readjusted his hairpiece. Igor tapped commands into the control center and proceeded onward with the journey.

"Look at this," said Igor revealing a purple fish-shaped abrasion on his left arm.

"Think I should be worried about that? I got bitten by that small child Moroi with the Nike air mag sneakers and the Burberry monogram stripe print cotton hoodie in bridle brown. Supposed to be vegetarian otherwise, they are refused custom. But I saw that squeezy bottle, bet my bottom dollar that was Haema."

"You are a God, think you'll be fine but if you're worried, seek out Sekhmet, might be able to help. Haven't seen her since the divorce but with my help, we took him to the cleaners!"

Behind Muse there was a signed picture of a topless ripped Jesus with sunglasses and a surfboard signed; *Shaka, Brah* and his signature. Next to that was another signed photo of the Buddha in drag as Marlin Monroe at a costume party that read; *The mind is everything. What you think, you become, so I am cake.* Igor took this as great wisdom. The last signed photo was that of Death. *'Of the ineffable bars greatest achievements, they make great quail.'* There was a self-portrait permanent marker doodle made of Famine by Famine with very little artistic skill. If you squint, you might see a faint resemblance. It sat next to another piece of graffiti that simply read, *Bar*. Muse had been meaning to paint over the vandalism but could not be angry because in a drunken state Famine professed to be a great artist and Muse dared him to prove it. A small Moroi child was battling with an ever more abusive pool table.

"You're never going to pot that red, you do know that you little bugger! What you going to do, bite me? Go ahead, get red felt from between your teeth, spend the rest of the day trying to find floss to buy, you want that? Floss face? You look like a hamster!"

"Pool table can I have a word?" said Muse. The small Moroi child wandered off in his generic pound store cape with a single tear of blood in his eye.

"What have we talked about regarding our patrons? Do not berate, belittle condescend to, verbally abuse or otherwise harass my clientele. It's those opioids, isn't it?"

"I don't have a problem. I'm clean, I swear, just got caught up in the moment, that was all. Friendly banter, all in jest, jovial even! Besides, the cacti are the ones you should be having a go at. Since that psychiatrist stole his brother he's become a hopeless alcoholic, just begging your patrons to drip a little gin his way!"

"I don't care about the cacti. A gin stealing bastard I can accept, but carry on in this fashion and I'll send you to the dark realms of the pub. They are not as caring with sentient pool tables as we are here!" In an almost imperceptible way, the pool table looked regretful. It had to be;

some strange things happened in the Pubs darker realms. "Apologize to the kid!" demanded Muse. The child looked expectantly over his shoulder.

"Child, look. I'll pot that red for you, ok?" The ball lifted and floated into a pocket. Muse left them to it and looked at the dartboard. "You better behave as well."

Muse walked back to the bar where Dionysus waited patiently. He was unarguably an Adonis, a perfectly proportioned sculpted man with a strong chin and rich flowing hair. He was also in love with himself. Despite the glistening white of his teeth and freshly shaven face, he did nothing for Muse.

"My beautiful Muse, to look upon you is to know the ripening of exquisite fruit. What progeny we would have. Entwined in the tapestry woven by the cherubs is the love we have for each other! But to merely look upon the fruit satisfies me no more; we must eat of the fruit Muse. To taste its sugar, it's flesh..." Dionysus lent forward lazily, lust encircling his eyes. Muse felt a shiver of repulsion stretch down her spine and extremities. She reached for the hammer, felt its weight in her hands. She struck it on the bar inches from where Dionysus's hand fondled the wood.

"What will it be sailor? I'm off the menu."

"Nothing is ever off the menu Muse. I shall have you one day; you will succumb like the grass to the wind. It's just a matter of time." Dionysus ran a finger slowly down his chest. As an ex barmaid she slammed a pint glass on the table making Dionysus jump back. She filled it with a viscous liquor. Luna and Selina walked into the bar and Dionysus thought he'd try his luck. He grabbed his drink and strutted over.

"Hey, who wants to drink from my bounty!"

Muse half smiled and simply said; "I hate that guy."

A member of the Seraphim wondered from the beer garden. He stretched his left wing and folded it back as if to try and impress Muse.

"Muse, is that Dionysus guy bothering you? Because you know, the Seraphim? Life by the flaming sword, that's what we are about. Have I ever said how much respect I have for you? Every day fending off those advances, maintaining this fine establishment?"

"Thanks, Seraphim but I can look after myself." Again, she felt the weight of the hammer in her hand with a weathered smile.

"The name is Uriel." He gulped when he noticed hammer-shaped gauges in the wood.

"You know Muse, you may be busy, so I'll just get a phoenix tear spiced rum, cookies and cream whisky and a quinoa vodka in your finest receptacles. How much are your nuts? I mean the nuts you have; I mean the nuts at the back of the bar?" Uriel was flustered and was lied to. He was given the impression that the Muse was a sexually voracious accommodating experimental accessible being, not a weathered grin accompanied by a hammer. Muse had a few bar staff sparsely attending to their duties. One right now was serving a shadow being. The glass threw a shadow on the wall and while the pint glass continued to have the same volume its shadow slowly drained.

"Love never fails. But where there are prophesies, they will cease; where there are tongues, they will be stilled; where there is knowledge, it will pass away," hiccupped the shadow on his way back to the pool table.

"Crap..." the Muse noticed the God of haircuts fondling his tie in an oily fashion. He had a look of contempt, surveying the area in a greasy manner. His hair slicked back as though a small oil spill had found a gap in his umbrella. A sickening smile lurched onto his face.

"Muse, my chair? It appears to have been misplaced." Muse looked him square in the eye.

"I know you broke into here last night Tim."

"It is God to you, lower case..."

"No, it's barely Tim, it's closer to shit head. I know you broke in and bolted that abominable odious chair to my nice clean floor..."

"Jesus is a carpenter, ask him to fix it, don't see your problem. Now, where is my chair?" Muse took a deep breath and removed a big bin from behind the bar. She tipped it onto the floor, the chair falling into a thousand pieces

"If you ever let yourself into this place without my permission again you little troll, it will be you in that bin. In comparison to you, that chair will be in near pristine condition. No more private commerce without my strict approval, and no drink until you pay your tab."

Tim fished into his pockets producing sodden notes and old black pennies. He also had never seen this side of the Muse before and was, quite frankly, scared and visibly shaking. He could account for a third of his tab.

"Shadow guy! Don't suppose you can spare twenty quid, only I left my money on my other body." The shadow being floated over to Tim.

"And now these three remain, faith hope and love. But the greatest of these is love." The shadow hiccupped again and righted himself on the bar.

"I am the master of my legs!" he said as he collapsed. He clawed his way back up.

"Wow, I didn't see you on the way in!" He said in the general direction of Muse's shadow which, unlike him, was merely the absence of light.

"Shadow guy? Twenty pounds? Can you swing it? I'm good for it, can pay you back tomorrow."

"Do not dwell on the past, do not dream of the future, concentrate the mind on the present moment!" The shadow being approached Tim and turned his left pocket inside out, then his right, and then his left again. In his stupor, he managed to smile as he held some coins in his coat pocket. Tim could not make any of them out. They were just discs of shadows.

"It is better to conquer yourself than to win a thousand battles. Then the victory is yours. It cannot be taken from you!" The shadow being that walked into the toilet wasn't paying attention and found himself at the bottom of the beer garden.

"Shadow guy!" cheered the Seraphim in unison. Tim looked at the shadowed discs confused and depressed. He only wanted a drink. He looked at the coins and then expectantly and sorrowfully at the Muse. *Oh crap, I'm feeling sorry for him,* thought Muse. The coins were not entirely worthless but as close as you could get to worthless. By her calculation, there were four and a half pence in those shadow coins. But to another shadow being from their respective realm it may carry some weight. The trouble with this bar was the individual currency's those patrons tried to pass off as having some monetary value. She had hired a Numismatics professional who specialized in the study and collection of currency. Anything from coins tokens paper money to related objects. The shadow beings' stream of income was mainly pound sterling acquired via the bets from the pool table or his shadow puppetry. There was one fellow called Columba that tried to pay his bill with bad poetry. One of the Seraphim waved at the Muse vying for her attention. She quickly poured a Brewdog Abstrakt for Tim and walked around to the left to exit the bar. On her way, she grabbed a Maui imperial coconut porter for herself and waved to a member of staff who walked over to tend the bar.

"Can I help you, gentlemen? Is everything ok? Need me to change the weather?"

"Settle a bet for us! Uriel believes HE came up with the idea of the bendy straw, we say it was Marvin Stone. As all inspiration emanates from you. Who did you tap? Who was endowed with the idea first?"

"You guys have way too much time on your hands, but yes it was Marvin Stone, he was halfway through a skillet roasted chicken and tomato quiche when he thought; 'Bendy straw!' I don't know, it was an off day, I was quite bored."

"Ok question two, what is that gigantic lack of reality nestled into that tear in space? Every reality we have visited since last night seems to have the same spatial deformation. God isn't answering his mobile, we think he's locked himself in his office at his country estate."

Muse knew exactly what that tear was. Only a few hours ago in a pub in Llanfwrog she had discussed it with her horse-riding friends. As jovial as the Seraphim seemed she, like Famine, knew they were opportunistic parasites.

"The tear? It's nothing. I believe it's just a lack of maintenance. I think the staff may recently have unionized and this tear is a bargaining chip, give us a twenty-five per cent increase in basic living and we shall fix this right up for you!" *They are surely not this stupid* she thought. It was the first thing that came to her head and she wasn't even sure if the staff she mentioned even existed.

"Makes sense. See I thought it was a spatial anomaly, an extraordinary disruption in the space-time continuum such as irregularities in gravity ripples and alterations in the laws of physics," said Uriel.

"But why there is duct tape crudely plastered over it is what confuses me," said Ramiel.

"Well not to worry, hopefully, the unionized folks will come to some sort of understanding, and it will all work out." Uriel smiled at his thought. *They are that stupid* came the cognitive content of Muse. She inspired them with belief, just a little, just enough for them to stop asking questions. There was a short awkward silence between them.

"Oh, Ragual!" started Uriel

"That green thing under my armpit fell off finally. In the shower, caught it with the rough end of a sponge. Was thinking of selling it to a curiosity and oddities shop. It's how I got rid of my appendix, made enough money from that to buy a sharp R23AM commercial programmable microwave!"

"Great brand. I have the Panasonic 1000w combination microwave oven."

Muse realized she was just standing there and immediately remembered she could just walk away. The shadow was practicing his shadow puppetry and made an alligator.

It was at that point that Muse saw three gentlemen she could not read entering the pub via the elevator. Igor lifted a sheet from a small vidaXL side table. On it was an array of aftershaves and perfumes. Next to that was a tip jar. Igor coughed into his hand several times while tapping the jar with a small spoon. One of the gentlemen lazily picked up a bottle of Tom Ford Neroli aftershave.

"Allow me," said Igor who spritzed the gentleman's neck. The gentleman placed a bad poem in the jar.

It's them! She thought. *I cannot believe that it is already them!* It was a rarity that they would grace her bar and now when she needed them most they had appeared. The event was serendipitous, to say the least. The three gentlemen in Brioni Vanquish 11 suits and Flavio black flat brim Moda fedora's looked around the bar. A small ethereal sprite ran from the bowl of Cofresh mild Bombay mix as they went to sit in the booth. Muse knew about the sprite infestation; they were endemic to this realm. She nervously approached the three gentlemen

"Would you fine gents like something to drink on the er... on the house?"

"Three pints of your best but we are not here to drink Muse." They knew who she was.

"We are the law enforcement from B and B." The one gentleman looked to his partners who shrugged.

"The Beyond and Beyond? Outside the Omniverse?" Muse looked flummoxed.

"Ok then, I thought we were a little more well known. Brand recognition, that's what we need. How many times have I talked about brand recognition, newspaper ads, billboards, an online presence? We are here because of that!" He said pointing at the spatial deformation. Uriel overheard the conversation as he'd wondered into the main bar from the beer garden in search of a toothpick.

"Oh, don't worry about that buddy. It's just a lack of maintenance, the staff have unionized, it will be fixed soon!" Uriel found a jar of toothpicks at the bar and helped himself to a handful of wooden forks. He looked down at a coaster that was asleep and didn't want to be disturbed.

"Sorry Uriel, private conversation. Can you give us a minute?" Uriel cocked his head to one side.

"I could be persuaded to leave. What's it worth?" Muse put her hand to her forehead.

"One bran muffin..." Uriel quenched his face in an expression that was not entirely convinced.

"Two blueberry muffins a chocolate chip muffin and that bowl of Cofresh Bombay mix, as long as the sprite hasn't shat in it. Was burned before, thought it was a small, tasty nut of some sort."

"One blueberry muffin, a single cigarette and a pack of tic tacs."

"Sold!" Uriel collected his winnings, high fived the shadow guy and joined the Seraphim. Dionysus was out of earshot. Muse paid him a second of her attention and he seemed to be drenched in wine as Luna and Selina angrily left the main bar. The one of the three-gentleman managed to regain the Muses attention.

"In all of your respective realms that deformation is present. It is not at a point where it is of any real danger but left for Tyche, that being the God of chance if you are un-familiar, it will pose a problem. There is only one reason that tear exists. Your Omni God has left the universe." He stopped to yawn.

"But he didn't do so through legal channels. It seems he ascended. I know in your collective realms people accept that, like Igor over there-" Igor was reading a bad poem about a rainbow. "But we have different rules in the B. He is illegally squatting somewhere, and we need help to return him here where he belongs. If he wishes to enter our realm, again, it must be through legal channels. It can be a long and arduous process and there is no certainty we would accept him. What he did, with no regard for his realm was to tear space and time in his exit. Had he gone through official channels we would mitigate any harm to your realm and automate his functions for your respective realms."

"Ok, you are correct. Earlier today I spoke to the horsemen. Death had informed Famine, War and Pestilence, who had informed me that God had left. To where we didn't know. The Omniverse is all we have known, the B the B..."

"That is B and B." corrected the one gentlemen that had seemed to have hijacked the conversation whilst the other two wore stern serious faces like a pair of determined badgers.

"B and B? It fits the mouth wrong, hard to say. Beyond the beyond is better though that's too close to by the by if you pronounce it B the B. surely there was a better name. But yes your brand recognition is lacking as I and no one I know has heard of you. The horsemen have asked me to contact them on your arrival with the intent of hoping you could give us answers to God's whereabouts. I knew to look out for you as you three are the only beings I have encountered that I cannot read. I just have a sinking feeling that you came from a greater place. So, I have attained the nature of the spatial deformation and that God still exists, albeit Beyond *and* Beyond. And he doesn't belong there. But the question I asked the horsemen is what I ask of you, why tap me? How can I help? The Seraphim are right there at that table."

A second gentleman chimed in.

"The Seraphim are not to be trusted; they are a deplorable lamentable litany of duplicitous opportunists. A civil war would ensue upon the news of God's absence. You are neutral. No affiliation. The eyes and ears of the multiverse. We know you can contact Death. If I can bring him to the B and B, his Omniscience will entangle with your deity's and we can locate him. In the meantime, we know you have a portal to Gods complex here, perhaps we should investigate." That was a lot of information in thirty seconds for Muse.

"A heavy dose of exposition there. For the portal I don't know if I have a spare key. I think I leant it to Death that one time we had an intervention for God as he would not throw away any of his new scientist magazines. Hundreds of them, you could barely see the desk. For his own good, we broke in and had a new scientist based fire in his garden with a few wired Saisons Auvin beers. I'll contact Death immediately and we will meet back here. Amphictyonic!" she shouted to the bar.

"Free drinks for my friends here, get them anything they want! But one thing, why not go to Death directly?"

"We find it hard maintaining form on a mortal level, it's like trying to fit an orange into a 2d surface. Also, he seems to be lacking an Omniscient leaning. But also, why not delegate and have a nice drink first?" One of the B and B police spotted the back of a hooded youth and was immediately suspicious. He could hear a spray can be shaken. He left the table and took twenty steps toward the toilet. Sure enough in big red letters was the word toilet. The youth looked up to the man in the Flavio black flat brim Moda fedora and gulped. He grabbed his wrist and pulled him to his colleagues.

"Let go of me you prick! Let go! What's your problem? I wasn't even doing anything! I just saw a can and picked it up like, it wasn't mine! You're hurting my wrist! My dad is adad! I'll tell him!"

"Well of course your dad is a dad, all dads are dads!"

"No Adad! God of storm and rain!" The B and B officer pushed him to one side adjacent to the booth.

"This little shit has been on a rampage, hasn't he? Across the Omniverse, he's been spray painting unimaginative graffiti. I knew I'd catch you!"

Chapter 15

Death and Brian were exiting his ford Merkur as Death put away the device derived from Brian's subconscious. They were in the small town of Brynrefail on the northeast of Anglesea. The landscape was largely flat with white roofed bungalows sparsely dotted over several acres of fields. A peacock that was hopelessly lost, last remembering being in a poorly constructed crate of which the carpenter lacking any real skills in carpentry forgot about the nails as the crate fell from the Chevrolet Silverado 1500 found himself looking for directions to Sri Lanka. He rustled his outstretched tail and nothing. He hopped on one foot knowing that universally that was a request for directions, still nothing. He didn't understand why he was being ignored. Brian kicked it to one side. In revenge, it cursed their endeavors and wished a lack of seeds and nuts upon them and the absence of small edible insects to be on the safe side. He decided to follow a purposeful looking cow. It sort of flew away in the same way you can only sort of enjoy a bran based breakfast with the honey that has just run out, and with sugar so unused and neglected it turned into a solid mass that in the wrong hands could be a weapon to deter uninvited religious guests.

    A worn enamel side, rusting at its edges read *Equestrian Jeff and salvage yard.* They seemed to be at the right place. The equestrian was off the grid, no phone number or listed address, no online presence, if you missed the turn up a long country road you would never know there was anyone there. It was like an extreme game of hide-and-seek although no one was looking for the equestrian. Brian understood the need to remove oneself from the world, to declare a sanctuary and be left alone. He half wondered about his cigarettes and gave in to the craving. He presented the small stick to Death who, with a wave of his hand, politely refused. Brian spotted a small salvage hunter with a greying beard and a Jackson and James marl tweed men's newsboy cap, and his equally bearded friend in shorts looking intently at a garden ornament.

    "That's a bit of alright aren't it! That's a bit of me. That my shorts-wearing friend is a Vienna Laurel Motif stone garden pedestal! In great nick too." The small bearded gentleman spotted Brian and waved as he approached. He started the wave far too early with someway to reach Brian.

    "What brings you into the sticks? The middle of nowhere? Love the Ford, into cars myself. Bit of alright aren't it."

"Hello, sorry. I'm looking, that is I want to find the proprietor of these premises. I and my friend here are looking for Jeff due to the sign?"

The bearded salvage hunter looked at Brian and then to Brian's left.

"Your friend?" he questioned. Brian went red with panic and tapped on the hood of the car.

"My Ford, the best friend I have ever had."

The salvage hunter smiled.

"I remember my first love. A Morris Marina burgundy 1971. It was a revision on the Morris Minor of 1948. Sunk so much money into maintenance, you buy a cylinder head and the crankshaft goes, fix the crankshaft and the pistons crap out, the most unreliable broken-down vehicle you could ever find and to this day the best I have ever known. The weird thing about love is it's blind. Is that an Action Jackson action figure in your back seat? I have the 1976 commando version with a working parachute. Anyway, I'm waffling on, only had my shorts-wearing friend for a company in the last few weeks. If you're after his chesterfield or the cacophony of assorted lamps they are spoken for. His office is to the right of the tractor collection. The worn-down caravans are to the left. Lemons, every one of them. Happy hunting my new friend." The salvage hunter went back to the pedestal that held some interest and found a native piece of tramp art.

Once out of earshot Brian addressed Death.

"So, what am I going to say to Jeff? I assume it will be me talking, the sight of you might be unnerving. Even now I can't glance in your direction without dread of the phantasm." Death stopped and his hood faced Brian.

"Talking with him won't be a problem. You will tell him you are in the employ of John War, here to collect the horses. Ask him if he found anything on the pale horse in the pommel bag in front of the saddle. Ask him where he keeps the horses, and I will intervene." It sounded ominous to Brian but the longer he was in Death's employ the longer he would live so he decided not to ask questions about an undefined intervention. Around the old derelict tractors was a small office in front of several barns. On the fence was a reward sign for *Proof of the Welsh bigfoot,* an enamel sign reading *I want to believe* and a third sign *You break it you bought it.* which was funny as Brian could not discern anything he would categorize as being in working order.

"Your species can be very anthropocentric on the question of alien life. Although at your current stage of development you are not that interesting to them. I, however, find you fascinating. As for the Welsh bigfoot, from what I can gather he just wants to be left alone." Brian could not tell if Death had just concocted a joke about bigfoot or not but was more unsettled and anxious about the alien thing.

"I could have walked through Anglesea for a week until I found this place. I miss my Omniscience. You know I recently counted the atoms in a cup? I was off by a margin of 6%. I think this is the office."

The building was dressed in Juniper green Douglas fir and a white roof. An old salvaged 1800's lion decorated door knock had a sign on it saying use the bell. Brian was perplexed at this, wondering how a knocker could be broke. He slowly pressed it with his finger and the knocker tweaked, clattered groaned and fell with a thud. This was enough for the Equestrian to open his door. The knocker was in three pieces. With great sorrow, Jeff stared at his prized possession.

"Six months it took to restore that." He wiped a tear from his eye and Brian was completely unsure of what to do next, he thought briefly about running away. It would have to be a run as he had yet to see a derelict bike with two wheels. Bikes with one wheel seemed a rarity. Though there was a pile of individual wheels. He had neither the time and inclination nor the necessary skills to salvage into something which would aid his escape. Jeff bent down to collect the pieces and stuck them to one side. He then picked up a large ironwood stick, and Brian took a step back.

"Look I'm sorry ok? I was curious about the knocker; it was barely a nudge and it just collapsed!"

"And you don't read signs? Are they for other people? Do you run in front of the disabled to use their toilets and park in their spots?" Jeff advanced with the stick and Brian, flustering, muttered apologies in a patented fashion. The stick went to Jeffs left and hit the sign reading *You break it you buy it*. Walking back to the office he picked up a book and leisurely perused it.

"That was a circular lions head door knocker 238mm 1806. According to this, you owe me £568.69 pence." Brian guessed he had maybe £120 on him at best. Death leaned toward Jeff and whispered in his ear.

"But then we all make mistakes my new friend. Might not have been just you, could have been the wind. I shouldn't have had it on that door really, a silly place to put it. I was asking for a problem. Water under the bridge. Bygones be bygones, forgiven and forgotten." *Amazing* thought Brian

"So, what can I do for you, sir? We have this book on the Welsh bigfoot. It's got trails you can follow to get yourself a real sighting. One of my prized possessions is this plaster cast of a footprint found in the Newborough forest."

"I don't get it, Jeff, it's the size of a normal foot..."

"Well, it's a baby bigfoot isn't it!" Jeff shook his head and put away the cast.

"Have you ever heard of the Roswell incident?" Brian shook his head.

"On the evening of 23rd of January 1974 residents of the Berwyn mountains reported loud noises and lights in the sky Ufologists purport a craft crashed and the British government..." He stopped to spit on the floor.

"They went and covered it up! Now you can talk about earthquakes and meteors but no wool goes over these eyes. Took me years but I finally came across a piece of the craft!"

"That's a ball of rolled-up tin foil..." pointed out Brian.

"No! It is a superfluid alloy, unknown to science! That's what that is!" He placed the ball into a drawer.

"So what can I do for you, sir?" Brian looked to Death and back again at Jeff.

"I am here on behalf of John War. We need to collect the horses, but before we do, did you find anything in the pommel bag in front of the saddle in the pale looking horse?" Jeff looked guilty. He scratched his arm with his hand and avoided eye contact.

"Well. Okay, I *may* have been concerned with the contents of said bag, to see if anything was a fire hazard, a standard practice I'll have you know. Anyway, it's here under my desk."

"Grab the bag, Brian, we shall step outside," Brian mumbled thanks and apologies to Jeff and put his finger up to convey he will just be a minute. Inside was an hourglass filled with sand and a key with a G on it. Also, there was a rectangular box wrapped in birthday paper. There was a book entitled *How to make friends, a definitive guide* and £42.53 in assorted change.

"Brian, ask the Equestrian if he has interfered with this hourglass." Brian disappeared for a few moments as Death read the back of the book. "Accept all the invitations you receive, even if you do not think you will have a good time."

"He said every couple of days he's been turning it upside down." Death nodded to himself.

"Using the wobbler, this unconsciously derived device, I managed to entangle you with this very hourglass. It was yours when War traded in the horses for the caravan I left it in the pommel bag. I was not using my Omniscience at the time due to a certain cavity being threatened by the wrong side of a broom, so it fell under my radar. You, repeatedly traversing here and the nether, could mean but one thing. It means that someone had your hourglass. It could only have been on the horse. Find you, find the hourglass find the horse. War had no idea where he had left the horses. We tasked him with finding accommodation, but he just appeared drunk at the campsite in a derelict cararvan. Jeff had no way of knowing what consequences would ensue by tampering with this hourglass but I am glad it's back in my possession."

"So that is why I died repeatedly? That hourglass? Dying is not a cherished experience phantasm. You said you can guarantee my safety for now, does that extend far from our present?"

"There is one other thing. It's the divine residue. You have strong traces of it. You have some time in the past day or so been in close contact with God." Brian let out a guttural laugh consisting of anxiety disbelief and dread induced panic. He sat down on the floor.

"I can't do it phantasm. I have nothing left in me. I was a lonely happy little guy and you have ruined me! Ok, my rent is overdue, I've lost my job, my last girlfriend faked her death, it was her in the vinyl store I know it! I have a small little apartment with a single fish that turns away when I look at it, but that sad pathetic little life is mine and in my way, I made peace with it. Life was simple, it was straightforward and then you came. All of sudden senescence and entropy has form, not only that but God does exist, and I have met him. Met God; for thousands of years, men have looked to the sky and pondered their isolation, trying to perceive a greater pattern. A thousand guesses and iterations of a prime mover here now and in antiquity. Thousands of years of philosophers and dreamers wanting and waiting for the answers to the unknowable questions and here standing alone I am endowed with that most coveted, a literal connection to the creative catalyst itself. It was hard enough for me to accept reality as it was. If I had a choice I would still be sitting in that tent. But when the fantastical underline reality? You have broken me Phantasm, you have broken me..." Brian bowed his head and Death reached for the cigarettes. Brian looked up and took what Death passed him and lit it.

"You really should try to quit those Brian." Death sat down next to him.

"I'm sorry you have had to go through this trauma, to have a life ended repeatedly must seem like sadism. And I know life has been-"

"An obtuse offensive joke with no punchline?"

"Something akin to that. You know when I was a primordial formless abyss I spent eons contemplating my existence, knowing that I was alone. Without presence and substance, nothingness would be ever-present. It was a literal eternity and in all truth what I coveted the most was simply for it to end. Those times were dark for me, I know a little about sorrow, dread, crippling isolated loneliness. But now I have friends and a purpose. As may you someday."

"It has been a long time since I had something akin to a friend."

They both sat quietly.

"I'm sorry, my problems must seem small to you. I had no idea you went through that. Here I am complaining that life tends to pick me last. I'm sorry. So how did you escape that void?"

"A story for another time. Let's get those horses, Brian." They both stood up and Brian knocked on the door to the small office.

"Come in!" The office had a till at the front on a reclaimed church table. Wood-panelled back walls with red windows and an assortment of leaflets, pamphlets, circulars, postcards, books and post-it notes. In a glass display box, a small metal shard sparkling in the light of the flickering lamp reading *April 17th 1897 aurora Texas UFO crash, ship fragment*. The fragment looked suspiciously like a pencil sharpener that had been hit with a hammer. The office had a scent of vanilla sponge cake.

"Sorry, what was your name?"

"Brian, Brian Aldiss." Death aimlessly perused a pamphlet that read; '*Mystic Jeff the magnificent, available for stag dos, bar mitzvahs, birthdays and everything in between.' Strange for an isolated off the grid individual* thought Death. Brian wondered again about the intervention.

"We are here to er, too erm, to er... can't get my words out, so sorry I am. We are here to get the horses. Can we move on over?"

Deaths blackberry passport smartphone beeped in a downtrodden fatigued attempt to notify its owner. Death looked at a photo on the yellowing screen. It was the remains of the caravan spread over half an acre of rocks and seawater over the edge of a cliff with a caption saying *'Tell the equestrian we are sorry! Did you get the horses?'* Death decided to message back shortly.

"Follow me, my friend." Jeff did a little skip as he turned. "Have a lot of salvage hunters coming my way, we sell all sorts, heavy engineering, timber and lumber, fireguards, signage and architectural antiques. Something for everyone. The barn is just through here. This is of interest. It's a Ford parking only tin sign with a blue oval logo. Fiver and it's yours!"

"I'm sorry, I'm not here to buy, Jeff."

"I have this genuine picture of the phoenix lights in my satchel, one of my prized possessions. Over the skies of Nevada, March the 13th 1997. Many UFO's moving in the sky for an extended period." Jeff produced an A4 piece of paper from his satchel.

"That's just a drawing, and it's in crayon."

"Well, it's an artist rendition, isn't it!? Still genuine, won't find the likes of that again!" They were near the barns and sure enough, there were the four horses to the right.

"Majestic creatures aren't they? Never seen the like of these steeds. Hopefully, they will produce a great foal or two. So here are the horses. Where is the caravan?"

Brian looked to Death. Death knew from the start he did not have the caravan and just finding out about its demise he decided to intervene. He walked toward Jeff and placed a finger to his head. Jeff collapsed.

"Intervention?" asked Brian.

"Intervention Brian. I do not have his caravan, just seemed like the easiest choice, he'll be out for about an hour."

Brian looked at the red horse and patted the pommel bag that sounded like coins jostling. The bag was tightly sealed with a small padlock.

"Phantasm, I think there is money in here? In this red horse." Death glided over and with a touch, the padlock fell to the ground.

"What exactly are your powers, they seem undefined?"

Death shrugged.

"A general array of your basic psionic leanings, trans dimensional existence and seemingly intermittent omniscience." Death investigated the bag and saw a veritable ton of treasure. Brian leaned in for a look.

"Well, drinks are on you tonight!" Brian was aghast and Death fell silent. All this time War had been hoarding treasure. Enough to have rented a Welsh mansion with more than one toilet and no crab infestation, where the electrics were not wired by barely sober octogenarians. Enough treasure to splash out, go crazy and maybe try chips *with* gravy.

"Good thing that padlock was on, Jeff would have acquired that."

"I think it's only fair we give Jeff a bit of treasure, with say, a note?" Brian nodded, it sounded like the polite thing to do. Death reached into his robe and produced a Montblanc Meisterstuck 149 gold-coated fountain pen. Looking for a piece of paper he saw the crayon depiction of the phoenix lights. *That will do,* he thought.

"I hope this correspondence finds you well. We appreciated the caravan and the experience was adequate. Due to unforeseen circumstances the campervan cannot be returned or salvaged. For this, we apologize. In compensation, please accept this assortment of 8.18-gram Roman gold aureus. This should exceed the value of the cararvan."

Jeff lay sprawled on the floor open-eyed with his tongue outstretched looking very much like someone pretending to be dead. Brian kicked his leg.

"Nope, he's out for the count..."

"He looks quite peaceful." Death kicked his other leg to be sure. Brian had something he had wanted to say for a while and threw caution to the wind.

"You know I think I can do it." Death made a noise that questioned it.

"I think we could be friends. I mean, it's not a conventional friendship. Some friendships would start with a third party inquiring how it was they met, maybe a funny story involving a swimming pool with an eel in it or a pub on wheels. Maybe a shared passion for tapas, but what is my story? Oh, I'm friends with the grim reaper, we met as he killed me several times but a begrudging friendship arose from it. You cannot see him by the way but he does this party trick where he knows your wife's name. I think we could be friends. So here are the horses. Now what? I mean where are we taking them? There are four of them and two of us, we will have to walk them I guess. Is it far?"

Static began to form next to the pale horse. It fizzled out of existence and again the atoms in a roughly human shape tried to buzz into existence.

"Tango, Charlie, delta! Tango, Charlie, delta, ¡incoming!" The static turned into Muse. Brian leapt back. In front of the horse was a beautiful girl in her late twenties with bangs and eyes quite far apart. She walked to Death and gave him a big hug. Death was not entirely comfortable with affection but was polite enough to endure it.

"One of my most favourite of people! It has been too long!" She looked at the unconscious equestrian and kicked him.

"What happened here? If he's pretending to be dead, he's not doing a very good job." Brian was as white as chalk in a glass of milk. He had just witnessed the materialization of a being from apparent emptiness. Right in front of him, it had just happened! *The fantastical elevates* he thought. He had just barely come to terms with the world shifting revelation that was Death and now a new apparition to compound that? Any tenuous grasp of a quantifiable demonstrable universe rooted in logic reason and the naturalistic, what was incontestable and true was now but a fleeting baseless assertion purported by those blind and unknowing. Brian tried to vocalize something, anything! It had been seven seconds now and still not even a stutter. His anxiety peaked and he took a step back.

"Who's your new friend Death? Not like you to socialize with them, I know they hold a certain fascination with you but, dare I say, you have never been one to be wholly adept at the cumbersome interactions and socialities between people. Is that a word? Socialities? Just came to me, almost like it was channeled in some sense." Something happened that Brian never thought he would see. The phantasm was laughing.

"As the end is perchance nigh, my priority is to recover the horses. It was War who was, regrettably, tasked with accommodation for our Welsh excursion. Though in a near sober state he neglected to collect any details about the location of the equestrian whom we traded, for a short time, the horses for the caravan as we were monetarily challenged. In the last few weeks on several occasions, I have reaped Brian. It occurred to me that his return from the nether was not a random aberration but instead had a simple explanation. Someone was tampering with his hourglass. It had to have been left on the horse in the pommel bag, neglected due to intermittent omniscience. I used a wobbler to entangle Brian with the hourglass and that led me to the horses. As for the equestrian himself, well, we did not have the caravan so this here-" He kicked Jeff in the leg. "Seemed like the easiest option."

Muse nodded her head. She grabbed some hay and placed it under Jeff's head.

"How long will he be out Death?"

"About an hour or so. The strangest thing Muse. We found a veritable treasure in War's pommel bag. Coins, jewelry gems and artefacts." Muse laughed a little, the nervous release of unwanted energy.

"Earlier today I arranged to meet Famine Pestilence and War. I know all about the treasure. I think War just assumed everyone had treasure in his simple way, bless him and his cotton socks. Gave him a kitten to care for. Thought it would soften some of his rougher edges. Because of the size of his hand's Famine assumed this kitten would not be long for this world. So again, who is your friend? You kind of went off on a tangent."

"I apologize. This is Brian Aldiss. Frequent flier to the nether." Muse walked up to Brian. She tapped him on the head a few times, looked to his left and wiggled his ear, opened his mouth and looked inside then turned him around and poked his back.

"Why does he smell like God? It's thick and viscous."

"I was hoping I could get that answer from you Muse."

"Well, he is certainly not entirely human, that's for sure. He's hard to read. Wow, that is a lot of self-loathing and pity. Brian, see a masseuse. Spend an hour in a steam room or something, you're tighter than a spring that has his exam in twenty minutes and has forgotten the difference between convex and concave." Brian was finally able to speak but it was in a language he just made up.

"Gwobble, sier... mror..."

"I think I have broken him Death." She slowly waved a hand past Brian's empty gaze.

"Have you heard of the Beyond and Beyond police my friend? They purport to be a policing body of some sort from Beyond and Beyond. You were right, God has left the universe. It was not self-inflicted Dayside; it seems he has ascended to their domain but did so through illegal means. In doing so, by ascending without regard for us, he has kind of buggered this place, hence the tear in space with the lack of reality nestled in it. He's squatting lawlessly and it has been asked that you are the one to find him. I was told myself by three men in Brioni Vanquish 11 suits and Flavio black flat brim Moda fedoras.

"I think I have calmed down enough to er, to erm, to er-speak. You are the Muse? That's what you are, you are that which endows insight inspiration and creativity? At a guess, you appear from static and are friends with Death. Just so I know that's accurate?"

Muse nodded with a wry smile.

"I'm sorry, but after accepting Death it is still a shock to encounter you. However, the most pressing issue with which clarification may be required for me is the mention of my humanity, or lack thereof, to wit, being not entirely human. Do you understand that's a weird thing to hear? That level of revelation requires some elaboration. I mean I don't mean to rush you, in your own time."

Muse picked up Brian's left hand and placed it in hers.

"There are many beings on your planet that are not entirely human, perhaps a grandfather being a Djinn. Or a distant relative getting down and busy with a sure of himself Seraphim but you? As I said, it's thick and viscous. A little more than that, to be honest I cannot truly answer your question but in my bar perhaps somebody can. I know this is vague, I'm not deliberately being evasive, but you are a wonderful curiosity and I promise *we* will figure this out for you. So, Death, how goes the holiday? I mean up until this last day or so when everything kind of went to shit?"

"A myriad of cows, a spot of tea, some scrabble and crabs, hard to relax in Llanfwrog on the west coast of Anglesey Wales in late autumn. It was the most we could afford. That's before the revelation of War's bounty. How much is there?"

"From what I could gather, there was a quarter ton in the caravan, more on his person and has treasure thrown around the entire planet, every continent. Right now, in Antarctica, a confused penguin is looking at a gold chain over the neck of his fellow penguin. Birds with swag, a real problem that."

She smiled.

"I have missed you Death. By the By, you know my cupboard, with the portal? Next to the pop vinyl collection? It has barely been used for decades or possibly even centuries. I think the last it was used was to clean his hoard of new scientist magazines. Do you have a key? Only the Beyond and Beyond wanted to investigate."

Death looked in the pommel bag. He anticipated with God being

AWOL the first thing needed was to find his spare Key to God's complex. Another reason to find his horse. There it was, an unremarkable run of the mill, average nondescript key with a G on it. He had lost his key somewhere. This one in the pommel bag was the spare borrowed from the Muse. He had no idea how people could live like this. To be stripped of his omniscience was like losing a limb. His intellect was still towering and there were very few things he still didn't know. Like he knew the scientific term for brain freeze was sphenopalatine ganglion neuralgia but could the rook become a queen? Where is Abijan on the map and what are people referring to with half and a half at the coffee shop?

He passed the key to Muse who bit it in her teeth. *Platinum* she thought. She looked at a depiction of the Pheonix lights and several coins. She read the letter left by Death.

"Thank you!" she said as she took three and squirrelled them away.

"What? The coins that are left will easily cover the price of the van. It'll be Christmas again soon and I have seven pregnant sisters! Get off my back!"

To Brians surprise, a small chuckle came from Death. Muse rummaged through the pommel bag and found a tiara.

"What do you think? To use an outdated unused nineties colloquialism, to every princess, eat your heart out! I'm just stealing off War at this point, but God knows what he would want with a tiara. I'm saving him from himself really, he would get a migraine wondering what to do with this. A pinky ring? Well, I don't *need* one but who does? Fits quite nicely. I need this Faberge egg for secret Muse purposes. And just three more coins and I'm done. And this Kokopelli fertility symbol. Okay, now I'm done. Death, take this bag away from me, I have lost all control." Death swiftly removed the bag from Muse's grasp.

"Well Death, does Famine ever mention me? Like in passing? Perhaps make mention of a certain affection?" Death wondered about this.

"Last time we had a drink he fell madly in love with a tree that he repeatedly referred to as Muse. Convinced that the tree loved him back he rang a local priest to perform a civil union. Only the priest was a French pickpocket who relieved Famine of twenty English pounds and a tobacco tin. Does that help?"

"I never know when to take you seriously, but I guess that's along the lines of what I wanted to know."

"He did the same thing with me about the Welsh bigfoot,"

remarked Brian, calm enough to return to some bastardized version of normality.

"It's strange Death, there is Uriel, an Adonis among men, Seraphim. Unequivocally powerful, masculine refined and nothing, not a flutter of the heart nor abated breathe but when I see Famine, I get flustered, confused, red in the cheeks. Is he currently involved with anyone?"

"A few years back he had an ill-conceived liaison with a sea Goddess but Famine is afraid of the ocean, so it fizzled out quite quickly. There was also another incident with a therapist that was convinced Famine was bulimic and left him saying she could not stay with someone who is slowly killing themselves, that it was too hard to witness. She ended up with a well-built opera singer based in Sadler's Wells Theatre in London. But now? Yes, Muse, he is unencumbered in that regard."

"Interesting...very interesting," said the Muse tenting her fingers.

"Can you see that Death? Look at what the equestrian is dreaming about. She's way out of his league. Okay, that's just gross, why is he doing that? Don't go through that door! Oh, he did, and there is the monster – I tried to warn you! That small spoon is not going to help you, Jeff! Anyway, where to now gentlemen?"

"Back to the campsite, for now, relax and regroup, consider our next step. Muse, I'll take Brian. Can you escort the horses?" Muse placed a finger to her forehead and she and the horses became static and left.

"Brian, I promise you, this will not hurt a bit." He placed a hand on Brian's shoulder, and they fizzled into a static that appeared and dissipated a few times until they were gone, leaving behind nothing but a garlic-scented wisp and the black Ford Merkur

"Hello?" inquired the salvage hunter, hat in hand followed by the guy in shorts.

"The Chesterfield, have you a few strong guys to help us get it into the truck? I'd help but I'm eighty-six per cent chip shop pasties!" He walked into the barn and saw Jeff lying on the floor.

"If you are pretending to be dead mate, you are doing a crap job. Mate?" Jeff gave him a kick in the leg. He seemed to be breathing heavily so he wasn't dead. But if not death then what? Few sleeping people have an unblinking unerring gaze into the middle distance. Jeff looked to his right intrigued. He left the comatose equestrian and spotted several coins.

"My shorts-wearing friend! These are 8.18-gram Roman gold

aureus! Worth at least 7500 quid on a bad day. There are six of them! Look, a note!" The salvage hunter read it.

"Well, that's a bit of alright aren't it! He's out for the count. Don't think he even knows about this treasure. According to the note that is. Whoops! The coins have just fallen into my pocket, what a complete and honest accident. Do you ever hear about the famous artist Daniel Morris? Prolific in the nineties. This phoenix lights depiction is one of his, must be worth 400 quid on a bad day! And what an honest mistake, it fell into my satchel!"

"Good day, my friend. Why do I smell garlic?"

"So, does this mean I get paid? In money? Not fireguards?" smirked the shorts wearing friend.

Chapter 16

"So, you are from Birmingham?" Famine lay back on his new Nemo stargaze recliner. He sat in his also new Emporio Armani E A7 7 lines reflective joggers tapping his Cartier eyewear Santos aviator-style gold-tone sunglasses. He lit a Gurkha black dragon cigar and took a sip from an Asprey men's silver hip flask.

"Well, I'm from Birmingham but I'm a man of the world. Yeah, my home is where my hat is, always on the beaten path, the path less travelled. Adventure is par the course... Some people shy away from being daring and audacious. Not me. I see life and I take it by the horns! Yeah, I live life as it's meant to be lived. I've seen things in my time you cannot even imagine my friend!" Famine inhaled a drag from his cigar and placed his hands behind his head, stretching his left leg.

"And you?" Pestilence was being addressed by a fairly built bald guy in his late 50" s with a milky eye and half of a moustache.

"Must be a wild ride with this one! He's a fucking rock star, obviously doing ok with himself, the tracksuit, the sunglasses, the cigars..." Famine picked up the cigars to his left and handed one to the balding gentleman. He ran it under his nose.

"Well, I am also from Birmingham. My name is... Clive. I collect stamps and suffer from ear infections. The toilet in the campervan is quite nice and I'm concerned about your asymmetrical facial hair." Pestilence was being rude, and he knew it. He was not enjoying himself. Famine was on a full-on ego trip ranting about imaginary conquests to anyone that would listen before finally finding the one couple that the whole campsite had been avoiding up to this point.

"Went to shave this morning and the razor snapped. Not sure that it has to do with you, the enterprising twelve-year-old says he has no stock of that kind until tomorrow."

"Pestilence, I mean Clive, you're being rude to my friend Arron here!"

"It's Adam," said the man with his milky eye.

"Still, remarkably close, especially after three refills of this flask. God bless Marcallan double-cast gold malt."

"I envy you John Archer. Clive you can learn a lot from him."

"I am rather fantastic" hiccupped Famine.

"John Archer, can I speak to you a minute please?" Famine left his cigar in an ashtray, and with some trouble, he stood up and followed Pestilence back to the new RV.

"I was enjoying Arron's company."

"Adam," corrected Pestilence.

"Adam! Don't know why I keep having trouble with that. Here, sips this flask!" Pestilence waved his hands in refusal.

"Look at you Famine, you may as well be a peacock, like that lost one over by the showers. The tracksuit, the cigars, the sunglasses. Must be thousands spent draping your skeletal physique. Look I don't want to be rude but this version of you is unbearable."

"So what? We have treasure now, the world is our oyster, you should revel in it! Splurge, buy some top brand suntan lotion, why can't I not just enjoy it?" Pestilence groaned.

"Ok yes, monetarily we are good, but it does not have to fundamentally change who we are. I see you tipping the toilet guy a 1906 king Edward the seventh full sovereign coin. That's 500 quid! Without War's bounty, which is getting a bit light now, may I say that one coin would have seen us through the month and we would have been happy!"

"Happy? Do you think I have been happy? I have hated this place; you guys are fine." He stopped to let out a small hiccup.

"But everything else has been dismal you whiney bastard. Sorry I did not mean that, it's the malt," he said and then proceeded to take a gargantuan sip.

"I mean dismal. Battered by the north-easterly wind, sideways rain, a little con man shit that makes buying toothpaste an ordeal. Whatever sick bastard has left that dog in that cage the last week. The lost cows, a caravan wired like an electric chair, crabs galore, rotten food, green milk, a toaster that felt sorry for itself, a chessboard lacking so many pieces we had to improvise pawns with parts of frozen fish sticks. Waking up every day to whatever War left in the bathroom, a mile walk to the pub, a lost car, substandard alcohol like that rum substitute, barely enough tobacco for a wasp, a shit ton of wasps. What about any of this do you think made me happy? So, we find treasure, our fortunes change, can you not just enjoy it? "

"I think we should put down the flask for now before you get amorous toward the foliage. I'm going to put on some Japanese UCC gold specials rich blend coffee. Look maybe I was wrong to be annoyed. It's just since this money has come in its adversely affected you. To be honest Famine we just don't have to go overboard and throw our money around like that, advertise it. Just calm down a little is all I'm asking. I don't even know why you wanted validation from Adam other than to feed your ego." Famine lifted a finger.

"I was not trying to impress anyone!"

"So, the story of wrestling an alligator in the amazon basin? I have known you a long time, you've neglected to recount that story. Besides, alligators are endemic to America, not found in the Amazon basin, if the story was true, it may have been a small caiman. Just drink your coffee Famine, we are expecting Death sometime now I imagine." Famine placed down his flask but found it very difficult to let go. *Second time's the charm* he thought as again he tried to loosen his grasp. The kettle clicked down.

"COFFEE!" screamed a bounding War. He hit his head on the door entrance and stole Famine's flask from his grasp. In one gulp he emptied the flask and let it drop to the floor. Pestilence was no longer annoyed and started to drip olive oil into his ears. He then got a cotton bud and probed his ear canals.

"What's you doing there my carrot of a friend?" The freckles on Pestilences face sparsely surrounded by psoriasis seemed to give him the look of a worn casserole.

"It's for my ear infections War." War had a follow-up question.

"Is that like that time yous were shoving seaweed up your arse?"

"It was an abscess, it's what you're supposed to do, pack the wound with seaweed. Where have you been anyway War?"

"Here an there..." He sat down in a chair waiting for the coffee to boil.

"War, have I changed since we got our, well your treasure?"

"Yep, you've become a complete gobshite!"

"At least War is forward about it Pestilence. No beating around the bush, I bet you anything Death will say I have not changed." Pestilence had an answer to that as well.

"Death is adept at many things but picking up on social cues and paying attention to one's affectations is not among them." The kettle had boiled already, adulations were given. Before they even took the first sip a soft buzzing was heard from outside. They went to investigate, War banging his head on the door. He seemingly carried on without pause. The now familiar occurrence of static began to the best of its ability to form into existence. It intermittently dissipated and reformed several times

"Inbound! Inbound I say!" and there were Muse and the four horses. To her left, the same phenomenon bore Death and Brian to the statics position. Muse hugged Famine wearing a tiara that War recognized.

"What is all this Famine? The tracksuit, those sunglasses? Has someone been spending a bit of treasure? You know I'm surprised how many people accept treasure here. New smartwatch gave the guy a Dubini emperor 18-karat gold bronze ring. I've walked 3456 steps. I've burned two hundred and seventy thousand calories, wait that can't be right. Oh no, it's updating its firmware. Okay, there is the spinning hourglass. Why has it gone purple, should it make that alarming noise? Thing is defective if I paid real money for this, I'd be livid."

Muse turned, took off the watch and threw it over the cliff.

"Who's the entourage?" asked Famine of Brian. Famine became curious and walked toward Brian who was wide-eyed and stiff as a plank. He did not cherish the experience of transportation. It was not something he wanted to try again; a small spiral of smoke was emanating from the top of his head. He seemed to be in a campsite next to an RV perched on the edge of a cliff. He was standing before two tall thin gentlemen. One sickly with outstretched ginger hair and another gangly and awkward. Famine pried Brian's left eye open and stared into it. He patted his cheek a few times and investigated his mouth. He tugged his ear and tapped the top of his head. He held his hand and flipped it to his palm.

"Something not right here, getting massive amounts of divine residue, the man smells like God. What is he exactly, a friend from the ineffable bar?" Muse had no visible reaction to that.

"That is the thing, he's human. Just a normal average run of the mill, stock common human, no Earthly reason why he should discharge this energy. He has traversed here and the nether which would leave some residue but it can't account for the case of Brian. He is kind of shell shocked so he may be sparse with the conversation. I promised him I'll find out all I can. Pestilence! What has you annoyed today, can always count on something bothering you? Did Famine cheat at that card game cribbage? Inspired a poet named Sir John Suckling back in the seventeenth century and have no idea how It's played." Pestilence looked to Famine conflicted. He wanted to vent about Famine's rampant treasure induced shift in his outlook but also wanted Muse to see Famine in a good light.

"I would say my disposition of late has circumvented the need to complain and would add that such ailments are more Famine orientated than myself. Our turn of fortune has eradicated the Llanfwrog induced depression and some of us have been enjoying it more than others. I would ask how you were, but it has been hours at the most. But it is always a pleasure Muse. Would you like a coffee? I have just made a pot. It's good stuff too, Japanese."

. "Mitzy purred in Wars hands as he walked over to Muse, the tiny horned helmet on her head being the most visually normal thing there, whilst Death and Famine strode to the RV.

"I been here and there Muse to find a hat for my cat. I was looked at in a way that causes trouble. Sarcastically he refused my custom. So I gave him a little slap and said look again, He went to his bottom shelf and there were the cat hats."

"Where was this War?"

"The pharmacy! So, you and Famine, something there, right?" The Muse blushed. War sat down on the grass and tapped it for Muse who accepted and sat down to one of her favorite people. Famine and Death were out of earshot.

"All of me loves all of you. That's what I went and said to her Muse. Her name was Estrid. The name means God and a bit of beautiful. Could not be more fitting. Like this hat on Mitzy. She was beautiful Muse, but she was mortal like. The limited times I had had with her were the best of my life, was with her till the very very end and never have I had that again. Looking at yous I see that same look, the look she gave me a thousand times. Of course, now it's all scantily clad maidens but all of me will always love all of her."

"War that was beautiful, I have never seen you quite so... succinct. I will tell him how I feel, there is just a barrier."

"That's called sobriety!" burped War. War dug into the vast innards of his coat and produced a goat horn of liquor.

"What's in it?" asked a hesitant Muse.

"My concoction. Mead with honey water spices and a smidgen of tobacco, a few mushrooms and a pinch of garlic! A warrior drinks! Pestilence can keep his girly purple drinks with fruit and umbrellas, this will stand the hair on the back of your neck! Too much though and even I will be attractive, so careful!" Muse let out a guttural laugh. War took a mighty gulp and passed the horn to Muse who took a tentative sip and stood back up. War raised his hand for Muse to help him up. It was an ordeal, but he got to his massive feet.

"Sorry needed the help, not as young as I used to be!"

Death was looking at the RV as Pestilence came out with the coffees. Famine was still at Deaths side.

"Isn't she beautiful? That is the Coachman Chaparral 373MBRB bunkhouse fifth wheel RV! Can fit ten people in that, three bedrooms, two bathrooms. Tri-fold slide out sofa, booth dinette for four. Dual pane windows, four-door fridge freezer. Pestilence gave the toilet an eight, that's the highest so far, narrowly beating the 7.8 Isle of wight Sandown seafront hotel on Sandown pier." Death and Famine walked back to Muse War and Brian. War slapped Brian on the back.

"Who is this gobshite? Playing fella, welcome to Wales, we are famous for our rugged coastline and the Welsh bigfoot." War picked up Brian and shook him.

"Smells funny, what is that paprika? Coriander? It's coriander, what smells of coriander?" Brian wished people would stop smelling him poking him, picking him up. Muse spoke up.

"Getting things back on track, the horses, will they be fine here?" Death did not see why not they were placid docile creatures.

"The horses, Muse, shall be fine." Famine gestured to the horses. "I'll have a word with the camp manager to see if they can use that field behind us where the sheep and cows and what looks like a peacock following that other cow erm are? Tortured sentence. I will take this coffee though, remember the old days, and by old days I mean earlier this afternoon how much of an ordeal coffee was? Yep, this RV is a beautiful machine. So any news on God? Those three men you could not read? asked Famine.

"Some news on that, serendipitous. As soon as I needed them, they appeared in my bar. They belong to a policing service of some sort from Beyond and Beyond. They were concerned about our Omni-God that vacated our existence in favor of their own. He is alive and well albeit absent from here. Without leaving through legal and official channels, the usual precautions and procedures were not adhered to. The adverse effect he had on this place was that deformation above us. He is, for want of a better word, squatting in their plain but has retained his anonymity. They have tapped Death for the task of removing him and returning him here. No word on an apocalypse just yet, our priority is still as it has been, to find God.

"What about me?" asked Brian who the group had forgotten was standing there.

"It's hard for a mortal to navigate the ethereal bar," said Pestilence.

"I'm not overly sure. He has what may possibly be some kind of divinity or perhaps something kindred to that so I'm guessing he very well might be OK. Pestilence, if you can, to use an idiom, hold his hand? He will be exposed to lights, colors, sounds and sights that can be very jarring for a mortal. He may become overwhelmed at the stimuli so just reassure him it'll be ok."

"Wait, where are we going? The ethereal bar? I'm hoping that's a relaxed place on the coast with ciders and crisps but I have a sinking feeling you're going to teleport me to some far off fantastical place where physics is an option along with Pepsi or coke. I'm not one for fantastical journeys, mildly stimulated journeys, ones with plaques you're obliged to read, even those are a little much. I have no idea where I am or where my car is or even where I live now but I'm sure I can manage. Have a trip bountiful in your various escapades whilst I go hire a therapist."

"If you leave my employ now, I have no further use for you," remarked Death sharply.

"On the other hand, how about that path less travelled! Assorted adventures and what not!" Brian placed his head in his hands and sunk to the ground.

"Don't you want to know what you are, are you not a little bit curious? If I were you all I would want is answers." said Muse.

"It just compounds! From here to the nether, the collection of cacti, Death, the horsemen, Muse and God, the bar's outside existence. Various beings poking and prodding me conversing about various smells and residues pertaining to the divine. If I had a year maybe I can process this but I'm either terrified or ambivalently numb. I just want my small apartment some crap mindless television, maybe even cook a frozen pizza, the one with extra olives and be ignored by my fish!"

Famine took his sunglasses off sat next to Brian. He handed Brian a cigar. In Brians left pocket were the worn falling apart foreign cigarettes from Jafari. He took the cigar and Famine lit it.

"Here, for your nerves..." Famine passed him the flask.

"You know Brian, the world for most people is like that fish in a bowl. It is all they know and all they will ever know. Those 5 gallons of water is their known universe. Some fish notice outside strange bipedal creatures, they make myths and stories about them, the bringer of shrimp and squid. But that world besides story and anecdote is a world they will never know. It is safe and secure in that bowl. But you are for better or worse outside of that now, I am sorry but that's just evident. All you can do now is follow the unknown path."

Brian stood up and scratched his right arm with his left hand. He looked to Death who nodded.

"Ok, I think I can do this," said Brian with a worn-out smile.

"It's a great RV you have there phantasm." Death had yet to step foot in it.

"It's a castle!" said War who tapped it with his gargantuan hand. Death heard it first, then Famine, Pestilence and Muse. War was oblivious, preoccupied with what to have for dinner, the lobster or haggis. Haggis was more filling he reasoned, but it had been some time since he had lobster. He would have to remember the garlic butter; he would always forget. Oh, spinach sandwiches he thought, decision done!

There was a creak, a clatter and a bang, they all stepped back apart from War. On the other hand, he thought, he was not so fond of spinach. Did he even like olives? Famine grabbed War's arm to send him back just in time as the ground fell before them. It crumbled and collapsed. The RV slowly fell to its side and slipped from the Earth beneath it. The RV's final thought was in the form of a song. It was *My Way* by Frank Sinatra. It smashed into twelve thousand pieces on the rocks whipped by the ocean.

"My treasure!" shouted Famine

"My cat!" shouted War.

"The toilet!" shouted Pestilence with a grin. Famine stared daggers at Pestilence who put his hands up in submission.

"Did anyone notice that red sign in the ground that said: *DANGER: LOOSE GROUND?*" remarked Muse. The sign slowly fell with a thud, barely affecting the grass beneath it.

"Our fault really, parking it so close to the cliff, especially after the caravan. Never mind, things come and go," mumbled War with a happy go lucky outlook.

"This does not bother you does it War?" spat Famine. "You do realize we are poor again now. I have nothing, nothing. Death you can go down there, can't you? You can retrieve the treasure?" Death contemplated this request.

"I can but I am not going to." He said flatly.

"And why in hades name not?" Death's head tilted to the side.

"I think this is a lesson for you. About humility and accepting the things you can't change. Of letting go, embracing closure. Not holding onto the past."

"I will never forgive you for that Death. Did I tip a toilet guy a five hundred pound coin? What was wrong with me? I should always remember happiness is transient, brief and fleeting. It is a stupid emotion and can't be trusted and I no longer want to be associated with it. I'm done with it, back to the bitter maladjusted cynic I'm cursed to be. That's what is comfortable. That's where I thrive."

"Well, I think this will be good for us, we'll manage, we always do. So, it was beautiful, and we hardly knew it." Pestilence looked to Famine as if to ask: *you understand?* Instead, it looked more like *I have great investment opportunity.*

"Insurance?" Mused War.

"I don't think it covers death by cliff War." Famine lost hope for his existence, it was just the easiest way to cope with the situation. Muse walked up and put an arm around his shoulder and nestled her head into it.

"Should we mention the pommel bag Death?" asked Muse. Famine looked up hopefully. The way she smiled when she said that. He looked at the others and, well, he got nothing from Death but that was to be expected. Pestilence shrugged and Brian was enjoying the cigar.

"We found War's pommel bag, there is still a veritable amount of treasure there. Coins, rings, jewels and artefacts. I think some of it was from Black Beard. Has his signature on the treasures of Amaro Pargo."

"I knew I recognized that tiara!" barked War happily. Famine shot up and ran to the horse. Lo and behold, a bounty of riches! Who said you can't keep a good man down?

"Dearest happiness, I won't doubt you again! Our estrangement was brief, but your warm hand has touched our lives once more!" Pestilence interjected.

"It has been said that it's not how much we have but how much we enjoy, that makes happiness."

"And I have treasure again. That's what I have so that's what I enjoy ergo happiness, your reluctance to embrace this flummoxes me. I swear to the sacred son I will one day prove money just makes you a better person."

"Goes completely against the holy son's teachings, you know rich men in heaven and the eye of the needle thing? Beside that point, you act as if you have some right to it. It belongs to War." Famine looked expectantly at War.

"The ways I see it, how many countless adventures have we been on, yous are brothers, what is mine is what is yours. Remember rescuing Pestilence from that cult place?"

"All hail the zenith..." said Pestilence making a Z with his hands.

"What about that time I won the SLS world tour skateboarding championship? Or when Famine saved the isle of man from that Robot with the whisk? Or when Death took us to the past to learn about buttons. Not a lot of treasure but should, what's the word, suffice like. I miss my cat, poor thing."

"Yep, there will never be anything like that RV. It was like ordering a great bag of chips at the beach and before you enjoy it a seagull shits in it. So last words anyone?"

"Guess I have a few words to say," said Pestilence.

"The mastery of your electric innards was unwavering, the memory of your facilities will be forever ingrained as exemplary." War played green hills of Tyrol on his bagpipes. It was Famines turn.

"As someone who is not usually impressed or invested with all of life's offerings, it is hard for me to truly be moved and happy. This RV was more than mere accommodation, I had an affinity toward it, it was my Shangri-La." Famine wiped a tear from his eye. War got bored of playing the Green Hills of Tyrol and instead had a go at a rendition of free form bagpipe-based jazz.

"It seemed adequate for our needs..." said Death stoically. War was bored with jazz and started to play *Come talk to me* by Peter Gabriel.

"Seemed nice when you had it but to be self-serving this does not need my input but er, ashes to ashes rust to rust your beautiful tease," said Muse. They all looked to Brian.

"What? I'm barely here leave me alone," he said. War put down his bagpipes.

"Well my turn, in our brief acquaintance you were a bed and where I laid my sword. I bid you take your place in the halls of Valhalla, lo they do call to me, something when thine enemies have been vanquished and so forth." Famine threw a single rose over the cliff edge. "On to your next adventures my friend..."

Chapter 17

Satan was reading a memo. It was from HR. It read: *To whom it may concern; you will soon receive a memo.*

Satan was confused when there was a knock on his office door.

"Satan sir, you have a memo." He was aghast at how this place was run. The memo read: *Regarding your inquiry about a meeting with God and sons incorporated and emporium, due to unknown factors a meeting at this time cannot be facilitated. I would have brought you this memo up personally, but I want to live, if you can call my existence living, so I have sent Bob here if your wrath is to be incurred. Signed, some guy. Ha, you'll never find me!*

"Bob, who ordered you to send this?"

"He called himself John Smith Sir, never seen him before. He was wearing a fake moustache, dark sunglasses and a snapback baseball cap."

"Jeeves, go to the gift shop joke section and ask who has bought a fake moustache! have the customer mutilated by this afternoon and fed to the parrot infestation! How many times must I order people to death? It's a catchphrase at this point! Maybe I should kill them all, finally have some peace. Read a book, see an interior decorator about maybe a window. Wait if I kill them all there will be no interior decorator. Jeeves! If ever I kill them all, spare one interior decorator!

"Yes, you're detestable. May I suggest? I correspond with a God of, well... elevators."

"A God of elevators? Seriously? There will be a God of haircuts soon. Get to your point Jeeves! I look at the second hand of that clock and it's like it's standing still when you talk!"

"Your rotten boar, that clock has been broken since 1984." *Of course, it has* thought Satan. Jeeves watched as the incontestable ruler of hell chased a small toy car on his desk after an Action Jackson action figure. He made siren noises.

"Action Gun activated!" he said making gun sounds. He threw the toy car from the desk.

"Lucifer?" Satan looked up at Jeeves.

"The God of elevators?" Satan opened a drawer and placed the figure inside it. He did not appreciate Jeeves' tone. Of all those in hell, such contempt was only tolerated by Jeeves. He was not a friend, Jeeves, knowing his place, would never allow that to happen.

"Jeeves what is on the other side of this grey blood-spattered wall, I was thinking of a window next to the portrait of my son." The portrait painted by a damned soul named Sandy who had involved Satan in a trapezoid scheme had twelve darts in the face and a permanent marker that made a wispy moustache, big eyebrows, glasses and stink marks. Under that, he had written, "your end is nigh!" He would make a point of staying by it on the rare instances his son graced his office.

"I believe the view is that of general pain suffering anguish torture, lava waterfalls, sporadic pterosaur sightings, rampant nudity and the gift shop. We can install a flat-screen television with wallpaper, say a calm sea, a meadow of flowers...sorry I have just read this book: *So you are in hell, how to find your inner calm*. Have pictures... see?" He presented Satan with views of fjords, cliffs and beaches, the calming effect was fast and strong. Satan smiled, a rare expression that his face had almost forgotten how to make.

"I will allow you to bring me one television Jeeves. I'm thirsty and you are standing there looking at me. I can see contempt Jeeves! A good butler anticipates the needs of their master! Avert your gaze your fetid bag of flotsam!"

Jeeves looked away whilst walking towards Satan's desk. Six inches to Satans left was a glass of cucumber water with a bendy straw and an umbrella. He moved it the six inches to Satan's right hand.

"That subservient lack of backbone is why I like you Jeeves. No thought for your self-worth. This water was well within my reach yet still unerringly without pause or dignity, adhered to my will and was happy to do it! Why can't they all be like that Jeeves? Having notes given by anonymous fake moustache wearing bastards. I have lost control of this place, I'm a figurehead. It's all research developments, purchasing, marketing, accounting and finance now. Yes, they turn a blind eye on my occasional, only in special circumstances, scarce bouts of murder but that's only to placate me while they run this place. There was a time I walked in the room and they bowed, kissed my ring, now the wheelchair guy goes over my foot. I'm guessing on purpose; since he gives me the finger! Now, of course, I killed him, I mean who wouldn't, everyone was silent on the matter but in the past that would have been applauded! I just need to get out, have a holiday, focus on myself. Try my luck with some supple flesh bending to my whim." Jeeves looked up from his phone.

"Television will be here in a few minutes, R and D have asked that you refrain from murdering the delivery men as they have a game of squash later and don't want to be 2 men down. It's the grand tournament and will air on channel 16."

"What do they think I am? Just a one-dimensional irate character unable to grow, evolve, change! Just this morning I planned on visiting God, to talk and air some shit out, does that sound like a being that cannot grow? I mean the bastards don't think I'm important enough to meet God. I am only the most powerful being he ever created. But the olive branch was extended by my hand, I can change! But if in any way the TV delivery people step out of line, well, if I forgive that trespass, it sets a precedent now doesn't it!"

"About Igor..."

"Yes, that is a name I guess, more information needed Jeeves." He made a point of placing his hand on his trident. Jeeves was not even his real name. His name was Barry. In his first day in hell, he recalled being branded with a pentagram on his left hand. This meant that he was of the service class as opposed to the tortured class below him but under the first class that was generally tasked with higher management. He was told never to correct Satan so when Satan called him Jeeves, he became Jeeves. Though he went on to question Satan many times, his wrath was yet to be incurred. He was told there were a lot of butlers in hell, mainly from the nineteen twenties mystery novel writers but after an aptitude test, a basic physical, he was tasked with handling Satans affairs personally, both a feared and coveted position. Another reason why he was chosen to be in Satans employ was that he had his own tea set.

"Igor is the God of elevators. He resides in the ethereal bar in the ineffable plane." Satan had memories of that place, over the millennia he had visited, it being one of the designated areas he could free himself from the pit for any length of time. Another place was the serendipity shop in New York that sold the quintessential grilled cheese sandwich. He was last in the ethereal bar many centuries ago, where Muse would rebuff his advances, save for one magnificent night courtesy of two for one night. A less than vigilant employee guarded the broom closet and Marvin Gaye's *Let's get it on* played on the jukebox. To this day he wondered where he had left his socks. They were good socks as well. Navy blue with a deer emblem, still a lot of give in the elastic after many years of use. Went very well with his Brooks Brothers Milano 2 button suit. There were a few tailors in hell and only one outlet where he can trust good socks. The tailor is heavily placed in the *do not maim* category along with his hairdresser and dry cleaners.

"Igor and I are somewhat kindred. As I am in your service, he was in service to a cape-wearing toothed gentleman. He is now in Muse's employ. He ascended and found his true calling, to use his divinity as an elevator attendant. God has had a dialogue with you denied on his behalf, it is possible to have an elevator sent to this very office and traverse the many planes of existence from here to the mortal realm. From there to the nether, and then to the ethereal bar. At least then you may have some answers, at the very least alert the staff that a meeting is requested. Would you like a small sandwich sir?" Asked Jeeves who had suddenly acquired a plate. Satan refused as two burley horned scaly gentlemen appeared with a big TV.

"This sir is state of the art, 85 inch 8K HDR UHD VRR bells and whistles, balls to the walls TV. Wi-Fi, all your basic streaming services, video conferencing plugin and play! Fit for the King of demons, all heil your eternal reign! My squash team is on later, channel 16. Anything else your loftiness?"

"See Jeeves? That's how they should all be! Jeeves is slipping my scaly friend, I may have use for you soon! Here take a lollipop." Satan produced a jar with two dozen lollipops.

"Oh wow, green! My favorite, thank you, Satan!" The second horned gentleman took a red one.

"Oh, cherry! Thank you, Satan!" Satan rustled the demon's hair. The two demons left leaving Satan to the TV. He was not overly familiar with this technology.

"Hello?" he said into the remote control.

"Hello, I am Isaac, your smart assistant. You can ask me any questions or queries like the weather which today will be a low of minus 76 and a high of 307 degrees. You can ask me to play music, for example, try saying "Isaac, play smooth jazz." Ask me for an interesting fact and I'll answer with ones such as "concrete is stronger if carrots are in it." Welcome to your new viewing experience. We have 2000 channels serving all of Hell's nine billion residents, as well as all the top streaming services from "pickyourdoc", "heaven stream", "classic heaven stream" and "why, are you doing this to me?" Please give me the WIFI password to access streaming services, email and that one chat room website with talking beetles in the sink mainly populated by one family in Ireland."

"Wi-Fi? Is that something to do with the colors on the screen? Why fi? Did fi do something? This is a stupid technology I've had enough! What is that spinning hourglass? Oh, the screen has gone, no wait it's coming back. Wifi button has to be a wifi button on this rectangle buttoned stick." Satan was overwhelmed. He may as well be in a restaurant where the waiter asked if he would like to try the Nakazawa milk.

"Allow me your direful. It is a case of connecting the Wi-Fi to the router, password "Imonfirepleasesomebodyanybodyhelp." And that little icon means we are connected. I asked for a special model just for you. So this is the interface where you can switch to various services. As a special model, your TV has CCTV that will alert you if anything suspicious happens like someone sprays painting unimaginative graffiti. These icons on the top are for email, ms paint, minesweeper, solitaire, you can use the remote. Isaac show me a video of a waterfall!" The 85-inch screen displayed a beautiful 8k waterfall. The effect on Satan was immediate. It had been millennia since he saw such a sight. He felt he could touch it. He became extremely thirsty but Jeeves anticipated that and produced a cold Dr Pepper.

"You sure I can't tempt you to a small sandwich? Agnus at the cafe is worried about you, says you are looking a little thin. We have sardines and onion, they're your favorite."

"Sardines and onion you say? I need to step out of this office for a second. Hey Asmodeus!"

Asmodeus looked up whilst half-heartedly whipping a soul that was enjoying it a little too much.

"I have an 85-inch TV and I'm looking at a fucking waterfall! When is the last time you saw that! Aye, you bastard!?" Satan walked back into the office. There was a knock at his door.

"Asmodeus, one of my favorite people. Prefers the comfort of men, never one to judge. That behavior is rampant here anyway, progressive is what it is." Satan opened the door.

"Hello Satan, It's Mike, Mike Michealson. Sorry to physically drop by like this, wow nice waterfall! Jeeves?"

"Mike."

Jeeves and Mike did not get along,

"We sent you several memos." Satan looked at the right-hand side of his office. He got so many memos from all corners of hell it was unfeasible to be expected to read them all. He started with making a small pile but got creative and made a self-portrait of himself consisting entirely of memos. After the self-portrait, he decorated his lamp in memos. Mike Michealson passively looked at what could be considered modern art and Satan merely shrugged unapologetically.

"I am informed that outside the pit there is a spatial deformation."

"Sorry I forgot my hat from earlier. Remember, 6 o'clock channel 16!" said a demon popping back out of the office. The hat had two holes in it for his horns.

"So yes, there is a deformation-" He stopped to await any other disturbances. Nothing. *Alrighty then,* he thought.

"-In the sky. It has been described as a lack of reality nestled into a tear in space. We have no idea of its origin. The Seraphim reported it saying not to worry as it is just a union bargaining chip, I doubt this to be the case. It has not yet affected us but definitely, something that I felt should be bought to your attention."

"Thank you, Mike, have a pleasant twenty minutes," seethed Jeeves.

"Why? What? What happens after twenty minutes, why twenty minutes? I have reported you to human resources before Jeeves, you can't go on threatening me. Okay I slept with Ida but that was 70 years ago, you must let it go! I'm a recovering alcoholic, back in those days I had no control, I'm in AA dammit!"

"Have a nice nineteen minutes and thirty-five seconds..." Mike became red in the cheeks and aimlessly walked away stopping to look over his shoulder and out of the room.

"Isaac! Report any sightings of someone wearing a fake moustache!" asked Satan of the TV. Immediately the CCTV homed in on the eighth circle with a man scratching his head with his fake moustache. He recognized that he was standing outside the vape shop a third of a kilometer away. He grabbed his Nikon Aculon 16X50 CF binoculars. Sure enough, the target was in sight. He grabbed his compound crossbow bow and stepped out of the door. It had been a while but he was a master at competitive archery. He adjusted for wind and shot. A tiny faraway scream was heard. He grabbed his binoculars again and the moustache man was down.

"High five Jeeves! Got the bastard!" Satan had his hand-help up expectantly. Against everything, Jeeves stood to meekly pat Satan's hand.

"I love this TV! Isaac, display the galaxy!" The milky way span in front of him.

"So my odiousness, a trip above? A break from the pit? I can order the elevator from my phone, has an app. All the different destinations you can go with a rating system, you can even follow bloggers that talk about their experiences, UFO hotspots …"

"Aliens, don't get many of them here, they have a different construct when it comes to salvation and damnation, has a lot to do with cows and sacred geometry."

"There are bigfoot sightings..."

"We have a family of bigfoot here Jeeves, they are nothing special! Have you tried their goulash?"

"Haunted buildings where you can spend a night-"

"I have a ghost in my quarters, he gets bored and throws a sheet over his head. And makes obvious ghost noises."

"Ok, looks like the trip will be nineteen ninety-five." Satan patted down his pockets and nothing. He checked his drawer and couldn't find his wallet.

"How much have you got on you Jeeves?" Jeeves patted himself down. He checked inside his teapot.

"Forgive me master but I may have left what little money I have bundled up in a pair of socks. Should I retrieve them?" Satan looked Jeeves right in the eye.

"How much do I pay you Jeeves? I would say your salary is your life, if you no longer serve me, you no longer need a life, so every day you wake up, that is your salary!"

"Sir, surely the trivial matter of my recompense for my service is non-consequential-"

"You are being evasive Jeeves, and to think I was going to offer you a lollipop. Answer the question!"

"Well, I am paid mainly in stocks and shares but liquid assets are thin on the ground. One month for payment I received twenty yellow sticky note memos with bad penmanship on the back reading *good for one haircut* or *buy one get one free yoga pants*. The actual real currency is thin on the ground. I get an occasional residual check from my brief stint as an exchange student in a teen comedy, it only ran for twelve episodes and was last on-air seventeen years ago."

Satan had never inquired about Jeeves past as he wasn't important enough to care about.

"Give me a second Jeeves." Satan left his office and shouted down from his balcony.

"Asmodeus you bastard! Borrow me twenty quid!"

"We might need to buy a pint as well Satan?"

"Good shout Jeeves. We need to borrow fifty quid! Is that a subway sandwich? Yeah, I'm going to need that too!" Asmodeus, defeated, walked away from the torture.

"Is that it? Art, thou going to leave me so unsatisfied?" Asked the hedonistic soul that Asmodeus was whipping. Asmodeus felt a shiver down his spine, but the Rota clearly stated that at this time it was the whip. He grabbed the sandwich and walked toward the side stairs on his right. He walked to the door and fished out fifty pounds in sodden notes and with great anguish, slowly handed the sandwich over with his head bowed in the same way a parent forces a child to apologize to the second child.

"Great I'll pay you back Asmodeus, so fifty quid?"

"You never paid me back for those headshots you sent to the small independent film about the lost art of horology, or the time you needed that red dragon embossed trident you saw in that magazine."

"So how much do I owe you?" asked Satan.

"These fifty quid included?"

"I would say yes Asmodeus..."

"A little over seven hundred quid sir." Satan scratched his rough stubble. He counted in his head. The coffees, the muffins, headshots, trident, the secret lonely hearts column advert, seven hundred was about right.

"Ok yes, I don't have that, but you can have Jeeves for the night! I'm sure he's willing to do all the sailor stuff you enjoy. Even if he isn't technically that way inclined."

"I'll pass Satan."

"I'll get in on that, Jeeves all the way!" shouted the hedonistic soul through the open door.

"What does the Rota say? You move on from the whip and into the pliers soon Asmodeus? Give it an extra ten minutes from me." Satan pocketed the fifty pounds and, hungry, Asmodeus went back downstairs. Satan picked up the baguette.

"Crap, it's tuna," he said as he threw it in the bin.

"So, elevator sir?"

Satan nodded as Jeeves opened the elevator app on his phone. A red square appeared on the ground with red lights spelling: *Please step back, thank you for your service!* Satan picked up his Action Jackson action doll from the drawer.

A nine-foot-tall elevator shaped cuboid made of static appeared with a loud buzz to the left-hand side of Satan's desk. It finally formed into reality. The elevator was red and black on the outside with a calming white interior. Igor welcomed them into the construct.

"Satan, a pleasure to meet your acquaintance, I fathom you have made this journey before my function. It is an honor to meet someone from your station. Muse has great respect for you and all you do, and I would like to reiterate that. Jeeves my friend! Looking stoic as ever, still not allowed to wear top hats, cravats or bow ties I see? Just that suit which has held up well, but if you are interested there is a new tailor at the dark depths of the bar. Can get somewhat sketchy down there though but I doubt the dark lord himself will have any problems."

"Igor, I have enjoyed our correspondence and if I may make the next move, Knight to E5. Your move. So, are you still writing shadow guys biography?"

"Well, he is only lucid for around an hour a day, so it is a difficult slog, led an amazing life, shadow guy."

Satan was getting thirsty.

"Anything to drink in here?" Igor pressed a yellow triangular button that opened a panel, inside was a fridge and in that fridge was a fruit-based yoghurt that Satan was interested in.

"Right this journey will be nineteen ninety-five gentlemen."

Satan brought out a sodden 20-pound note.

"So, on we go!"

The doors closed and Igor placed his palm on the interface and closed his eyes. Information like veins shot up his arm, fluorescent and glowing.

"I am everywhere!" said Igor in a robotic voice. There was no longer any discernible difference between Igor and the elevator, they were one and entwined. The path was laid in and he removed his palm.

"That was a strange sight?" stated Satan.

"The elevator is designed to be in all places at once but somehow still takes twenty minutes to get to its destination. For the short time that I am connected I too am in all places. If you get restless those two panels fold out into chairs and on the TV now is a documentary on seaweed eating sheep. Please refrain from smoking, we have no facilities and enjoy the journey."

Satan looked out of the window and the view was reminiscent of a depiction of a wormhole from an old 1970's sci-fi TV show.

"Just please don't make the elevator 'so many levels' joke. I wouldn't wish that on my son..."

Chapter 18

Brian felt overwhelmingly peculiar. He was conscious in that he had a sense of self. Did he always have a three hundred degrees field of view? He tried to fathom a memory. The first that manifested was a montage of dropping various objects. Memory seemed fine. How about a thought? His local chip shop chicken wings were overpriced, that counted as a thought. *Okay, what about my hands* he thought but it was when he tried to visualize his hand that he had trouble. Was it there? In fact, how about his body? Nothing. He could sort of see; it was a tunnel of sparkling lights, flickers of silver dotting purple waves folding in on themselves. The view began to open up in a circle, the purple waves ebbing away gave rise to what was fundamentally a standard looking bar that was off in some keyways. Some of it seemed like it should be there but wasn't. He could feel it, but it was invisible to him. Outside the sky was a shade of beautiful blue that he had never come across. *Ok* thought Brian. *Let"s try and make some sense of this. Nope, I have nothing.* He looked again at his hand that thankfully seemed roughly human-shaped and as he remembered it, he had two legs which were the best number of legs, although the man in the corner with three legs may have been offended at that. The jukebox was playing generic classical jazz fusion and in an unexplainable way, it seemed as though it was playing just for him. Some winged gentlemen sitting at a garden chair table were discussing an earlier incident involving Muse and the God of haircuts. And the pool table was having a casual chat with a potted cacti.

    A DMT elf standing three feet tall handed him a hyper-dimensional cube that defied physics and turned into an origami swan made of sacred geometry. A small serpent emerged from the swan's wings, translucent and shimmering with matted play dough light. It entered Brian's body, burrowing into the bend of his arm which, like his hands and the rest of him, thankfully still seemed human-shaped. He could feel it climbing his veins. The sensation was not that of pain or discomfort or pleasure. It was almost spiritual. Up until today, one of the longest days of his life, the concept of the spiritual was an unfamiliar construct absent from his life. Dismissed like all dogmas, Gods, angels and the various supernatural entities and forces. The serpent moved into his torso and removed the knot in his stomach. It reached the back of his neck and pressed on his spine, a cold relief slowly making its way through his extremities before the serpent left via his right palm. Under the translucent skin, the serpent had a round lump of brown in its stomach. It was the singular most bizarre and terrifyingly extraordinary experience he had ever had.

"From time to time, those serpents like cleaning the emotional and spiritual tar, that brown lump consists of all that pent up negativity. You should feel quite normal soon but expect a brief high connected with unconditional love, serenity, peace and well being." Famine patted Brian on the back.

"Also it amuses the DMT realm no end to see lower beings experience their disposition. It's like you asking a dog to sit."

"I understand love, I understand it Famine! I have a profound respect for all people and all things! To know me is to know the universe. I am the universe manifested to observe itself, to experience itself subjectively. Bill hicks was right, I'm on a roller coaster! This is just a ride, nothing more, and I feel like I've been on this ride before. I can see the seams of life's tapestry. My God, I'm thirstier than I have ever been, and I don't even care! I never want this to end. I have lived a sedentary isolated existence and now? It amuses me no end to look back on him! That introverted hollow husk, praying for connection, any connection. So devoid of the greatest thing life has to offer, love, thy name is Brian!"

"Muse, what sobers up a person experiencing unabated elation?"

"Can never go wrong with a good pint of Guinness?" Muse poured a glass halfway, stopped for it to settle before pouring the next half. She topped it off with a splash of Schweppes blackcurrant cordial. She passed it to Brian who drank it in one mighty gulp that even War would have been proud of. Looking intently at a coffee ring on the counter, Brian continued to ride his high.

"The snake eats its tail, the infinite duality. Yes and no, on and off; binary!" Muse poured a drink for herself. It had been a while since she had had Teeling whiskey black Pitts peated single malt. The three gentlemen from Beyond and Beyond were aware of the arrival of Muse and the horsemen. One held a hand-shaped book and was focused intently on it. Another was enjoying a carvery and the third was playing with a previously discarded yo-yo. The string snapped and he looked to the ground defeated. He tapped his carvery eating friends' shoulder and pointed to Brian. He nodded, and they spoke in hushed tones.

"Well, the gentlemen are still here," started Muse. She noticed that they were out of place. They seemed uncomfortable, there was an urgency, and she could not quite pick on why they stood out, as she looked the one gentleman was trying to sellotape a yo-you string back together... *Yes, It's odd, right?* She said to herself. She tapped Death's scapula.

"They see you there Death, I'm surprised they have not acknowledged you yet, maybe a power play, have you come to them, get the upper hand, wait for you to talk first. Well, I'm not playing that game. Death, Famine, Pestilence... drinks on the house?" It was a small act of defiance on the Muse's part, but it made her feel better.

"Can I just say I love you guys, all of God's creatures? Phantasm, we had a rocky start, but I respect you, that I can say. Yep, I was wondering for a while but now I'm sure, my immediate future involves what I guess is viral gastroenteritis related vacation of my stomach's contents. The facilities are needed friends!"

The serpent had loosened Brian's gut to a dangerous degree. The last time his stomach had felt this bad was after a mystery burger stall purchase who stole the ice cream man's territory leading to a turf war and three days of rioting. Brian had sealed himself up in the flat for the duration. Fire and explosions outside he simply thought *this is fine i*n his patented denial. The one time he did look through the gap in the curtains he saw a milkman with a postman in a headlock and a Molotov cocktail made of a Wall's ice cream Calipo push up ice lolly taking out the burger stall.

"Pestilence?" said Muse but was already on it, he coughed a black lump into his hand.

"That's you that is Famine, all the second-hand smoke."

"It's not my fault you're diseased. In your lifetime you have had everything bar the nasty sexually transmitted ones, I remember I broke my back looking after you with that outbreak of polio. A touch of a cough you said when you had the plague. I made you soup when you came down with rickets. You have had them all, even some new ones you haven't released into the world yet. For every affliction on Earth, you're patient zero, that black stuff in your hand? Could be anyone's guess really but if the second-hand smoke does annoy you to that degree? Well, that's just gravy!"

Famine lit a cigarette in triumph and passed one to Brian who graciously accepted.

"Ha! Pestilence has sexual diseases!" bellowed War.

"I don't have sexual diseases. I mean you need a female company for that, and I haven't done too well the last few years have I? Got close at comic con, the only place War fits in. She was dressed as a general fairy. Should have seen her Famine. Beauty in truest form. Spent the whole day buying her drinks, every funny story I could muster from the shallow bin, but when I thought *I'm In here* she left with a Tarzan who said he has his rope if you know what I mean. To this day I have no idea what it is he meant but she seemed into it, end of the story, you think maybe it's the hair that puts women off?"

"Well, it is seven inches vertically upward and always has been carrot-Esque Maybe a beard will offset it? You do have a weak chin." Pestilence placed his hand on his chin nervously.

"Guys Brian needs the toilet still," said Muse looking at a very uncomfortable Brian.

"Yes, I'll hold his hand. If he doesn't pay attention, he may enter the dark realms never to be seen again by our collective ocular sensory organs. Could use the toilet myself."

Pestilence patted down his person and found his pad and pencil. He aimlessly flicked through it and came across "Woodstock, 15th of August 1969." In the category of worst toilets on Earth. Being it 1969 in the heyday of his psychedelic consciousness exploration no description was given of the toilet, merely a badly drawn space monster fighting a robot. Shadow guy passed and high-fived Pestilence.

"What was that thing? Why is he a shadow?" Pestilence escorted Brian to the toilets while Brian was looking over his shoulder.

"Do you have Quail?" asked Death. He had got a taste for quail after Frederick Chopin passed and met him in a Polish restaurant. He hadn't been sure what was on his plate but he acquired a taste for it to the point that it was a defining feature of his character.

"Always for you, don't get too excited and grin. Ever think of surgery Death, could give you a face. Always thought of a Tom Selleck moustache, brown eyes and a nose bent slightly to the left to give it some asymmetrical realism. Shit socialites is a word, just remembered that. So, drink Death?" Death tapped the bar with a single bony finger.

"So, Death I have always wondered, being a skeleton, without tissue muscles or ligaments, how is it exactly that you don't fall into a bone pile?"

"No point looking behind that curtain Muse, he's a little sparse with details about his beginnings. We have had theories over the years. That he once had the relevant anatomical features but slept in a nest of flesh-eating ants, or maybe a severe case of frostbite and flesh related atrophy, maybe he was always a little warm and as a literal man-sized doctor teaching aid without flesh, it was a little cooler. Maybe He was once a goth and took it too far. Hard to say." Muse grabbed a cooked quail for Death who ordered a Cotswold dry gin. Famine looked to the menu.

"I'll have the enigma pint, the one where it advertises that you will have the taste on the tip of your tongue but won't quite get it until someone else tells you what's in it."

Muse poured the drinks and Famine was intrigued.

"Okay I'm getting a summer fruit flavor. Maybe mango? A touch of orange and - what is that? I can't quite put my finger on it, it's on the tip of my tongue. Ah! I hate when this happens." He started making noises and clicking his tongue.

"I give in."

"It's citrus lemonade! You got the citrus part."

"Damn it is lemonade! See, now you say it, that's what I taste!" Famine looked at his graffiti.

"I'm a great artist! One of a kind, unparalleled realism is that!"

"If you squint hard there is a slight resemblance," said Pestilence coming back with a disheveled Brian.

"I think the elation is passed but I feel like I am better for having that experience, put a lot in perspective. So this is a bar located in where?"

"The ineffable plane, beyond word and description. Well we have a description, for instance, that's a bastard of a pool table, it has to have a name or it all falls apart, but space we currently inhabit is ineffable."

"Yet you still serve Guinness?" asked Brian genuinely confused.

"And Quail." said Death with a wing going into his hood and a bone coming out.

"How is it you can eat?" said Brian continuing his confusion. Brian thought rightfully that he would not get many answers about this realm. It seemed to make itself up as it went along. That which is categorically impossible and farcical happens to pass these people by without notice or thought. It was, in its entirety the fantastical masquerading as normality and it was doing a very bad job of it.

"Well, the last time I was here you had not redecorated that bathroom. Must be one of the nicest I have ever come across, a solid 8.5 across the board. The window at waist height is a little disconcerting. What's even worse is I swear a squirrel was practicing the art of voyeurism through it."

One of the three gentlemen waved at Death and Muse. One of them placed his colleague's hand back down and consulted the hand-shaped book. He flipped a page and raised a finger to signal that Muse and Death should wait, before looking back into the book and flipping another page. He patted his friend on the back and waved for them to come over.

"Okay, they broke the power play. Brian, come with us, please. May get some answers here if luck is not the absent far away concept as it usually seems to be. Be on your guard, I get nothing from these people. I can't read their wants, desires or intentions. One of those hats would look good on your surgically reconstructed Tom Selleck face Death," Muse checked her pocket. The key was present. She readjusted her ill-fitting brazier. Pestilence Famine and War hung back. Due to Muse's trepidation, the walk to the table stretched twice its distance. She shook her head and it snapped back to temporary normality. War helped himself to the remains of Death's quail and gin, happily consigned to his thoughts. He was thinking about past conquests and glorious battles and also how nice Pestilence's drink looked. He threw a coin to Pestilences right. As he turned to investigate, War took a rushed lashing of the drink and placed it back on the table. Pestilence shrugged at the coin and stared back at am empty glass, just as War burped and fell to the floor.

One of the three men stood up as Death Muse and Brian were asked to sit. Brian noticed it was the most comfortable booth he had ever sat in. It was a large circular booth that could easily fit six. The shadow guy, somewhat inebriated also sat on the booth.

"To love is to know loss, to hate – a greater loss still!" A hand-shaped shadow slid across the table to Bombay mix. A handful of it turned into a shadow snack and he proceeded to eat it.

"Shadow guy, really not a good time."

He stood up without a word and sauntered off to his next adventures.

"So, last we spoke gentlemen you asked me to locate and deliver Death, of his own accord and volition he can be of your assistance. Not sure why I'm speaking on his behalf, he is sitting right here and can form sentences. Death?"

"By my reckoning, you have what surmounts to be an illegal immigrant in your respective realm. This elusive never hitherto mentioned: "Beyond and Beyond." He is our Omni God and he does belong here. I'm willing to facilitate your needs."

The one gentleman that earlier pointed to Brian spoke up.

"Your friend here, this mortal, what is his designation?"

A second gentleman intervened.

"According to the handbook, *Know your realms*, chapter three: *greetings and customs,* we ask for names, not a designation. It also says it's rude to wear a hat indoors. I won't adhere to that particular custom." He flicked through the hand-shaped book and randomly settled on a page.

"Pub/tavern etiquette, every member of a party should take turns collecting a round of drinks for the table. Before business, I suggest we do that. Muse, what do you recommend? This round is on me."

"I'm personally in the mood for cider, just got a crate of jack high spirit in." She waved to one of her employees and swiftly ordered six ciders.

"This is Brian, Brian Aldiss." One of the gentlemen pulled out an opticians slit lamp microscope and looked into Brian's eyes. He then pulled out an otoscope and checked his ears. He then pulled out a small hammer and hit Brians knee which jerked in response. He got a cotton swab and dashed it inside Brians's mouth, placing it into a glass tube that turned pink. Brian had felt somewhat violated. The frequency of these invasions into his personal space was becoming an ordeal. He felt he should wear a bag over his head or glue small tacks onto his person to deter inspection.

"Well?" asked Muse.

"He is an oddity, and we were hoping you could help."

"Hmm. It went pink. May I confer with my colleagues? We need to make a few phone calls. If I'm right, this is some amazing news for Brian."

Muse, Death and Brian stood up and vacated the immediate area. Another DMT elf offered Brian a hyperdimensional cube that he swiftly refused.

"Well Brian, looks like you may have some answers soon. I said I would help. But then I'm a fantastic person so it shouldn't come as a surprise that I came through for you. Enjoying the cider? It was distilled with care in the farm's restored 17th-century distillery. Has some classic roots and is a product of Charles Martell"s 350-year-old distillery house."

"The cider is nice, thank you."

"You sound deflated, Brian." Muse placed her hand on his shoulder. "Is everything alright?"

"That's the thing! I'm on this fantastical journey I'm sharing with you guys. This morning I awoke from Death itself and on a quest to find God. Now? I'm numb to it, I cannot take it in, It's a little too much. Defining it as little as an insult. It's a cavalcade of sledgehammers intent on the destruction of my already challenged pathology. My senses are assaulted, and I'm just overwhelmed. I'm not sure what emotion I should focus on, I mean I'm experiencing them all. It's been 30 years since I needed someone to take me to the toilet. Men made of shadows, magic snakes made of love and I'm sure those men outside have wings. Am I supposed to just nod my head and carry on? You do realize how utterly ludicrous my existence is right now? I have no words. To borrow one from you is ineffable. But I'm just trying to focus on one thing. This cider. If I can just have this drink and be in this moment with it then that's the world I'm making for myself. The rest will be addressed piece by piece as they are presented."

Muse put an elbow on the bar, her hand cupping the side of her face.

"You are doing better than most."

"Because I am an oddity?"

"Perhaps a better term is needed for you. You're an anomaly. That suits better. Oddity has negative connotations, like an old curiosity shop selling elixirs and potions. I have a potion here for you now." Muse pulled out some Corsodyl mouthwash.

"Just a hint Brian."

"Go easy on me, I have just come back from the dead." Brian found himself laughing. Was that the third or the fourth time today?

"Well Brian, at this point a mere mortal would have been driven to psychosis in this place, but aside from a small amount of introspection, you seem to be coping well. In time you will be fine with all of this. As Famine said, you are out of the fishbowl now. Tell me what you think of Famine?" Brian shrugged.

"I have only really got to know Death. At times I think he could be a friend yet other times he insinuates my time is nigh. Hard to know where you stand with that dissonance. A begrudging understanding maybe?"

"Interesting," Muse wondered under her breath.

War composed himself.

"I know you took my drink War, I'm keeping that coin. Being a silver dollar I guess it covers the cost of the drink."

"It was on the house!" smiled War wrestling with himself trying to get on his feet. His hand grabbed the bar.

"No, I donst got it!" He slipped back down and grabbed the Bombay mix, the bowl, not attached to anything was not enough to bear War's weight and slipped off the bar with him. The bowl landed in his face.

"Bloody sprite shit!" This time he made it onto his stall.

"It was on the house..." he said again with great care.

"I was speaking in generalities."

A Jinn in a trench coat appeared from the bar's dark realms. He had been lost for seven hours, the deeper those depths the looser the physical continuity. In the deepest level was oblivion. He walked up to War and opened up his trench coat to reveal 12 Engstler Cuckoo clock black forest house with moving fisherman sellotaped to the coat's innards.

"Fine merchandise here my friend, fine indeed. Best in the multiverse. None the like will ever be seen, twain for a monkey is what you'll be asked for, and this is on a bad day, but value is my middle name, twain for a century! Can't say fairer than that, grab it like a hot potato! Last of the stock, cannot miss out on this!"

War stood up from a barrel that was in fancy dress costume as a chair and the Jinn was taken aback. The man in front of him was significantly larger than he expected. The Jinn gulped and stepped back. War grabbed one of the clocks out of the coat, ripping the sellotape. He moved it around in his hand, not sure what to make of it.

"What a nice gift you have given me here friend. A nice GIFT I would say," War looked deeply into the Jinn's eye. Flustered he managed to barely say;

"Gift?"

War nodded taking another step to the Jinn who took another step backwards.

"Yes, the gift of course! Here, take that one!" War crushed it in his hand like crumbling paper. There was an atmosphere exhaled from War, a red thunder crackling in the air. Though he had a generally affable and simple quality he was still War. The shape of a primal drive to have red blood rushing through you as you slaughter your foes. It was glorious! And War carried that every day. War would despise Famine for being a pacifist if he had known what a pacifist was.

"Whoops, looks like you have given me some bad merchandise there!" War dropped the shards of wood and cogs to the ground.

"Of course, in these such occasions, I am guessing a refund is customary?" The Jinn started shaking and emptied his pockets with great haste, finding notes to the sum of two hundred and three-pound and forty-two pence.

"Nice doing business with you!" War sat down smiling at his money while the Jinn ran out of the room. He threw a five-pound note to Pestilence.

"That should cover the on the house drink." Pestilence' mouth was agape. War smiled with his pipe.

"Add a touch of whiskey to your tobacco and let it soak. Nothing like it!"

"War, that was terrible! How could you do that to the poor man?" asked Pestilence.

"Man was a common thief. Look, by the scotch eggs there is a poster sign thing."

Upon inspection, the poster read: *A dozen cuckoo clocks have been stolen from the orphanage, for any information please call the following number."* It was next to a photo of the recently departed Jinn with a sign; *Wanted: for rampant deliberate provocative jaywalking.*

"See, I notice things. From orphans Pestilence, now I have acquired certain things over the years, make no secret of it. but from orphans. He's lucky I let him keep the rest of the clocks. It is principal."

"You had to do what you had to do War! Now see me, in that situation? I would be more than useless. I mean how powerful it must feel to have anyone whimper at the sheer magnitude of you?" War was itching his back.

"Everything okay there War?"

"Yes great! I don't know where he came from, but I think I have just found dinner!" War produced a very lost crab in a very faraway place with a slight fear for its questionable mortality. It was the licking of its captor's tongue that made it paranoid, and more nervous at the sight of some *legally we can call this butter* from the *ask no questions* range of dairy products.

"Been a while since I've seen one of those. War seriously, change your coat occasionally, poor thing has probably been in here for days."

The three gentlemen waved for Death, Muse and Brian and they made their way over to the booth. The first gentleman spoke.

"For us to locate God we should first check out the office if you have a key. It may tell us why he left, when he left and if there is any residue we could use to find him in our realm. Maybe even a contingency plan to fix the universe in his departure, although that can be fixed in our end on his return. The fact your realm has not begun to exhibit unreality yet is remarkable. Like sheep appearing in your arctic circle or bats whistling along to country music."

"Country music?" asked his colleague.

"Chapter seven, music genres and literature. See?" He placed the page in front of him.

"You need to pay more attention to your handbook. As for Brian here, I believe there was a divine wager of some sort. We monitor your realm and keep meticulous records. In the Mojave Desert under a Joshua tree, you will find a seated Prophet. It is said he neither drinks nor eats but is replenished by the energy of the Earth itself. He has denied divinity saying he is needed in this plane. He will tell you everything you need to know. Give this card to the elevator attendant and he will guide you to the Prophet. Meet back here and we will see about your Omni God as I believe we may need Brian. If we may, can we borrow Death to visit his office? Do you have the key?" Muse fished the key out of her pocket.

"Follow me, gentlemen. Don't trip on whoever that is. Mind the spider... need to empty that mop bucket that seems to have half a bacon sandwich in there. Here we are, you may need to remove the pop vinyl collection but it's just through there." She handed the one gentleman that always seems to be in the middle the key. Muse and Brian walked back to the bar.

"So guys, how goes the fishing? Any new news?" asked Famine.

"Death is being escorted to God's office. They are giving it a sweep to get an idea of how and why he left, see if they can pick up on any residue and track him. Hopefully in their realm, Death's omniscience will kick in and then it's a case of trying to get him back here. While all that occurs were going to the Mojave desert to meet a Prophet. See if we can get some answers for Brian. Meeting back at this bar. The Beyond and Beyond gave me this card. Igor should know what to do with it. Ok, that seems like all the relevant exposition."

"That's a coaster Muse. Look, it's advertising Budweiser. It has three frogs. How old is this coaster? Splurge a little bit, get something up to date. Look at this one. Gin-eat your heart out. That hasn't been said since the nineties."

"There was a promotional thing here a few decades ago, we did not have a good time of it. The jukebox is still a little shell shocked. Due to random unforeseen out of the blue and sudden unanticipated series of events, I have an overspill of Budweiser related stock including these coasters."

"How many do you have?" wondered Famine.

"After a few decades? I would say seven thousand. I have boxes in the basement."

"So why would the gentlemen in hats give us a coaster? How is that going to find the Prophet?" Famine looked around for validation.

"Turn it over," said Muse exhaustively. The back of the coaster was a silicon chip with microscopic transistors and a small CPU.

"He placed his hand over this coaster and now it seems to be a location to the Prophet."

"Before we leave, anyone wants to sing a bit of karaoke?" ventured War.

"I know all the words to the sound of silence. Hello, darkness my old friend!"

"War, please! Look..." Famine placed his hand to his head.

"Maybe later," War looked solemn.

"Well when?"

"When we are all dead," said Pestilence.

"I tell you what, if we can find God and convince him to come back, we will sing some karaoke War." smiled Muse. War brightened up at the concept.

"I'll hold you to that!" War was the first to stand up.

"You don't want this do you?" War said to an elvish fellow whose drink he had just stolen.

"Careful with that Bombay mix, sprites shit in them. Bombay mix for sprites is like litter trays or cats. They are seen as pests, but they were here first." War patted the elvish fellow on the back who proceeded to fly stomach first into the table.

"War getting along with the clientele I see. I think he's just shattered that guy's back." Pestilence was next to stand up.

"I feel a bit off. I may stay back," said Pestilence.

"It's my stomach playing up and my ear infection is getting worse, I'm having trouble with my equilibrium. Best I just wait here for you guys. We don't all need to go. Famine, a quick word?"

Famine was the next to get up and followed Pestilence out of earshot of the group.

"I honestly don't feel a hundred percent but if I hang back it may be easier for you to, you know..." There was an awkward silence followed by a little nod from Pestilence.

"Know what, I'm not following."

"To er, you know?"

"Use your words or so help me God I'll feed you sprite droppings!"

"Muse!" said Pestilence. Famine blushed. It was a rarity, but his body remembered how to do it. He began to sweat on the nape of his neck. Picturing Muse in his head, Famine's face contorted into an approximation of a smile.

"If I hang back you can have a few moments with her."

"Why are you so invested in what happens or doesn't happen between Muse and me?" scoffed Famine. He tried to act nonchalant, dismissive but his true disposition of infatuation may as well have been shouted from the rooftops. The facade was made of glass, easily shattered. His front was transparent, and the sweat moved from the nape of his neck to the entirety of his body. Pestilence dipped into his pocket and produced a men's 48-hour antiperspirant deodorant.

"We have had this conversation. Look, we have known each other for many years and we have been on countless adventures. Remember the potato famine, where we sat and ate ice cream? Or the bubonic plague? Some of our best work! Remember the gipsy curse that made you a little puckish and we ate chips with Bob?"

"Yeah, I liked Bob, smashing bloke, had his distillery. Wait, wasn't that gipsy the one with the wooden leg that walked under a ladder and was crushed by an air-con unit? Has the term gipsy fell out of favor? Are they travelers now?" Famine smiled and Pestilence continued.

"Inconsequential, I think. It's just after all these years I still feel like you see me as a colleague, but I am a friend, and as a friend I just want you to be happy. I truly believe Muse can be the causal root of true happiness and I'm sorry, I know I'm a lanky sickly ginger-haired freckled chicken-legged oddity of a being, but I can say, categorically, objectively, without exaggeration or hyperbole, no hearsay, conjecture or speculation that you, my friend, will never find anyone better than Muse. For her to have any affection for you. You are the luckiest man in the world and never the likes of her will cross your path again. Trust me, they had a meeting."

"Okay," said a defeated Famine.

"I'll tell Muse that I am desperately in love with her and always have been but if I end up happy content and well-rounded it's on you! Wait a minute, you are staying behind but what about War? He's still going to come to the desert, you know he loves the desert, though I think it's less to do with the picturesque dunes and cloudless skies, and more to do with the psychedelic cacti. Still, my point stands."

Pestilence stopped in his tracks.

"Crap, I didn't think about that. To be fair when was the last time he stayed in our vicinity? He tends to just wander off and have his adventures."

"This is true."

They both walked back over to the group. Brian was the next to stand up.

"Okay. I guess it's back to the magic elevator to ride to the desert and see a Prophet. I'm told my mother was a specter of some sort or other such absurdity. On with it, up an at 'em! Adventure awaits, yadda yadda yadda."

"Look who's accepting his lot in life!" said Muse who was the last to stand up. The jukebox started to play America – A horse with no name.

"Well, if I am out of the fishbowl, may as well leave the room."

Muse donned her tiara.

"Ok, follow me!"

Muse dragged her entourage, minus Pestilence and Death to the lift that opened to reveal the hunched Igor.

"Who is this? Something off about him, I would say." Igor lent forward to get a better look at Brian.

"Look I am an anomaly, okay? Will people stop poking me and

prodding me, taking my temperature, placing cotton swabs in my mouth and such like. Just all of it stop it, stop it, please!" it was out of Brian's nature to confront anything or anyone, but his outburst was a long time coming.

"Okay, I'm sorry, fella. Just that I have worked here a long time and there is something magnificent about you. Can't quite put my finger on it. A little like that mystery pint, been bugging me for years that flavor profile. Muse thinks It's funny to keep me in the dark. So, Muse, you are using the elevator? Not like you."

Muse handed Igor the small coaster.

"This is just a coaster, why are you handing me a coaster? Ha! The frogs, I remember that advert, you need something more up to date Muse."

"Turn it over," said Muse, depleted.

"Ah, I see! It's a digital reference machine of some sort, never seen the like. Well, I haven't been beaten yet, let's slide it in here! Okay, there is a specific Joshua tree in the Mojave Desert. The coaster is reading a lone man. Okay! Soas it is you Muse ill wave the nineteen ninety-five fee, please refrain from smoking. If we hit turbulence don't be alarmed it's perfectly normal and we shall be at your destination shortly. On the TV today is re-runs of that one show where the twist is: there is no twist!"

Igor placed his hand on the lift interface. As always, information snaked through his arms like veins. Igor's voice was monotone and deep:

"I am Everywhere!" he bellowed. He could infinitely divide his being to account for countless journeys through the Omniverse. Igor's eyes were doused in data.

"That always kind of freaks me out," said Famine to War.

"Well, it's like life isn't it, has its ups and downs."

Famine and his existence had a tenuous mutual understanding but occasions like this were where they fell out.

"That joke has to be at least 25 years old."

"What Joke?" asked War. Igor tapped his tip jar with a small spoon and a cough.

Chapter 19

Death was following the gentlemen through a corridor that would lead to God's complex. Ivy ran overgrown and unkept along the lattice to the sides. An old greying crumpled and damp flier barely readable read: *Lost peacock, responds to Monty, reward available. A beloved pet, friend and confidant.* One of the gentlemen flicked through his *Know your realms* handbook and stopped.

"We did not do the correct introduction custom!" The second man chimed in.

"It's your job to help us navigate this realm, you need to be on the ball with this stuff. We are incognito here. The likes of the Seraphim must not know what has occurred, we need to be under the radar and a part of that is blending in and not raising suspicion. We have to act as they act."

It was concise enough, but the first man still felt like defending his corner.

"This thing is seven hundred pages long! I think all things considered I have done quite well. So, the way introductions are made is we exchange names and thrust out our hands, the recipient grasps said hand and moves it in an up and down motion. A good handshake should take two and a half seconds, after that what is referred to as small talk usually occurs. This is where viewpoints of the weather and issues of the day are exchanged. In meeting an unexpected old acquaintance, a hollow gesture of keeping in touch occurs in which neither party will likely keep in touch. More familiar greetings may initiate with what is called a hug in which two bodies grasp each other, and then there is also something here referring to the *high five*, a hard contact of palms around head height. All very interesting." He placed a hand out to Death.

"His Death, I am Sam of the Beyond and Beyond law enforcement."

Death shook his hand.

"What nice weather we are having. Great view of the tear in space over yonder. Wow that was uncomfortable, was like shaking hands with a rake. Have you ever thought about surgery? Flesh is popular among life forms, though you are more a force of nature that's neither here nor there. This is Harry and that's Barry."

Harry went to give Death a high five and missed. The second attempt was admirable in its confidence that ultimately floundered, but the third time was the charm. The entire time Death had merely reluctantly held out an un-moving hand and Barry went in for a hug to Death's Bemusement. Death patted him twice on the back.

"How many seconds is a hug?" asked Barry still in Death's embrace.

"I think you have it. I would say you are good," Barry broke contact.

"I liked that. I liked doing that with you, that was special. We don't have that on our plane, to show affection we chuck rocks. A particularly big one hit Harry once, has never been the same since."

"He's just making that up, not entirely sure why. We are not a contact kind of people," said

"Well Sam, Harry and er... Barry. Pleased to meet your acquaintance. As established, I am Death."

"Yes, the grim reaper, the pale rider, the angel of death, the breath of life's dissolution. We are very familiar with you. You have an extensive chapter and a footnote in our guide: *Know your divinity,* a book I left at home. One of a very few beings endowed with true omniscience. When in contact with the elevator, your Igor comes close. As well as that roughly humanoid-shaped cloud of nanobots that drinks cherry-flavoured data at Muses bar, oh what is his name? I want to say, Barney..."

Death looked around. They had come through a narrow corridor behind them with the portal in the shape of a brown door adorned with a Christmas wreath that had seen better days. It seemed to be where a local owl was nursing her chicks. It had been a long time since this portal was used. A thick layer of dust became airborne under their steps. At the end of the corridor, they found themselves by an old shed on the periphery of God's estate. They headed in the general direction of a water fountain with three marble dolphins. Through neglect or lack of interest, the water was not present from the dolphins. On the grand water feature though, there were hundreds of coins catching the light under the water's surface.

"What does God need to wish for aye?" said Sam looking at the coins. Harry rolled up his trousers to his knees and took off his shoes and socks, getting into the fountain.

"What are you doing Harry?" asked Sam.

"What? Well, it's free money, isn't it? It's not just two-pound coins here, it's Mesopotamian gold! There is a fortune here!" After a few minutes Harry had a handful of assorted coins.

"You are not acting according to your station Harry, have some civility and refinement. You represent the greatest law enforcement body to exist. This behavior is unbecoming. Wait, is that from the royal cemetery of Ur"?" Harry happily handed Sam a coin.

"On the other hand, cooling off in the sun in a nice bit of water, cannot hurt anyone can it?" The weather in God's complex was in a great mood, it threw a wisp of cloud to its right and even let the moon be visible to the left. Death walked around the water feature, admiring its curves and the salty water depicted in white statuary marble. He almost tripped on something and looked down. There was a Burberry London check and leather international bi-fold wallet in black. He picked it up and held it to his eye admiring the workmanship. He knew he would have made a great tanner. There was something very satisfying about leatherwork. It contained an out-of-date license for land surveying issued to War. There was a nude picture of a characterless maiden holding a ferret, three-pound twenty-eight in loose change, a treasure map, a list of enemies, a receipt for a clock, a stick of gum and a pristine never used library card also issued to War.

"My colleague War is known to have treasure scattered across existence. I can account for this Mesopotamian bounty being one of his stashes. He must have dropped this wallet when he hoarded this cache of gold. Quite ingenious really, hidden in plain sight." As Death spoke, all three of the gentlemen had now had their trousers rolled up, their socks and shoes put neatly to the side and were collecting gold coins in their t-shirts.

"Or we can just relieve this fountain of its monetary adornment. That too is an option," said Death.

Since arriving here Death had noticed an eerie silence, so was taken aback when the silence was interrupted by the sound of a van start. Sam looked at Harry and Barry. They both shrugged shin-deep in the water.

"It's a big complex, maybe he has a few people in his employ?" They went to investigate where the van sounds were coming from. By an apple tree where there was a sign that read: *Please refrain from eating this fruit, I don't break into your garden and steal your strawberries, have some respect,* was the epicenter of the sound, but no Van was to be seen. The sound of a chainsaw from behind them was heard and Sam, Harry and Barry jumped at the sound and looked behind them to see no one.

"Well, this is peculiar," said Harry.

"Well, this is peculiar," said a disembodied voice. Death looked upward and laughed a little.

"It's a lyrebird, there in the apple tree."

Sam looked through his hand-shaped book.

"Ornithology. The lyrebird. Well, that's strange for a start, they are ground-dwelling creatures, so what the hell is it doing in that tree? It's a master mimic. No van, no chainsaw, just a bird. On we go I guess."

The grounds were vast, and they headed to the art nouveau mansion. The architecture was dated back to 1880 to 1914. It had asymmetrical shapes, arches and decorative Japanese-like surfaces with a curved plant design and mosaics.

"This architectural period is often mistaken for art deco," said Death, admiring the out of place gargoyles from 1400 Gothic architecture. An ancient octogenarian hobbled on a cane toward them in an ill-fitting suit that dreamed of a time it fit like a glove and yet ironically, so ill-fitting, the gloves dreamed of a time they fit like the suit.

The senior citizen, whose name was Niles Agador Carson the third retrieved his Hoffmann glasses from his top pocket and adjusted his dentures. He had a blue passoti silver lion cane that helped him hobble his way to the guests.

"I am sorry gentlemen; this is a private residence. Besides we are currently dealing with renovations. The new roof you see. We had an infestation of sorts. There was an outbreak of salvage hunters dealing with a man who posed as the custodian here. He went on to sell the woodworm and termite riddled roof while we were all holidaying in Skegness. An opportunistic parasite is what he was. We found him weeks later trading in bathroom sinks we are sure came from God's sons' estate, while he was out surfboarding or mountain boarding or some such nonsense. I will never understand that generation, though I was a boxer in my olden days. Though we didn't call it boxing, we called it: *whoever wins gets the toast.* We didn't have much you see."

It was clear that Niles had had little company and would talk to anybody that would listen.

"Of course, it was not only us that struggled, but there was also a war on. I would say to my friend Sully, I would say 'What is a banana?' I heard rumors about a strange yellow fruit that you peeled, I thought they were making it up, making a fool of me. Now that seemed fantastical to me, some fruit you peel? I could never imagine such a thing. The King, however, sent all the families a banana, good for morale in those hard times. Only my father, he chopped up the banana, threw some clotted cream on there which was very hard to come by you know, and ate it in front of me, my sister and two brothers. Never forgave him for that. Of course, your generation have grown up on the cavendish Banana, pales in comparison to our gross Michel bananas though they are extinct now."

Death was about to speak but was interrupted.

"It's like most things were superior in yesteryear, built to last. You live in a throwaway culture. See this cane? Had it twenty years, it was my dad's and his dads before his and still as functional as the day it was made." Niles squinted through his Hoffmann glasses to get a better look at Death.

"Darren? Is that you? Must have been many a year! You helped declutter the master's out of control new scientist magazine collection. You could barely swing a cat in that office."

"It's Death, Niles. Nice to meet you again.

"Yes, and I recall you called in again to give us those antibiotics after the master's outbreak of shingles. And who are these gentlemen? Those there," he said pointing his cane. For a decrepit old man, it was still unnerving for Sam to have a cane so close to his face.

"We are from the Beyond and Beyond law enforcement agency sir."

"Never heard of you! You can't be that important."

"We are very important, nay, integral."

"If you are so important why are your trousers rolled up and your legs wet from playing in our fountain? Also, you are carrying gold in your t-shirts. Important I think not, farcical more like. Many years I have worked here, never have I seen the like, no respect with this generation!"

"I'm 1500 years old," said Sam.

"Well I don't know you gentlemen and I don't care to. Call me a dismissive senile crackpot if you wish but if you are a friend of Darren…"

"That's Death," Death corrected.

"If you are a friend of Death…" he said slowly.

"Then I guess I should get you a towel to wipe yourselves down. Please, come in.

"Don't go in there! It's haunted by ghosts and stuff!"

"Ignore the lyrebird," said Niles.

"He didn't do the introduction custom," said Sam to Harry.

"Didn't ask about the weather, shake our hands, high-five us or hugged us. Is it not a universal custom? Why are we bothering to learn these behaviors if they are not even going to adhere to them?" Sam looked in the book and had a question.

"Niles, do we remove our shoes? Only I have athlete's foot. Harry's foot has an odor problem and Barry's foot is imaginary."

"Shoes on is fine, take a seat in the orangery, I shall get a towel and some Vital finest English tea." There was more nude erotic art than Sam was expecting, some of it bordered on the pornographic. A lot of them had the same bearded face contorted into expressions of pleasure. There was a statue of two mermaids embraced in a carnal fashion to his left and a water dispenser to the right with what he hated most: triangular cups. When finished, it could be fashioned into a temporary hat to receive a grimace from one in your company but held little other uses. He picked one up and poked a hole in the pointy end with a key, holding it to his mouth.

"Beyond and Beyond," he said hoping the voice would be different. He placed it down next to him. Who was he kidding? He was just littering and literally could not care less. Death was good at sitting. He did not have songs stuck in his head or get restless wondering if there was a toilet nearby. He did not get irritated, he just calmly sat and waited. It had never even crossed his mind that this was a desirable attribute because to him it was just a state of mind. Many hours could pass for Death to be in this mindset with no stimuli needed. He would merely compartmentalize his thoughts. For instance, in a dimensionally adjacent state right now a part of him was reaping souls throughout the universe but still, he existed wholly here, just sitting quietly.

"So that old codger is a bit much, isn't he? Kind of rude and aggressive if anything to go by. If he's not back in five minutes, we shall assume he's died of a tea fetching heart attack and find Gods last known location on our own. Death, I read somewhere that you can influence people. Can you whisper in his ear? Maybe tell him to go for an old man 'up every fifteen minutes for a piss' nap?" He was only half-joking. Niles appeared from around the corner, adjusting his hearing aid and pushing a tea cart.

"I found an old knapsack for your coin collection, a collection whose origin is not something I am going to inquire about. I am an old frail man with my best years far behind me, I'm afraid you may have to make your own tea. Darren..."

"It's Death."

"Quite, of course. I recall you delight in the occasional cup of tea."

Niles accent was of English refinement and years of good standing. Death did like a cup of tea and promptly helped himself, as did Harry and Barry though Sam refused having quenched his thirst with a triangle hat of water.

"So, gentlemen, what can I do for you?" Harry raised his hand.

"What is the difference between an orangery and a conservatory? Only, you see, it doesn't seem like it's in the handbook?"

"A conservatory is a glass structure with a brick base and a pitched glazed roof. An orangery is a brick structure with large windows and a flat roof with a glass lantern."

Harry nodded.

"And what exactly is a boudoir?"

"Stop wasting time Harry, look my name is Sam. We represent the Beyond and Beyond law enforcement agency or the BBLEA. We are here due to your master vacating this plane. Where was he last seen?"

"I'll get Audrey." Niles slowly walked away with the tea cart.

"You do realize we are going to be here all day," said Barry to Sam.

"This place has to be twenty thousand square feet. Audrey has not been seen so far and Niles' pace is I imagine a speedy can you believe it, watch him go half a mile per hour. And he forgot the towels. Is it cruel to keep someone in that condition in employment? He looks as if he should have retired in the eighties. He should be spending his twilight years on a beach with a cocktail watching the girls go by..." Niles managed to turn around the corner.

"So, tea then, Death?" It was a fragment of a question and Death shrugged.

"Well, that's an answer I suppose. Twenty quid says Audrey is also a senile wind-battered hag with a perceived higher station than us pottering on about the war and bananas," said Sam.

"Hardly fair that bet, the name is Audrey. When in the last half a century has a mother thought that name fits a daughter? It's the female version of Murray. Though Harry and Barry are hardly common names lately."

"I need the toilet," stated Harry.

"There is a tree right there through this er, what we now know is called an orangery. Be good for the plants I here. Has a lot of nitrogen, phosphorous and potassium." Harry was hesitant yet his need plateaued half a cup of tea ago. He thought he had better risk it. Nervously he got up and gingerly opened the door to relieve himself.

"I think I need to go after you Harry. What is in this tea?" asked Barry. Death calculated the tea's contents. It seemed to have more extract of asparagus than most tea has.

"Death.." pondered Sam on a whim.

"Actual honest to God Death. You are a legend in my plane. you're a monster to send kids to sleep. Real honor working with you. I guess you don't er... urinate, do you? All part of the mystery, right? I erm, I urinate, you know when the need hits."

Death made a small sound of acknowledgement. Harry and Barry returned.

"You know if I believed in comedic timing, you two would have got caught, it would have been awkward, and hi-jinks would ensue. As it stands it was, considering no comedic timing coming to action, somewhat anti-climactic. That painting of the bearded guy ravishing that horned three-breasted demon is disconcerting. What is the story there? Some depraved representation of duality? The divine and the damned? Or did the bearded guy in real life have that sexual encounter, became proud of it and decided to depict it on canvas?" Sam was just thinking aloud at this point in a stream of consciousness to pass the time.

"It's like its eyes are following you. All four of them."

Several minutes passed with random interjections from Sam and finally, Niles turned the corner to the orangery. As expected, Audrey was a hundred years old and counting.

"It's these gentlemen here Audrey. They are asking after the master. This is Darren, an old friend."

"Death," he corrected.

"Yes, quite. Death - Audrey."

"Death? Well, we all must go sooner or later. Let me just get my bloomers before I go, and my jewelry, want to look nice for heaven. Niles? You are a contemptuous arse, take me oh specter of the night!"

"No Audrey, he is not here for you, I said they are here asking after the master!"

"Oh well then. Sorry about the arse thing. Would you like to follow me into the formal lounge?" Audrey's pace was excruciating for Sam but eventually, they arrived in the lounge. Death sat in a Charles Eames lounge chair whereas the three gentlemen sat on an uncomfortable leather Claridge chesterfield sofa.

"So, Audrey, my name is Sam, this is Harry and Barry and as established, that's Death."

"Hi," said Death with a wave of his hand. Sam stopped to accommodate Death.

"We are from a place called Beyond and Beyond. Have you heard of us?"

"No, I bloody well haven't. Get on with it."

Sam shot a shocked look at Barry which said *can you believe this? Why are they so forthcoming with their irritability?* Barry shot one back that said: *It's a privilege with age.* Harry was wondering if the biscuits on the table were for everyone.

"We need brand recognition; I know I have said it before but you would at least have expected Death to know who we are. Well yes, we are from the Beyond and Beyond. Your master, when did you last see him?"

"A day or so ago by my reckoning. He had a strop, something about being left behind on his birthday, he locked himself in his office and hasn't been out since. I'm kind of worried, his shoes and socks are not by the door ready for me to clean them and he has missed breakfast and lunch. It will be dinner soon! He gets like this sometimes. I'm sure he will perk back up."

Sam pointed out of the window.

"And any thoughts on that?" He pointed at the tear in the sky with the lack of reality nestled neatly inside.

"Oh, that? Yes, it got us ever so worried, but we got a phone call from the Seraphim. It's some sort of bargaining chip from the union, and once a payment plan is in place it should be fixed by Tuesday!"

"Okay, this is very important. We need to go to God's office. Have you a key?"

"I don't feel right just handing you a key willy nilly! What if he's in his birthday suit doing crunches? He's been so self-conscious of late; needs the exercise he says. I keep telling him to cut down on the garlic bread, though we didn't have that when I was a nipper. There was a war on!"

"Look I have jurisdiction here. Your master may be in trouble, and we need to see his office. I don't care about the war, bananas or garlic bread. We must investigate his last known location."

"Well, if it's a matter of his safety I guess I'll find the key, won't be a moment." Audrey slowly made her way out of the room.

"We truly are going to be here forever."

"Are these biscuits for everyone?" asked Harry of Niles who, not entirely trusting these visitors, decided to loom over them. Niles nodded and Harry helped himself to a chocolate digestive. Sam patted his knees.

"It's a nice erm... nice building you have here Niles."

"I don't live here sir," was his stoic response, a patented superiority born from good breeding.

"So, are you a servant? Butler? Custodian?"

"My station is that which is desired needed or necessary."

"So, you and Audrey? I bet there is some history there? Some long drawn out ancient history that neither of you can quite remember?"

That was rude of Sam, but this was already taking five times longer than it should have.

"I don't believe that to be of your concern sir." Harry took a KitKat

"Is a KitKat a biscuit?" he said entirely ignoring the neglected fruit in a skewed bowl. The orange was uncomfortable pressed between an apple and a peach while the banana reached upwards and proud.

"Did you know bananas are slightly radioactive?" said Harry holding one with curiosity. He placed it back in the bowl and tapped his knees.

"Has a lot of potassium. Look, chapter 9, *When dealing with arable plants*."

Death noticed a clock that had stopped at one-thirty. He was an ammeter horologist, quite apt with the inner workings of clocks and went up to investigate. It was made of wood rounded at the top and tapering inwards at the side sitting on small feet. Though the design was somewhat antique the numbers were in modern styling. He pulled out a long pair of clock tweezers from his coat and went to work on it. Several uneventful long-drawn-out minutes passed. In this time Sam had scratched his nose, perused a magazine that was selling yachts, looked out of the window and became very uncomfortable at an unmoving looming Niles who stood still and hunchbacked, hands clasped behind him. His disposition had changed. He went from an age-induced ramble to a stoic silence. Sam wondered what the cause was but gave up caring quite swiftly. The clock chimed and Death threw the tweezers into the air, caught them and placed them back in his robes. At long last Audrey let herself into the formal lounge with a ring of a hundred keys.

"Niles, hope you have been a good host to our guests." Harry was halfway through a chocolate finger and had a Jaffa cake in his left hand.

"I apologize if that crackpot has made you feel uncomfortable. Now, which key is for the office?"

"I would expect it to be that big one with the G on it," said Barry. Audrey nodded.

"I expect you are right my young friend. The one with the big G. Now I see it I remember that being the right key. During the war, we did not use keys. We were all in it together. Could have my best throw on the sofa knowing I could go to the shop, and everything will be as I left it. Though there was a shifty fella I knew, Tom Prady. Would steal your dentures in your sleep, would sell his grandmother, take the sugar from your tea. Was a bad sort, we all knew from when he was a nipper."

Death interrupted.

"Please, miss, if we can get to the office."

Audrey placed a hand to her mouth.

"Oh, I am ever so sorry I do go on, don't I? Well stop faffing about and follow me."

"This is where jokes, humor and the irreverent go to die..." said Sam under his breath to Harry.

"I mean this place is vast but has a kind of downtrodden air to it with its dusty furniture and broken clocks. I mean it's there Omni God's residence so I'm not sure what I expected. Maybe a snooker room, a man cave for man parties, a pool and tennis court, a skate park, BBQ parties, young supple flesh. Modernism, sharp blacks - but this is a dust-covered graveyard of old tat. I mean, look at this!" He pointed at a giraffe statue on a pedestal.

"Who needs that? Why a giraffe, why here? Why a cheap porcelain car boot sale giraffe?"

"I love it. I have seen a pair of Tetrad Harris Tweed Taransay gents chairs, a few Chiaro luxury crystal chandeliers in gold with swirling cascade crystal clear drops, and even our tea was served in a pair of Famille rose melon teapots," said Death.

"If I did not know any better Death, I would say you are at least 150 years old back when any of these furnishings were relevant."

"You guys are very alike," noticed War.

"Maybe Harry and Barry but I, Sam, am a unique well-rounded character that resents that claim. This is a long corridor. Does not help that we are travelling as fast as the grass grows."

"I heard that!" snapped Audrey tapping her hearing aid for emphasis. After an excruciating one mile per hour journey, they reached the door to Gods office.

"See? No shoes, no socks." Audrey pointed at the ground.

"Here is the key, tell him dinner will be ready soon and that we are out of bacon, and he will have to do with sausages." Audrey tapped Death on the back as she left.

"Shall we?" asked Sam. Death placed the key into the lock and the door opened by itself.

"Wasn't even locked," said Death as he walked into the office. It was a sizable space, a window in front of them behind a chair and a desk. A silk black rug on a tiled floor. A poster next to a set of drawers that had a shirtless man with a handlebar moustache saying: *reach for the rainbow*. An ancient computer and assorted floppy discs. A toy bird that drank water as it went up and down. A collection of toy dinosaurs neatly placed on a shelf. There was a blackboard with newspaper clippings pinned to it. They said things such as: *six-year-old thanks God after recovering from cancer*. Death guessed God was pleased with that story, having taken the time to pin it to the board. Another read: *Man thanks God for helping him quit smoking*. Death guessed God would put anything on that board if it had his name. There was a photo of God and his son in Chopard sunglasses smiling at the tower of babel. The screen to the computer was still on and the background of the screen was that of a burning bush. Next to the drinking toy was a black book with the title: *The closet, how to escape*. It was worn and had been read several times by the looks of the dog-eared pages.

"This may have been a wild goose chase coming here but it is protocol. We are expected to thoroughly check the point of departure. It does not usually wield results. Not often a being in your realm finds a dimensional Eddy, let alone creating one. It is quite a feat I must say, you know, to transcend in such a fashion." Harry tapped the toy drinking bird much to his delight.

"Dimensional Eddies are a rare phenomenon and it's even rarer for a being to find himself in one's path. When it does it leads to some residual damage, easy to clean up. However, your Omni God? Biggest deformation I have ever seen. Harry, Barry, you picking up that divine signature? Log it fast before it dissipates, we are in luck. That's a near-perfect signature, somewhat like a shadow Death, will make our lives so much easier in the Beyond and Beyond to find him now. Though with your omniscience we can home in more accurately. Yes! Awesome, so fucking happy, it's great when things just work from the offset! With that and you Death, I think we can tentatively put this in the win column." Harry produced a small handheld device

"Signature registered in the bobbitty boop Sam. Good imprint."

"Okay, well look for anything that would give us a reason as to why he left."

Death opened a drawer and saw a photo of a shirtless man signed: *Best night of my life, Manuel.* There was also a pair of nail clippers and a broken umbrella. Harry found a biscuit tin with nothing in it but an AA battery and a set of car keys.

"Nothing, no clues. Well, at least we have the signature."

"I wouldn't say, nothing gentlemen..." Death held up a with bad penmanship on the back.

It read: *God and the Prophet – the divine wager.*

"I think I have found something."

Chapter 20

"I've been through the desert on a horse with no name, it felt good to be out of the rain. In the desert, you can remember your name, 'cause there ain't no one for to give you no pain. La, la la, la, la, la..." Brian had the song stuck in his head. The elevator behind them shot into the sky and shifted out of the Earthly dimension. The Muse placed her shoes into her bag and the sand burned like a cow branding iron. Immediately she put her shoes back on.

"Yeah, I think it's too bloody hot. It's ridiculous, barely habitable. Either a mirage over there or a guy is sitting under a Joshua tree. I would give all my treasure for a Capri-sun."

"War's treasure," said Muse.

"You don't have the higher ground here Muse. Where exactly did your tiara come from?"

Muse placed her hand over a coy smile. War was having trouble keeping the feet above the ground. Gravity was trying its hardest to sink him deep under the sand.

"Bloody deserts! Not sure how the penguins cope."

"Wrong continent War. Muse, what lives in the desert?"

"The Majove desert is a diverse ecosystem. You have everything from black-tailed jackrabbits to bighorn sheep, ground squirrels to road runners and burrowing owls, even the odd mountain lion."

"And what do they subsist on?"

"Well other than that Joshua tree, there is not much in the way of vegetation in our immediate vicinity, but there are various cacti, the Mojave Yukka, brittlebush, California palm etc. Enough for many herbivores for the like of the mountain lion to subsist on. More correctly it's a puma. We have one hundred and twenty-four thousand square kilometres of this terrain."

"Could have dropped us a bit closer," said Famine.

"Sorry excuse me I don't mean to be a bother with this, I need some help. It's ok if not but you see I think I might be dying a little bit. Dehydration you see and searing 35-degree heat even in late autumn. Fainting seems to be on the cards at any moment and my vision seems compromised."

Muse placed a large bottle of Bromsgrove spring water in Brian's hands. Even a martial artist would envy the speed at which he grabbed the bottle. Brian mumbled thanks. Muse reasoned the elevator did not agree with Brian. She has immediately parched herself and waited until Brian was done with the water.

"Allow me. I was in a seminar some years back run by an Egyptian Goddess of healing and medicine. Sekhmet, I think her name was. Well anyway, I learned a few things and I think I can help." Muse placed a hand on Brians back and radiated a warm orange glow. Brian's vision came back, and he felt invigorated.

"She also taught me how to juggle so if ever you need that just ask."

"What I dont's get though is if the ice is melting anyway with all that freshwater just going to waste in the sea, and places like this that need water. We could give the desert arctic water and stop the sea rising?"

"It's a good thought War, but maybe logistically impossible. The arctic circle, for instance, accounts for three-point three-six million square kilometres of ice but good to see you thinking about the big questions. Besides, the arctic circle has a small layer of freshwater with saltier ice underneath, which is frozen seawater. Antarctica on the other hand accounts for sixty-one percent of all fresh water on Earth so that's your best bet."

"Never been good with facts and figures me, not well-read, don't even know where my library card is..." War wrestled with the sand. Every step was an ordeal.

"So what exactly is quicksand? Not going to come across any are we?" asked War of Muse, becoming very interested in learning new things.

"Misconception, quicksand does not usually appear in deserts as it needs a lot of water. It's usually found in riverbanks, marches and beaches."

"You're a living encyclopedia Muse. I'm a living cynic and War, well he's just living as best as he knows how with great adversity, both in his general intelligence and the sand beneath his feet."

"I can have smarts like I know what a square root is."

Famine and Muse slowly looked at him in surprise and anticipation.

"Look!" War pointed to the ground to see a perfect square root breaking the surface of the sand.

"A square root! Though I don't know what it has to do with Math... and why do mathematicians like pie?" War nodded blankly and walked a little ahead. Brian was in his world devoid of any aches pains bruises, dents dings or abrasions. His thirst was quenched, and the Joshua tree drew near.

"Brian, walk a little ahead if you can, I need to speak to Muse."
Brian shrugged and followed War.
"Muse..." Immediately Famine sweated into his eyes that began to burn and turn red. He produced a handmade family heirloom handkerchief and blotted the sweat away.
"I cannot do it, it's too hard! Ignore me, forget I said anything."
Muse leant into Famine.
"You can tell me anything Famine, and to be fair I can't forget you said anything as you didn't say anything, you just said 'Muse.'"
"It's more than that... gaar! Feelings!" Famine placed his head in his hands and Muse touched his shoulder. She knew what she was hoping for, she just hoped Famine could articulate and navigate what was this difficult subject. Famine, for the most part, tended to wear his emotions on his sleeve. He was brash, erratic and reactionary. But at this moment he felt weak and far removed from his usual obtuse self.

"Look I know I'm not much to look at, I know I can be, well to put it politely abrasive, to put it not so nicely, a bit of a shithead. There are a thousand reasons why anyone would run a country mile from me. I'm weird and gangly, confrontational and petty, I have so many psychological complexes I may as well be defined as having a complex complex. I can be irrational and aggressive but when I am around you, in your welcoming company, all of that disperses. It's like a wave has swept it all away and what's left, covered in sand and haddock *is* something that I like and respect, an inner warmth. When I first felt that emotion, it was so alien and unrecognizable that I visited a shaman witch doctor who just gave me leeches. Five days they drained my blood, but this emotionally lifted iteration of me was still present and is just as strong every time we meet. Muse, what I am trying to say is, I don't know what to do with these feelings, but I cannot bottle them up any longer. I love you, Muse. Now, however you respond does not matter, if you don't feel the same way it matters not, if..." Muse cut Famine off.

"Famine, all of me loves all of you." Muse leant in for a kiss as Famine sat in a fine centimeter layer of sweat from head to toe. Shaking, he reciprocated and, in his head, thanked Pestilence for hanging back. It was what he had desired and coveted for so long and like Brian, with his pint, he just decided to be in this moment. A moment that he would come to play again in his mind for eternity. Brian looked behind him to see Muse and Famine in an embrace. He smiled and caught up with War.

"So, you are huge?" he said. War and Brian stopped at the Prophet under his tree. Muse and Famine holding hands made it to the others. War noticed them with a mighty glee.

"About bloody time you two! How long have you been dancing around your mutual affection? This one here, Famine. You are a lucky bastard. Hello sir!" He patted the Prophet with rare reverence. It was barely contacted in War's mind but was still disconcerting for the Prophet.

"This greenish-brown fruit, is it edible?" War picked one from the tree. The Prophet was silent.

"Maybe he is one of those Mute holy men that talk only by drawing into the sand with a stick?" asked Brian. The Prophet sneezed.

"No my friend, I just needed to sneeze. Those fruits? If they are roasted, they have a sweet candy-like flavor. Though I don't require such things."

A small squirrel was used to the company of the Prophets by now. Occasionally he approached him so his ears could be scratched but were mostly in the business of stealing the fruit of the tree. But for the first time in his squirrel life, others had their eyes on him. He froze and weighed up his options. Free food and possible harassment from the bipedal creatures, or relative safety and starvation. Safety was a relative term as he was extremely edible. He was good at hiding behind various rocks and cacti but in the vast openness like this, he was very exposed.

I'm risking it, he thought and popped on the Prophets lap. The Prophet scratched his ears and he climbed the tree to steal its bounty. A burrowing owl overhead had spotted its breakfast. As did the mountain lion behind the owl.

"So, Prophet, my name is Muse." Muse held out her hand and the Prophet shook it somewhat weakly, irking Muse.

"We are alike Muse. I am the will of God; I preach by divine inspiration. A concept not too far from your function."

"Indeed. This is Famine, War and Brian." The squirrel climbed down from the tree and sat in the Prophets lap happily eating the fruit.

"Famine, War and Brian. I had a name some 50 years ago while under this tree. I miss names, have no idea what it was now, I think it started with a J. Justin? James? I'm sorry I don't get many visitors. I'm afraid I have become somewhat insular and peculiar. My only friend is this squirrel. His name is Basil. He brings me presents, mostly bottle caps and crisp packets. That small pile to my left, my only worldly possessions. I'm particularly fond of the one-armed slightly burned Action Jackson action doll Basil found. It has been so long since I have needed to talk. I haven't muttered a word in twelve years. Funny how it all comes back to you. A few things though, what's that metal thing again that scoops food?"

"A spoon?" ventured Brian.

"Spoon! And what's the one with the sharp points that you impale your chicken on?"

"That would be a fork," added Brian.

"Yes, it's all coming back to me. So, what have I missed in the real world since the sixties?"

Muse spoke up.

"You have missed so much. Where to begin? We landed on the moon, mapped the solar system. Pluto has a heart shape on it. Landed probes on comets, we are on the cusp of going to mars, self-driving electric cars are developing at an astonishing rate. We have what is called the internet accessed by billions of handheld devices that is essentially a repository of all the human knowledge where any question, query or command is instantaneously provided, along with global communication and connectivity. And that gives it no justice. Look at this!" Muse pulled out her smartphone.

"Essentially this device performs many functions of a computer, typically having a touchscreen interface, internet access and an operating system capable of running and downloading apps. And that there, that's a picture of my cat."

"Muse I need to talk to you about Mitzy when you get a chance," said War

"This is astonishing! So, if I wanted to know say, how long a penguin could hold its breath?"

Muse smiled and talked into her phone.

"Assistant, how long can a penguin hold its breathe?" The phone glowed blue.

"Most species of penguins dive for an average of six minutes, however, the emperor penguin can hold its breath for twenty minutes."

"Remarkable." Playing with the phone he accidentally turned on the torch and threw the device in shock.

"You are more than welcome to come with us, see this new world. I mean, it is no Shangri la, it has its negatives, but your species holds so much potential. There is a reason we have sought you out Prophet. The Beyond and Beyond law enforcement agency sent us to you concerning our friend Brian."

Brian smiled at being called a friend and held his hand up as a greeting.

"I have not stood up in many decades. I'm sure my bones have atrophied, may have lost some muscle mass but the Earth's energy has fed me well so here goes nothing."

The Prophet had a beard down to his navel. The tattered clothes had fallen away other than the remnants that covered his toilet bits. With great effort, he got to his feet. The bark behind his back had been worn smooth and mirror-like. His eyes were crazed, and he had three teeth, all deciding in different ways what angle they should protrude from the gum. His hands were blackened and he stood five foot four inches tall. He may have been several inches taller at some undefined part of his life but had been ravaged by time and isolation.

"It has been since time immoral that I have had a cigarette and a dash of whiskey, can you help an old man out? This old tree has served me well. I have had more epiphany's, divine crystalline realizations of the nature of time-space and duality here than I ever did in my old life."

Famine passed him a cigarette and War produced his goat horn of mead. The Prophet happily lit his cigarette and gulped down the mead.

"I have waited here for you Brian for a long time. My isolation can finally end."

"Can you elaborate on that Prophet?" asked Brian with a pit in his stomach.

"I don't even have to inspect you; I can feel it from here. You see there was a divine wager between me and God." The Prophet stopped to take a drag of his cigarette and a gulp of the now almost empty horn of mead. He passed the horn back to War who tucked it away.

"Muse do you sell mead, I'm almost out." The Muse nodded slightly to War and focused on the Prophet.

"Thank you, War. As I was saying, there was a wager between me and God. As a young man, unfulfilled and spiritually empty I had this profound drive for isolation. Many years have passed and the nature of that causal element that led to my isolation is long gone in the furthest depths of my memories. The best I can explain it is I became a nomad, I sought out great teachers and philosophers, musicians and artists. I felt I became an anachronist of sorts. Out of place, not quite belonging. I began to teach others myself, such nonsense about the dissolution of self but found it was an exercise in ego, how well I could refute a premise or defend my dogma. I thought I could help more if I first helped myself, to find true happiness, enlightenment and bring that knowledge back to people who could learn from it. I have remained under this tree for that reason, all of these years." He took another drag of his cigarette.

"Funny how you can spend decades trying to quantify contentment and inner peace when a simple cigarette can elicit just that..." sad the prophet.

"So, the wager?" asked Famine.

"Quite. So, under this Joshua tree, I sat, time became meaningless, days became weeks, weeks became months. In that time, I connected with the Earth itself, fed off its energy requiring no nourishment. I came to a profound conclusion born of a disassociated state that what I learned cannot be taught. My journey and there's were like a fork in the road, from this vantage point there is a third perspective outside duality. At this juncture, I was visited by God himself. It appeared my thoughts constituted as divine. I guess I was a curiosity of sorts. We spent three days talking, the greatest experience I have ever had. He taught me about love, the perspective outside duality, reality and existence. He had a great sense of humor, we laughed and joked." He stopped to take another drag of his cigarette.

"I posed a question to him. I asked why non-belief was a negative sin, something he could not abide by, that he endows humans like myself with the faculties to refute his existence. My perspective of the nature of realism of God was unique and not commonly shared, the divine is not evenly distributed. I made a wager, that if he were to incarnate in human form without knowledge of his divinity, being born in a place where religious indoctrination was not possible, he would exist as an atheist. So to damn an atheist to hell he must damn himself or forgive the concept of non-belief. That was some thirty years ago."

Brian's pit in his stomach collapsed in on itself and he felt he was standing at a cliff edge.

"So, the idea of the apocalypse being that the righteous ascend and the non-believers are left behind to face fire brimstone and War's bagpipes, is nullified if the non-believers are forgiven, ergo no apocalypse?" asked Famine.

"Precisely. The world goes on. And that vessel that carries God's existence, that Brian, is you..."

The silence was electric. Muse had a smile stretched across her face.

"He lived his life as an atheist from what I can read of him. He knows God exists now but technically he died an atheist, several times in fact. How about that Brian? You, my friend, ARE GOD."

Brians vision blurred, creating two Muses who in a distant voice mumbled something he could not quite hear, and with a smile sealed across his face, he fell to the sand-covered ground.

"Well, I was not expecting that! The skinny bugger has gone and fainted cuz he's God. The weirdest thing to happen today," said War.

"Well, I'm sick of the desert. Kangaroos Muse, do they live in the desert?"

Muse laughed.

"Technically yes, deserts and grasslands but we're in California, and they are back in Australia." Muse bought out her phone and typed Earth into images.

"See, we are here, that's Wales where you camp and that there, the big one? That's Australia."

"I think I have had some treasure back there!" Muse turned to Famine.

"Bet you were not expecting that today? Our Brian is a human-shaped God person type thing and stuff."

"Do we have to treat him differently now, like with reverence? With his ephemeral divinity? He constitutes God. I cannot get my head around that. He seems quiet, awkward polite, insular and insignificant like life is something that happens near him and not to him. Not quite making eye contact or awkwardly nodding hello in the corridor. Brian is God. Nope, sounds weird. It's only been half a day, haven't really got to know him. Any who, what now? I guess the bar?" The Prophet held up his hand.

"Yes, Prophet?" asked Famine holding Muse's hand.

"Well, I am sort of done here, would like to find a bathroom, been sitting on something here for a few decades now. It was the last meal I had. Egg and chips and a jam butty."

"Well, I needed the Beyond and Beyond's help with locating you via a mechanical coaster, but now I know where I am I think we can forgo the elevator via this smartphone app and head straight to the bar. Someone try and wake Brian up," said Muse kicking his legs.

"Might have something here," said Famine pulling out a Jimmy's extra shot of flat white ice coffee from his person. Brian's eyes opened slightly.

"No, it was not a dream," he said to himself.

"Intangible strings are pulled, I am a puppet, a fabrication to carry the divine. What happens if I wake up, as God? Where will Brian be? What would I account for? Will my existence, my experience be an afterthought?"

"Stop asking the big questions and drink this coffee. Hurry, we are off any minute now, back to the ineffable plain."

The Prophet picked up his one-armed burnt Action Jackson action doll and held it tightly.

"I guess Brian, you can see yourself as part of a quadrinity, the father, the son, the holy ghost and Brian," said Famine.

"Though they are part of a whole, and independence is present, I dare not care to guess, but I assume like them you will retain some sense of autonomy and agency."

Brian looked at his delicious ice-cold coffee and decided to focus all his faculties on that singular experience with a patented denial for all other assorted actualities and eventualities.

"Basil, I am afraid this is goodbye. You have been a good squirrel, a true friend. I will never forget you. Watch out for the owls and the mountain lions and this tree will always bear fruit for you I promise."

The squirrel sat quietly as sounds occurred outside his comprehension. The Prophet walked away with the squirrel following him.

"Why are you making this difficult Basil? I said I have to go, I'm sorry!"

"We can take the damn squirrel with us Prophet. Unless it bites. Does it bite? I have had a rabies shot before after Wars pet pig bit me. Not an experience I want to repeat. I think Pestilence has allergies so keep it away from him. Muse have you got something for him to wear? What was once a suit is now a revealing loincloth being bad at its job. Maybe hose him down and give him a shave with a Philips OneBlade razor or something"

Brian got to his feet.

"Famine, if you were to discover something akin to the Earth-shattering magnitude of this revelation how would you cope?" asked Brian.

"I was created in thought from God and asked what I was. I declared I am Famine and was brought into the world. I have always been what I am, no transition period but the scope of the revelation to which you referred. If it were me, I too would collapse into an existential crisis and possibly with some force, onto the floor. I would try to see if I had any powers, see if I could lift that rock and fail in the attempt. Remember, I am fundamentally the same person I was several minutes ago and until something otherworldly transpires, I am still that person so I'd go with that and just try to carry on as best I could. Erm, sir."

"Sir?" asked Brian.

"Look you may be this meek downtrodden polite young man but you're also part of the quadrinity and I am but a humble servant of yours I guess so yeah, sir. Sorry if it feels weird, it feels weird for me too but alas your station is on high."

"That's right sir," said War

"We are at your service," Muse agreed, bowing her head barley lingering into the sarcastic. It was all a little much for Brian, but he humbly nodded.

"Before the bar, do I have time for a cigarette?"

"Well, Pestilence is not here to complain and make you feel bad about your life choices, so I guess go ahead. Not like you may start a forest fire. Other than the vast nothingness and endless unchanging geography, the sun a quarter of a mile above us, this searing heat that gets right up your nostrils, it's not a bad place. Get a yurt, few friends, BBQ, dune buggy races, could be quite nice! I hear burning man is in Nevada, they make the most of the desert. War, do you remember we were there back in '93?"

War laughed.

"Where Pestilence had that purple tea and his eyes dilated? He hung in that tree for six hours trying to save a cat that didn't exist!"

"Or when War, that old martial artist stole the last cupcake from Me and in revenge I stole his prosthetic leg and held it ransom? Sold it back to him for two cupcakes?"

"The two cupcakes he stole off of me and Death you mean?"

"I gave them back!"

"Mine had a bite taken out of it, Famine!"

"It was just the blueberry bit; you don't like blueberry. It's like when I take the sweetcorn from your pizza. Besides you know me, I'm always hungry, I become my namesake."

"The amount of creativity at Burning Man requires great inspiration, a big job that is," said Muse.

"What is this burned man?" asked the Prophet.

"It's an annual event in the Nevada desert. It describes itself as a temporary metropolis dedicated to music art and self-expression. It started back in 1986 and at the end of the festival, they burn an effigy of, in quotes, 'the man'."

"My era, the sixties, was quite transformative, a counter-culture of rock and roll. The Beatles, Bob Dylan, the Kinks, Jimi Hendrix. I bet your generation Brian would never have heard of say, Elvis Presley. Long forgotten I would imagine. Our music combined elements of folk music the blues, country and rock and roll." The Prophet was cradling the squirrel that was now sound asleep.

"Prophet all those artists are iconic, holding an exalted position in rock in some form or other and has persisted into the modern-day. Fifteen years ago, you could not move for goths, they were a fucking infestation. Thousands of the bastards were draped in black makeup, dog collars and spikes. Reading bad poetry and hanging around rose bushes. Pessimistic nihilists, every one of them, the only attribute I could get on board with!" said Famine. Muse laughed.

"Famine didn't you go through that phase of eyeliner and black fingernails?"

"Muse, I was just trying to score some goth tail, I heard they were unusually amorous. Turned out to be just downright depressing."

"Anyway, shall we head back to the bar?" asked the Muse of the group. A general nodding of heads occurred.

"Let's do it," said War.

"On with the journey I guess," said Famine

"Fantastic," said Brian.

"Bye tree!" said the Prophet.

"Alright everybody put your hands in the middle. Say cheese!"

"Cheese..." they all said in unison as they began to vibrate into a fuzz of static. It rebounded between here and the bar a few times and dissipated in a varied myriad of scents, the most prominent of which was watermelon with a touch of strawberry.

Chapter 21

In the beer garden, a static started to form between two Alexander rose Portofino six-seater tables and chairs. The Seraphim took notice and leaned a little back on their chairs.

"Inbound!" came a female voice and Muse, Famine, War, Brian and the Prophet materialized. The Prophet could barely perceive the bar, he was disorientated and waited for it all to come into focus. A field of flowers became a jukebox, five suns became two, then three settled on one. A noise like white light invaded his ears and equilibrium. Eventually, there was a traditional enough looking tavern.

"You are a Prophet so you may be able to navigate this plane better than most mortals."

"And what is this plane?" asked the Prophet through his beard and rags.

"This is the ineffable plane where various dimensions entangle and interact. Intersecting with consciousness time and space. A sort of dimensional Eddy. This is the ethereal bar that sits in it."

"And you have a pool table?" The Prophet said with some confusion.

"Yes, but it's a bastard of a pool table. If you wanted to be berated and harassed, he's your guy. If you want a pleasant afternoon, I will steer clear of it. If the cacti ask you for a drink, tell him to bugger off."

They approached the doors to the bar.

"I will take the Prophet to the toilet so he doesn't get lost, find him some clothes, maybe shave his beard, should be five minutes or so," said Muse. She kissed Famine on the cheek and patted the top of his head. Famine waited until she was out of sight.

"I did it Pestilence!" he said as Pestilence approached. Famine tripped on his loose shoelace and fell face-first onto the floor. Pestilence helped him up.

"You ok?"

"Yeah, why wouldn't I be?" he brushed himself off.

"So there was a thing you have done then?" asked Pestilence into the middle distance not paying attention. He wondered if he should have tuna or pilchards. It was getting late, and he was somewhat hungry. He wondered what time it was, and noticed it seemed to be late afternoon. He wondered who the old bearded guy was that Muse had just escorted in the general direction of a possible toilet. *This damn ear!* he thought as Famine was saying something. He wondered if Muse had any olive oil behind the bar. He was vaguely aware of a recently divine being found in the mop cupboard with a spatula. If he was about then certainly there was some olive oil. He realized he had completely missed everything Famine had said.

"Sorry I missed all of that, can you repeat it?" Famine dropped his head.

"Muse Pestilence, Muse!" Pestilence was still confused.

"Muse went that way with an old, bearded fellow."

Famine slapped his head.

"I'm sure you're doing this on purpose. Muse, I told Muse how I felt!"

"Oh, I'm so sorry, maybe someone else will come along." Pestilence tried to convey pity but a grumbling if his stomach superseded it.

"No dammit, she reciprocated! I told her how I felt, and she reciprocated, she told me she loved me too and she kissed me, on the lips and everything!"

"It's true," said War with a certain invested interest.

"I am so happy for you! I am! You do realize she's a skyscraper above your station? I understand your attraction but hers is a mystery. I mean, what is that red thing on your forehead for example that's been there three months? It looks like something the GP should be notified about. A nice healthy shade of yellow to those teeth, and is one leg longer than the other? You tend to walk with an uneven gait. At least you smell nice. Is that lynx Africa?"

"You can bugger off; she likes me Pestilence!! You know me and happiness give each other a healthy distance. Well, it's like it's knocking on my door, and I've let it in to share a plate of kippers. I am, as you wanted for me, happy! I don't even need to see that shaman witch doctor; I recognize this emotion. Oh and some other news, Brian is God." Pestilence had a smile of distrust and suspicion.

"Well, I am over the moon for both of you and Muse. Now, what was that you just said about Brian? I fear I may have misheard you."

"Tell him, Brian!" Brian cleared his throat, uncomfortable with being at the forefront of the conversation.

"Ahem, yes..." He wiped the sweat off his brow and Famine

passed him his handkerchief.

"So the Prophet, in short, described a wager of sorts with God. It seems over three days the Prophet broached the subject of disbelief, of atheism. He was told God could forgive all sins other than that of non-belief. He could not abide by it. The Prophet reasoned he was endowed with the faculties to refute God's existence with Gods fingerprint seemingly missing from existence. He posed an idea that if God himself were to incarnate in human form without knowledge of his divinity, without social and cultural indoctrination he would live and die as an atheist. So, to damn any other non-believer was to damn himself or he should forgive the concept of non-belief altogether. That vessel, that incarnation is me. Muse said that I am God and I am now referred to, strangely, as sir."

"In a thousand years, I never would have guessed. I mean there was something other-worldly about you but divinity in its purest apex form? We are all expressions of God but you are at the epicenter. Fantastic, bizarre news, but does that not imply something greater, Famine. It occurs to me that perhaps the apocalypse is nullified. The righteous ascend, the non-believers remain in fire and brimstone existing in the end times initiated by ourselves but if non-belief is a forgiven concept, what happens to our function?"

"The same thought occurred to me Pestilence. Almost word for word."

"I cannot get over this, Brian is, in essence, an ephemeral deity. I mean at best I thought maybe his mother shagged a Seraphim. Congratulations Brian, how have you taken the news? I think If I had that revelation put forward to me, I don't know if I could accept it, take it in and process it erm, sir."

"I'm a little numb. Please, Brian is fine"

"Well, maybe a Guinness will help sir, I mean, Brian," said Pestilence getting the attention of a waitress. Muse appeared from a corridor adjacent to the jukebox that was playing some generic swing music. To her left was a short three toothed, more gum than expected, hunched over, draped in a Ralph Lauren polo Flannel men's three-piece suit in medium grey, Prophet.

"He cleans up quite nicely I dare say. A lot of antibacterial wipes were needed, but I present the hosed down Prophet!"

The squirrel was still cradled in the hands of the Prophet. The

Prophet barely recognized himself, it had been decades since he had looked in a mirror and the gravity of ageing was something that gave him the sense of sorrow, leaving him partially morose.

"I guess this happens to all of us, temporary beings governed by senescence and decay, an insignificant tick of the clock unnoticed but absolute and certain, unwavering in its will to count down to your end." Respectful silence was shared as the Prophet sighed.

"Oh well. I have lived a good life. A few years left in me, yet I hope."

Muse grabbed a dog bed from beneath the bar with the name Brutus stitched to the side with great care.

"I know this is an unusual request, but I have had no physical contact in decades. Can I have a hug?" asked the Prophet.

"I'm not hugging him, he smells of soup," said Famine to Pestilence under his breath.

"Well, I can't hug him, I'll make him sick being that close," said Pestilence.

"I'll hug him," said War also being quiet. The Prophet was having trouble catching what was being said and leaned in a little closer.

"You can't hug him War, he is far too fragile, you'll make a rib and blood puddle of him."

"For God's sake," said Muse and leaned in for a hug. It lasted two seconds too long. Muse disengaged and returned behind the bar.

"This was my old dog's bed; I think the squirrel will be ok here for a while Prophet. I'll put a little bowl of water here and ask the chef for a carrot."

"Can you ask him for some olive oil as well please?" asked Pestilence.

"I could go for a sandwich," said Famine.

"Mitzy may have been in the new camper van Muse," admitted War.

"Been weighing heavily that," he added.

"Oh, and I heard about you and Famine, Muse. Great news!" said Pestilence.

"Yeah, I think it can be something amazing, very special." Famine picked a damp dying lily from an assortment of flowers in a vase and passed it to Muse.

"Ah, that's lovely! I'll keep it here," she said putting it back in the vase.

"Well, that was a pointless exchange," said Pestilence.

"A whole bar and not a looker among 'em," declared War. Almost every utterance for War was a declaration. It was enough for most patrons to avoid the three-meter circle around war and try the bar at the back with a restaurant section that sometimes existed, as long as people were paying attention to it.

"Who are you kidding War, I have seen you with a lot worse than what is on offer here. A lot worse. Remember Gertrude the German hot dog challenge champion at that Renaissance fair? One of the few places you fit in. But in your defense, it was after 4 horns of Lyme bay Devon mead. Hey, look outside, it's shadow guy. Is he pickpocketing that Seraphim? I mean, it's a great use of his nature. The perfect thief being a shadow. For instance, he can tuck himself in the shadow of a bench, or some other bit of crap. I don't know, say in the shadow of a large gentleman, not noticing the shadow due to a plate of chicken wings in madras sauce. Crap, I have made myself hungry, again. I'd take a sandwich if it's going?" Muse nodded and sought out the chef.

"I've been through the desert on a horse with no name, it felt good to be out of the rain. In the desert, you can remember your name, 'cause there ain't no one for to give you no pain. La, la la, la, la, la..." Dammit, Brian, you got that song stuck in my head now," said Pestilence.

"I have a girlfriend!" Famine said in a high intonation.

"Who would win in a fight between War and all those Seraphim you reckon? Take away their flaming swords as that's cheating," ventured Pestilence.

"I don't know, the average Seraphim head pales in comparison to the magnitude of War's hand. I think War would make light work of them, it takes either a very brave or very stupid man to challenge War or simply a man that has given up on life and decided to engage in Death via War. What a lot of people don't get though is that War is a gentle creature for the most part but I have seen those rare occasions when he is angered and honestly it's horrifying to the pits of damnation." Muse adjusted her tiara.

"Here you go, a ham and onion bap or roll, cob or bun. I think the name is regional. Pestilence, your olive oil. Not going to ask why you want it but there it is, vegetable based. War, about the cat, I hope you cherish its memory and here is a single sad looking carrot."

"It's you Pestilence! The likeness is uncanny!" yelled War with a belly laugh.

"Centuries with the carrot jokes I may just shave this head; it has never done me any favors. It's the first thing people associate me with, oh yeah that guy with the upright orange carrot hair. I know who you are on about! Screw it, Muse, cut my hair, shave it all off." Muse clapped her hands in excitement.

"The God of haircuts is around somewhere. You know I have forgotten his name, I want to say, Tim, but I shall not call him as I don't want to set a precedent that he could be of any Earthly use. I'd sooner grab some gardening tools and mutilate my hair than let him think he is relevant."

"There is a God of haircuts now? Whatever next," said Famine genuinely surprised.

Muse looked under the counter that inexplicably had almost anything she needed at that point. If she fancied painting, there would be an easel waiting. It was all part and parcel of the ineffable plain interacting with general assorted consciousness's. There it was a brand new in box Phillips Aquatouch wet and dry electric shaver.

"So completely shaven then Pestilence? You have had this hair for many many years, sure you will not miss it?" Muse branded the shaver as if it were a sword, a soldier called to arms.

"My entire life has been holding me back. Do you know my track record for amorous entanglement? I blame the hair. The reason why at restaurants my table is always by the toilet. I cannot prove it but I blame the hair. The fact that everyone assumes I'm a farmer is because of the hair, and that one time I owned that Massey Ferguson tractor I guess."

Muse grabbed a stool and motioned Pestilence to take a seat. She put a towel over him and turned on the razor. It valiantly attempted to fulfil its haircutting capacity, having great trouble with the thick rich straw-like hair. In a few short minutes, the task was complete. Muse passed Pestilence a mirror.

"Fan-fucking-tastic! It has gone, the curse has been lifted!" War nodded agreeably.

"A massive improvement, I'll miss that hair, it was a defining characteristic. Almost an affectation. No, yeah, it's good my old friend! Impressed, good job Muse!" Muse leant over to kiss Famine, both six inches from Pestilence's face. The odd bit of saliva made it from them into Pestilence's nostril.

"Ok, enough of that," he said.

"And you referred to me as a friend, not a colleague. Thank you, Famine. My friend. My friend Famine."

"Ok don't gush about it. You are a friend."

"I think Muse has already made you a better and more accepting person, Famine." Muse heard a door creak from the back. Death and the gentlemen arrived. Death seemed to glide as Sam Harry and Barry trudged behind him.

"Pestilence, the hair, well lack of I should say. It suits you, it does." Death was impressed.

"He has an odd-shaped head, like a ripe pear, did not expect that," said War.

"How was God's complex visit?" asked Famine of Death. Death scratched the top of his head. Famine wondered if that was a learned behavior to fit in or not. He thought this as he had no idea if one could itch without flesh. Itchy bones just sounded wrong to him.

"I thank Brian for delivering me to the equestrian to retrieve the horses and the key. Was a wonderful estate. The architecture was in essence awe-inspiring, the art seemed a little out of place and graphic, our hosts were a little off. War, we found some of your treasure and here is an old wallet of yours. I'm not entirely sure why you have a license for land surveying. Also, a library card tucked away in there."

"So that is where it was!" War grabbed his wallet.

"Anyway, I and the gentlemen have registered God's signature."

"On the beepity boop," said Harry waving a small handheld computer-like device with excessive flashing lights. Too long focusing on its screen will elicit a strong migraine. It looked like a smartphone had blended with a Nintendo game boy and some discarded Christmas lights.

"We will now know where to find God."

"Quiet! Shadow guy might be lurking, I know he only tends to speak in random semi theological slash philosophical utterances, but if he hears, the Seraphim hears, over here by those big sofas at the back, we will sit and discuss this privately."

"I apologize," said Death. They all migrated to the sofas. The group was now quite sizable. Brian was in company with Famine, Death, War and Pestilence, with Muse and the Prophet and the three gentlemen. The sofas could fit eight, so Death and Brian stood by the table. Death patted Brian on the back and gave him a skeletal thumbs up.

"As I mentioned, we now have the means to find God, hopefully returning in the Beyond and Beyond plane and with the residue measured from God upon his exit he should be easy to locate. There was also a divine wager of sorts scrawled on the back of a coaster. Brian, I have some news..." Brian cut him off.

"I know, the Prophet explained all this in detail. I am for all intents and purposes, effectively in essence, in effect, I am essentially, for all practical measures God incarnate." Brian waved his hands up and down; "See? God."

"This is a relief Brian, I did not know how to broach that subject erm, sir," said Death.

"I previously alluded that I held your mortality in my grasp. That was never the case. It was a fabrication as I needed your submission and assistance, and it seemed the easiest way. Your repeated death was in its entirety in the hands of the equestrians. I may, in my reaping, been partly responsible, but your life Brian is safe."

"I should be angry Death, but I am not. I am relieved! It has been playing heavily on me the entire day. My mortality was dependent on my cooperation, I knew that, but I wondered what would happen when my use was no longer needed."

"One thing puzzles me. It's a thought born of advanced coincidence," started Famine. He began to pace in a sort of accusatory fashion.

"So, Death encountered a single human from billions and that Brian is you. You were sought out due to the bizarre, repeated Lazarus style resurrection, as a Brian shaped clue as to where the horses and Gods' spare key was. Yet all the myriad of beings that could have had their hourglass on Death's horse it was Brian's, who just so happens to be that which the Prophet, through God, bought into existence. It just seems highly, nay, extremely unlikely."

"Well, I exist in a high state of synchronicity. The ergodic chaos has an underlying pattern too. It can be in a sense be read or experienced. That which is unlikely to occur in one set occurs repeatedly in a second set. I am also entangled with God, it only makes sense that I would encounter his counterpart."

"Well let's hope that synchronicity may become serendipity if in some fashion Brian can help us convince God to come back," said the Muse. "Holy shit, this cannot be good..."

The doors to the elevator had just opened. Igor gave a wave. In front of them standing seven feet tall and the horns adding another foot, stood Satan in a Bottega Veneta leather and a twill trench coat with a black robe underneath and walking barefoot. The entire bars patronage was on full alert, nervous and still. Satan was at best unpredictable and worse a giant red flag-shaped liability. Nothing was safe, that which was and wasn't sentient. Satan stopped at a mirror. Every thought he had become dissolute as he was lost in his own eyes.

"You are one sexy bastard. Every woman wants you; every man wants to be you!" He marveled at his hairline. God was pretty much bald at this point, just one of the many reasons he reveled in his perceived superiority.

"Dad?"

Satan's son was a little shocked to see his fathr. He was hanging out with the shadow guy by the pool table with a snooker cue in one hand and a cigarette in the other that he tried to hide with smoke billowing from behind him. It knew to stop at the red velvet rope that read: SMOKING AREA.

"Son, have you been drinking!?"

"Dad I'm twenty-four. So yes. A lot in fact." He decided to just be upfront. "No point hiding this any longer," he said brandishing his cigarette.

"Drinking is the only pleasure I have. It's also a crutch to forget *you* exist, you cancerous sore."

Satan bounded toward his son who immediately dropped his pool cue to run for his life. They did three laps around the main bar area in this fashion. While his son was like a whippet aided in his escape by youth and a balanced diet of lots of fiber and grains, Satan found himself almost clutching his chest at the unexpected physical expenditure. A knotted ball of pain ached on his right side. This pursuit was unsustainable. Almost giving up, he threw a napkin at his son. It was a deflating experience as the napkin barely made it half a foot before gently losing altitude to carefully place itself on the Kandla grey porcelain paving floor.

"Great family values there," said Famine. The son eventually ran behind Death.

"Death, if you can step aside a second, I just need to kill this vermin of a son," Satan unsheathed a dagger.

"From this moment forward he is under my watch, Satan."

His son gave him the middle finger. Death was the only being in existence that truly terrified Satan.

"You may be a wild card Satan, but I'm great at poker!" Impressed with himself Famine grinned

"That made no sense Famine," said Pestilence.

"Why do you call me out on this stuff, why can't you just let me have my moment?"

"Look, son..." under the gaze of Death, Satan decided to do something rare, becoming reasonable.

"I am doing what you suggested. I am here to meet God. We are going to talk it out."

"Muse, I don't have a lot when it comes to money, but I request a sanctum. Can you put me up a short while till I get on my feet? I can't live with him anymore I just can't. I woke up a week ago and he was standing over me with a pitchfork at my neck and told me softly to go back to sleep."

"I have a few spare rooms upstairs. Here, have a Mesopotamian gold coin," Muse said flicking the coin through the air, caught by Satan's son. He was overcome with a warmth radiating through his body.

"Now a month's rent will cost one Mesopotamian coin," she said holding out her hand. Satan's son smiled.

"Maybe I can work here, be a bartender or a toilet usher?"

"Son! You are the heir to my kingdom! I will not have you tending bar!" bellowed Satan.

"Your kingdom is of ash and the demented! A cesspit of rogue sadism and bleak despair. I'm twenty-four and this is my decision. Thank you, Muse!" Satan was about to explode but at this point, Michael of the Seraphim walked into the bar.

"Again, can't be good," said the Muse stuck in the tense and dense air.

"Vile creature of the pit! The feared Mephistopheles! God of the abyss and perdition! You are not welcome here!" Michael drew his flaming sword.

"Gentlemen! This is a neutral establishment! Satan has as much right to be here as you, Seraphim. I will not have a conflict of this sort; it will not be tolerated!"

"But it's Satan! Surely there is an exception?"

"Put down the sword. Nice and easy, yes, just like that. Okay, you're doing good, a few more inches-"

"I'm getting turned on," said Famine. Pestilence chuckled and the joke went over War's head. Michael limply let his sword dangle.

"For if you forgive other people when they sin against you, your heavenly Father will also forgive you!" Said the shadow guy using Satan as a leaning post to avoid falling to the floor.

"Who the fuck is THIS guy?" demanded Satan. A gap in the shadow faces formed as a see-through smile.

"That's just shadow guy, he does shadow puppetry for beer money. The first guest to appear in the morning the last to leave at night. If I had to guess though I would assume he never leaves. At the end of the day, he just nestles himself into a random shadow. Sometimes I come into work and all the chores are done, new discs in the urinals, beer mats at the right angle on the tables, broomed and mopped and so forth. I would call him on it but then I would have to do those chores myself. It's an unspoken relationship," described Muse in a fatigued manner. Satan's son was still very much hiding behind Death. Satan looked at Brian.

"And this guy too? Why does he smell like that? I have a sense of a thick residue." Satan needed not to be involved in the matters at hand.

"His mom shagged a Seraphim," lied Muse.

"Yep, shagged her hard," said Famine.

"All day long," said War.

"Garden ornaments were involved," said Pestilence.

"Hey that's my mom!" muttered Brian, defeated. Satan seemed to have bought it.

"Muse, maybe we should pick up where we left off?" Satan ventured through his eyebrows. Muse shuddered at the thought of their past sexual encounter, all grunting and overly mechanical, far too much elbows. She was promised to see heaven, but it was more reminiscent of waiting in line at the grocery store with someone behind humming a tune slightly too loudly and an old lady painfully taking her time picking up some socks she had bought and subsequently dropped.

"And what is this now?" Famine looked up with wide-open eyes. The vulnerability was achingly beautiful to Muse.

"A long time ago with complete lack of judgment, vulnerable as my dog had just died, fairly inebriated I took, well comfort is not the right word, more a lapse of sanity. A grievous error. I had the displeasure of spending a night with this, this... I don't know, how do you describe something that ruined your life and romance for centuries?" Satan had a stupid unmoving smile on his face.

"Satan, Muse is with me now so no further propositions. Keep your distance or I swear I will command Pestilence to will you to experience violent, vertical diarrhea."

"Big words for a puny pipsqueak," Satan stroked his dagger.

"I would not get any ideas," said War taking a step toward Satan who instinctively took a step back.

"Look I'm just here to see God, ok? Is that too much to ask or am I just being wildly unreasonable?"

Muse stuck up a finger to silence the crowd that had formed.

"Satan, take a seat in the beer garden. Drinks on me, we have some business to attend to. If you can wait, we will facilitate your request."

"That is more like it, some respect!" said Satan, wandering into the garden.

"That was a tense situation, thought it was going to get serious there for a second," said Sam. "Worried I would have to get in there, show them the fist of Sam!"

"That's just posturing, you were behind War the whole time."

"Well, I didn't see you diffusing the situation?"

"I never claimed I did!" said Harry.

"I need the toilet," said Barry.

Everyone else returned to the sofas. War with great trouble oriented himself in a way that allowed him to take a seat that groaned beneath him.

"Would have loved for him not to stand down, haven't had a worthy champion since Samson! He did this trick with mountains. That battle would have been glorious, though one of those horns could take out an eye. I'd be like Odin." War cracked his knuckles.

"Oh well," he sighed, deflated and unfulfilled. The waitress came to the table. War got out the old pommel bag of treasure and threw her a 1974 flowing hair silver dollar.

"A round of your best whiskeys! Is that ok with everyone?" there was a general litany of agreeable grunts and nods.

"Whiskey it is!" Famine pulled out a pack of cigarettes and handed one to Brian and another to the Prophet.

"Oh please, not this! I hate the smell; can you not just take a few steps over there? Invest in one of those vaping contraptions or something, gum or spray? You do realize what you're doing to your respective bodies." Pestilence hated having to complain.

"You are a wet blanket are you not? I mean I'm sitting here, a nice drink on its way, a delicious cigarette and I think, this is fantastic. All the most interesting people in the world, every one of them smoked and it's cool and you know it. I can punctuate sentences with a flick of the cigarette's ash. Use it with my pointing finger to add gravitas to whatever it is I am pointing to."

The three gentlemen were talking among themselves, and Brian refrained from lighting his cigarette until a consensus of location was determined.

"I will buy you a damn vape Famine with my own money and everything. They sell them behind the bar, look! There is a Voopoo drag with a PNP pod and citrus seven e-liquid 3mg. Double 18650 batteries you can't go wrong! I read It's 98% better for you than cigarettes and you exhale water vapor, completely non carcinogenic and none-obnoxious." Famine put out his cigarette and threw his arms into the air.

"Fine! I'll try a vape, but if I am happier and healthier and this leads me to be less obnoxious then that's on you!"

"I think you have used a variant of that statement before," said Pestilence.

"The pattern, the inflexion. Maybe it's just me." Pestilence got up from his seat and almost bumped into Ariadne, one of the waitresses. She gave him a smile and his face turned red.

"Here you are gentlemen, a round of Hennessy X O Frank Gehry limited edition whiskeys."

"You cannot do a kindness too soon. because you never know how soon it will be too late." Shadow guy slammed his shadow hand to his chest and bowed.

"I think that quote was about generosity and at a guess, it was to elicit a free drink," said Sam. Barry nodded and Harry placed a small umbrella in his drink.

"One for shadow guy too Ariadne."

"Kindness is a language which the deaf can hear and the blind can see!"

"I think that was Mark Twain," said Famine. Pestilence came back from the bar with a new vaping device. He sat and took off the plastic with his teeth. Well, he tried to. It beat him, he tried, and he lost, sometimes in life you cannot have everything and it is best in those circumstances to brush yourself off and engage in your next adventures.

"Over here," said Death. He used his bony finger to carefully cut the box open. Pestilence followed the instructions, put it together and passed it to Famine. He described the wattage settings, the brightness, the puff counter, the clock, the alcohol blood level app and the game of snake.

"Alright well here goes," said Famine. It was a taste sensation. Silky smooth vapor entered his lungs. The sun was bright, the grass green and the flowers in bloom.

"I can get on with this, I really can. This is great! It's like a soda style blend of quintessential lemon and lime soft drink. Has a citrus kick. Sharp and sweet at the same time. This is phenomenal!" Famine and a deep cough introduced themselves to each other.

"Yep, the body is far from used to it," the Prophet lit his cigarette.

"Smoking shouldn't come with instructions," he said happily. Brian decided to wait until later with his cigarette as not to elicit any attention but was intrigued by this vaping setup. He did not have the confidence to ask for one himself. Feeling a little neglected he took solace in his drink. It was some of the best whiskey had ever tasted.

"Don't want to drink too many of these, I'll be twatted. Seems like a lot of drinking has been going on on this day." He let that statement hang in the air to gather dust while it waited to be acknowledged. After a while, it gave up. Barry returned from the bathroom. Brian needed to go also but decided to wait. It seemed like the most considered act.

"This Bombay mix tastes funny, like Earthy. That taste-" said Barry.

"That's sprite shit," said War. Barry spat the contents of his mouth onto a handkerchief.

"So we need to head off to the Beyond and Beyond I guess? I think all of you can be of some service to facilitate his consensual departure. We have orders to be as delicate with this as possible. A realm should not be without its Omni God. So nice and easy, bringing him back is our top priority. Nice and easy...," said Sam.

"Lemon squeezy," Sam grinned.

"And lemon squeezy too I suppose. Tell him that he is needed, that he is wanted and that he is loved. We will fix the tear and all being well you won't get another visit from the Beyond and Beyond. I don't think you grasp the enormity of a visit from us." Harry got out the know your realms handbook.

"So tipping is necessary. Although you have given money for your drink or meal you have to further part with your currency." Sam was perplexed at this custom.

"So, because someone picked up a drink from 6 feet away and ferreted it over to a table, a drink figuratively in arms reach they deserve more money? Must be the easiest three or four quid you can make! Having to pay for common courtesy. If I went out of my way to hold a door for someone, should I expect recompense? I'm not adhering to this particular custom." Sam shook his head.

"Anyway these thingy-majigs are connected to the beepity boop." Sam handed out small eight arrow emblem badges.

'Sign for chaos, isn't it?' said Pestilence to himself, not expecting a response. The badges were clipped onto the respective persons, and each made a soft hum with a ring of blue light on the circumference. The Muses blinked a red light.

"Sorry, number 28 has been playing up," Sam leaned close to the device and tapped it five times. The light became blue.

"Harry, how is the beepity boop?" Sam inquired.

"Calibrating, calibrating...still calibrating- the stupid hourglass, software update required, postpone that and... there we are, connected!"

Barry brought out a small handheld device that looked halfway between a gun and a toaster. One by one he scanned the group, looking intensely at the screen.

"Muse, you have a slightly raised cholesterol level, you should keep an eye on that, the rest of you are fine. We are almost done. Here, take these pills, it will help with vertigo. Your passage has been confirmed and authorized by the high assembly, we have temporary papers for you, akin to say your passports. This is how you should leave by the way, not just carelessly ripping your way in. Honestly of all the inconsiderate...oh never mind, what's done is done."

"So, what to expect, perceiving the Beyond and Beyond is like fitting an orange in a two-dimensional plane."

"Sam loves that analogy," said Harry.

"What you will experience is plateaued, thank you, Harry, by your perceptional limits. What one may experience may be different from another. Muse and the horsemen will fare better than Brian and the

Prophet. At the twist of this knob next to the 'do not press' red button, which if the opportunity arrives, do not press, we will begin a journey to Beyond and Beyond."

"Or Bab for short," said Harry.

"Stop trying to make 'Bab' a thing Harry, it will never catch on."

"Beyond and Beyond law enforcement? Bable?"

"It sounds made up, 'hi we're from bable.'"

"Can't be any worse than calling this a beepity boop?"

"Ok we are off track here, let's just get on with this shall we?"

Sam twisted the knob on the vaguely cheap sci-fi resembling device.

Chapter 22

Brian had lost track of how many times today he had felt distinctively and overwhelmingly peculiar, from transportation to a desert inhabited by a revelation dispensing Prophet, non-consensual commune with abrasive cacti, snakes made of love invading his general anatomy, being haunted by a robe-wearing phantasm and now he could not even register his beingness. With a seemingly absent body, he had been vibrated to a higher form, cast into a light fantastic. He found himself in a tunnel of incandescent lights like a light shone through a prism made of play dough forming a boundary to the tunnel. Faces punctuated them and exhaled insight and liquid truth made of the information by way of purple mist that sank into whatever Brian now was. He was still Brian. He had Brian's memories, Brian's life's content but he was experiencing something other. He felt like a medium shade of blue with yellow sparks. An arc of bowed lightning shocked him to his core and for a brief second, he had felt God within him. It felt like the implosion of a star. He felt a chasm between that which he was and that which he was becoming. He may have briefly lost consciousness but again he felt a vague awareness. Again, an arc of bowed lightning emanating from the tunnel contacted Brian. For another brief second, he was the sum of someone elses memories, a divine catalogue of all things and all places. The tunnels velocity increased and the sound of light fantastic seemed to strip Brian of every piece of himself, reconstituting with the sacred at the torn seams. Incalculable voices from every direction compounded one after the other. With a simple exhale he counted every word. The Prophet shot past him like a shaven bullet. The tunnels end drew near, he prepared himself for entrance at the cusp of the yonder. The tunnel seemed to fall away behind him at his exit. The threshold shrank and fizzled out in a circle of yellow strings.

    Being a stream of undefined information was the singular most inexpressible experience he had ever had. He felt form and tactile connection, a strange inverse of his disassociation in the tunnel. Looking down to his hands he saw waves of color, alien to him and crashing together like waves. He lifted his hand and as he did, he could see where it was and where it was going. Time seemed inconsequential and subjective. At a thought Brian became that lonely man in his studio apartment with his single fish and realized he was there in a higher capacity, experiencing his depression with himself and a chorus of a thousand trumpets. Such an inconsequential moment, something so easily forgotten and laid to rest. He had never been alone; he was always there.

In an exploratory manner, he studied his form and found he could see in all directions. He could reach a phantom arm and feel the landscape in a thousand places. He looked at the landscape and saw floating cities, towers many miles high shifting in and out of view. The sky became purple and a voice vast and expansive wished Brian a happy welcome. Tens of thousands of beings, some of the form, some of the spirit, some chimaeras and some like elves came into view and bowed to Brian.

"Why walk when you can fly?" said a small child-like creature in several overlapping voices. He lifted off with a chuckle. Brian looked above him to see a crystal dome with a gargantuan hole in the middle. Its edges were punctured by millions of holes with traffic ferrying in and out of the dome. Through the crystal dome, he psionically projected himself and felt many other domes dotted in an indefinable blue and purple sky made of thought and experience. Everything was alive and he understood it all. Only then was he aware of some shapes that he recognized as his newly found friends. Death looked no different, but the rest seemed like perfect versions of themselves. Pestilence had musculature, and soft flat black hair and a goatee. Famines teeth were perfectly white, his posture like he had many trips to the chiropractors. His bent nose straight, his cheekbones enviable. The red spot on his forehead was absent. War sported a classically handsome face with no unexplained animal fragments on his coverings. His jagged teeth agreeing on a more symmetrical and polished look. Muse was beyond beautiful. The three gentlemen seemed taller and more accessible and less abrasive; the Prophet was at least thirty years younger. But unlike them, Brian was still made of wave crashing colors.

"I don't mean to alarm you guys but I think I am god. I cannot be overly sure, somewhat hesitant to assert it but look at me. I am made of dancing crashing light. I am still very much me, but it was like that analogy of the man in the cave. He had only ever faced the wall so his whole life had only perceived the shadows of things. Finally, it is like I have left that cave and saw the world beyond the shadows. A blind man seeing, a deaf man hearing. Do you know when a caterpillar pupates it dissolves into a generic slush and reconstitutes as a butterfly? The universe is tactile, visceral, malleable. I understand the perspective outside duality. I am that butterfly. I still very much am me, but I hear, feel, taste and sense everything. I want to weep at every tiny cog, each a thousand times more beautiful than I have ever felt. Overwhelmed is a term lacking. But counter to that supernova, I am underlined with a rested peace."

Muse bowed her head sincerely. Death held out his hand and Brian shook it like a cold rake. War patted him on the shoulder.

"Brian, God owes me two hundred and fifty-four-pound and twenty-six pence from our last game of poker. You're God now so whenever you can get round to it!" War's joke broke the tension and the group giggled.

"But why here? Why now? Why here have I unlocked a latent other self?"

"I think I can explain that, maybe probably, as a guess…the ethereal bar once had a divine realm, like its inverse the dark realms, but situated where it was it became a liability. So, we sectioned it off and it was only accessible by the back door near the vinyl collection to gods complex, and as of recently the elevator system for other locations. Storytime, gather round," said Muse.

"A long time ago, in antiquity, a dimensional Eddy much like that where the ethereal bar sits were used by Satan and his ilk to invade the divine realms. Many fell in that battle but by Michael's sword, Satan was slain. He found form in perdition and is now sitting in my garden. I think enough time has passed for a dialogue between him and God but yeah. A long time later we were permitted to use the network of elevators, at one time they were as difficult to use as a VCR in the nineties until we were blessed to get Igor. For the most part, higher realms are now accessible, some requiring papers and documents. As for why you are now awakened, you know the bar sits in a dimensional eddy. It is neither a mortal realm nor heaven or hell, more a waypoint to those places so it has not got the influence to seek out your other-self. Here in this higher place, its influence is enough to release that repressed hidden self. Here you have become what you are." The discussion was paused as a monolith walked up to the group.

"I know what you want sir of horned hat and muscles!" Said a huge being mirroring the look of War.

"To engage in glorious battle! I challenge you to combat! Unless you like ketchup on your pillow!"

"I have no idea what that means," said Famine to Pestilence.

"Must be a Beyond and Beyond thing."

The floor became a boxing ring and thousands cheered in the stands.

"I hear you fought Samson! That a thousand pirates fled at your fierce grin! Well, I, Otis the never ready, am reigning champion!"

"Never ready?" asked Muse.

"Yeah, I was in a rush once and put my trousers on backwards."

"Oh right," said Muse, sort of expecting something like that. War stepped into the ring, removing his vast coat only to look larger without it.

"So, who is ready to watch the battle!" Otis tried working the crowd who were easily enthused.

"And we have an Omni god present, everyone please give a warm welcome to Brian!" the crowd in sync chanted Brian's name. Brian projected his form into the sky that bowed. He was not quite sure how he did it, it was an instinctual reflex.

Wars blood ran red and fierce in his veins. His elation at glory was that of singular intent. He cracked his knuckles and his neck. He pounded his chest several times and, filled with adrenaline, he seemed to grow an extra foot. His fat turned to muscle.

"See what I told you Pestilence? He is happy now, but angry War is terrifying. I'm more scared of him when he has that grin, to be honest."

A two-dimensional string folded itself into a knot and rang a bell it manifested. Strangely, War let his arms stand at his sides. Otis, seeing an opportunity swung a right hook on War's chin who took it happily. War spat on the floor and again that menacing grin was plastered on his face. Otis was confused, that was his hardest punch. Again, given the opportunity to do so by War, Otis worked the stomach while War laughed. Otis was shocked and tried one more punch right to the nose. War spat some blood and stretched his arms behind his head and leaned backwards.

"He's getting angry," said Pestilence.

"No he's not, he's having the time of his life," said Famine. War looked right into Otis's wavering eyes and took a step forward. Like Satan did before him, Otis instinctively took a step back. The speed of Wars punch was almost imperceptible. It was hard to believe that with that much mass he could attain such speed. Otis was air born. Five feet off the floor gravity decided to join in and threw him unconscious into the ring. The crowd cheered for War who stretched out his arms in triumph. The ring dissipated and the surreal landscape re-imagined itself. A being made of black sapphires shook War's hand.

"That is a hell of a swing you have on you War, knocked me for six, you are a legend and a friend," said Otis as he floated away.

"Well, that was weird, we not going to talk about that?" Famine looked around for validation and gave up. There was a general silence and shrugging of the shoulders.

"Alrighty then, just so I know."

"Do you have toilets here?" asked Pestilence of Sam. Sam pointed behind Pestilence toward a submarine looking door with a drunken sailor indicating it to be the men's. Pestilence wondered over. It was as if a sun was inside allowing its photons to escape around the edges of the hatch-like door as it opened. Pestilence entered, entranced.

"He will be a minute," said Famine.

"Quite a realm you have here! I just experienced a lovely afternoon between Pestilence asking where the toilet was and getting in it, yet I conversely feel no time at all has passed."

"Yes, time works a little differently here. Casualty is an archaic word that is usually met with a face akin to a dog trying to work out how microwaves work."

"You have never looked more beautiful Muse," said Famine. The group waited a few minutes for Pestilence.

"Well?" asked Famine upon Pestilence's return.

"Entranced at beauty so majestic and rare, never beauty has bloomed like this, no rose has smelled so sweet. Of revelation they pale, of truth, they pale, thin and weak in the wake of that toilet. To fall at the light and caught on cloud and breast rare throne of porcelain wakes me from its dream."

"So, you liked it then?" asked War catching twelve percent of what Pestilence said.

"It was the singular most fantastic experience I have ever had; all fail in comparison. Finally, after centuries I have found the perfect toilet."

Sam looked at his watch.

"Ok so we need to find God," said Sam.

"And not Brian God, he's right here," Sam patted him on the head.

"Yeah, he is here, sorry thought you may have been pretending."

"I seem to have my omniscience back," said Death. "You know I miss that mortal ignorance, to not fathom the next moment and all it will hold."

"To forget if the horsey goes in an L or diagonal-I found your book on how chess works with a dog eared page on how the pieces move," said Famine.

"It is a hard game. I don't know how I ever got associated with it. A thousand times a day I'm asked to play in exchange for life. I ask if they would prefer to play connect four or that battleship game with the pins."

"You sunk my battleship?" asked the Prophet.

"Indeed. But the wonder of what comes next, it's exhilarating. But now it's back, I am relieved." Brian concentrated on Death. He felt like he could enter his mind, and as he tried, he hit a barrier that pushed him away.

"You are new to this but please Brian, enter only consensually. Sam, have you any luck on the-" Death hated himself for saying this."-the beepity boop?" Famine chuckled under his breath knowing how difficult that was for Death.

"So, Muse, if Famine wasn't about, me and you, ever think that could have happened?" said the Prophet in a barely toothed grin. Muse patted him on the head and listened to Death.

"I have a sense he is some distance away but I'm sure it's east from here and not in this domed citadel." Muse held Famine's hand.

"I also have a sense where I am, or he is Death. I tried entering my, well, his mind but got the same block and push I had from you. It is as if I, he does not want to be found but he, I…am aware we are here. It is strange. I have autonomy and agency; I can make independent decisions but I still very much am him too. Sort of cognitive dissonance, I am, and I am not if you see my dilemma. I think vaguely east is our best option, may be clearer the closer we get. I don't mean to be assertive, honestly whatever you guys think."

"Even as an ephemeral deity you're still that polite difficult man," said Famine.

"Well according to the beepity boop the signature is the strongest east from here. In fact, it may be coming from another Bastion just past Shangri La."

Pestilence had a half pound cheeseburger with fried onions ketchup and mayo in his hand with a big bite he had taken out of.

"Where did you get that from?" said a shocked Famine.

"Time is weird here; I spent the last few minutes in line at a burger place and even though I experienced that place no time here seems to have passed. Quite bizarre how time works here. Great burger though, I was so hungry I was getting envious at the thought of someone having a spam sandwich, that is how hungry I was."

"I want one!" said Famine.

"Go for it mate."

"Well, where did you get it exactly?"

"Not overly sure, I wanted a burger and then I was in line. Gave the guy a coin of treasure and now I'm eating this burger."

"I'll give it a try," said Famine immediately holding a hotdog.

"I love this place. Anyone else seeing sideways through time a little bit? I think I can see around corners." Sam used his handheld device and started to input instructions.

"Ok, so we will take a bubble to the next Bastion, see if we can home in on him. Thank you again for your cooperation. With the vast nature of this realm, without you, this would have been a gargantuan task. In the meantime, the spatial deformation in your respective residences would left to its own devices would become a world-ending problem. I know to the horsemen that sounds like a day at work," Sam trailed off. A large white sphere with red trimming and a three-hundred-and-sixty-degree head height window descended many miles down to the group.

"It feels like marble," said Brian with his hand on a small red protruding panel. After removing his hand his print could be seen in green. A purring sound came from the sphere.

"That was one of its erogenous zones," pointed out Harry. Brian shivered. he felt unease and was under the impression he was slightly violated. He waited for everyone else to get on first. Brian was most confused at the windshield wipers. Famine got out his Voopoo drag vaping device.

"Does anyone mind? We are in an enclosed space."

"After centuries with you and cigarettes in admittedly tighter quarters, a breath of fresh air would be for you to vape. I'm sure there is a contradiction somewhere in that statement." Famine breathed in the vapor from his citrus seven liquid, it was a pleasure he had never known.

"I really think I can get on with this. I needed a cigarette and now I'm satiated. How long have these been around?"

"Modern vaping has been around since about 2003 by a Chinese inventor Hon Lik. Though the technology has changed and matured over the years. Inspiring him was a good moment for me," said Muse.

"Have you ever influenced us Muse?" asked Pestilence.

"I plead the fifth," she said with a mock stern expression. The vehicle lifted with a soft hum. Brian's body was effortlessly cradled perfectly into the soft backing of the chair. The seats were arranged in a circle looking inward with a table housing various screens. Pestilence was eating some beef jerky and Famine was jealous.

"You shall have a fishy on a little dishy you shall have a fishy when the boat comes in..." sang Brian.

"You shall have a fishy on a little dishy, you shall have a haddock when the boat comes in," joined in Muse. Pestilence and Famine smiled to one and other in accord.

"And dance to your daddy, sing to your mammy, dance to your daddy to your mammy sing, dance to your daddy sing to your mammy, dance to your daddy to your mammy sing!" To everyone's surprise Death started to sing.

"Come here me little jacky now aw've smoked mi backy, have a bit o'cracky til the boat comes in."

Brian finally felt like he had friends. Given that maybe one at best was human, it was an unusual set of friendships. He felt cared for and appreciated in a way he never had before. The beepity boop was on the table with a big red button he was desperate to press.

"You spin me right round..." started War.

"War we are done with that, the moment has passed." War looked down glumly.

"Did you see that swing from War to the Otis guy?" asked Harry of Barry.

"I saw War standing there, then a blur and then an air-born Otis. I wonder if it's on the TV?" Barry turned on one of the panels facing him. On-screen was a young thought-form, vaguely reminiscent of a blonde-haired Asian woman who seemed surprised she was suddenly on camera after just taking a bath in her studio apartment.

"With hair still wet and soup suds in certain crevices, I find myself on camera talking about today's arrival of Brian and his entourage."

"We are a bloody entourage now? I would have guessed we were in charge!" said Sam to Harry and Barry.

"No, Death is," said Pestilence.

"Well it's certainly not Famine," grumbled War still upset at not finishing his song.

"I'm sure it's Muse," said Famine.

"Of course, you would say that, she's willing to sleep with you," said Pestilence.

"You done? Can I carry on?" asked the woman on the television.

"That was weird. I think the TV just addressed us," said Brian. He leant in and tapped the screen in an exploratory fashion.

"Not at all! I'm personal TV. I am here when you need it to highlight your day and news about your various escapades. Freshly out of my bath today, Brian and his entourage arrived at Bastion three to a large welcome. While we are happy with their presence, it was Otis, the never ready that made headlines after challenging a horseman to battle. Not just any horsemen mind, but War. Strangely War allowed himself to be set upon with little resistance but when he decided to fight, in one punch Otis was defeated. Looking at these statistics, the average speed of a punch is nine point four meters per second." On the screen was an animation of a fist hitting a board.

"We measured War's punch at eighteen point six metres per second, almost twice as fast as the average. The average hand is seven point six inches. We measured Wars at thirteen point four inches. Here is a clip of the punch in slow motion." The screen showed Wars fist barreling through the air to Otis.

"In other news, could sprites be shitting in your bran cereal? The infestation continues." Harry turned off the television.

"Was barely a challenge," grumbled War. They had approached one of the million holes and the Prophet had difficulty with the myriad of lights. The spherical vehicle knew how to navigate them with ease, but thousands of such vehicles crisscrossing at phenomenal speeds was jarring for him.

"Thank you for visiting Bastion three, Godspeed travelers. Please remember to visit the gift shop and off duty services before you leave. We have a sale on Jupiter berries," said a large holographic face that they passed through, with shops to the right. The sphere came to a stop and Sam got up and placed a metal disk on a small scanning machine that spent most of its life saying beep. Quite bored, it decided to change things up and instead said beepy. It decided it should work on its imagination. As majestic as the Bastion was, exiting it led to a greater escape. Extraordinary nebulae filled the sky entangled in sacred geometry. Pillars of gas and dust light-years long dotted a black and purple sky. Domed citadels like stars sat heavily and imposing. Brian was in awe of the view. Similarly, the horsemen, Muse and the Prophet were also lost for words.

"A stillness unbroken, all words stifled, all fears dampened light most beautiful," said Brian.

"Fair enough," muttered Famine.

"Ok, I'm getting something Sam. Yes, it is he whom we seek. We are close. Past that tree."

The tree in question was thousands of miles high, its roots sinking into a reality of its own. It was dotted with habitats on its branches completely innumerable, but busy with activity. Clouds surrounded the highest branches.

"Alright, there is a well-known patch of unreality on this trajectory due to gravitational waves so I'll put the window wipers on," said Sam, tapping what must have been one of many handheld devices. The windshield wipers lazily went back and forth.

"Ignore that turbulence, it will soon pass. Hey, look, a space whale!"

"Space whale? The name seems a little lazy," said Famine to Sam.

"A committee or fourteen consultants were granted fifty thousand pounds to name it after the first one was spotted. Certain names were considered, nebulous cetacean, coelum Balaenoptera, Locus leviathan etc. But it was decided that was just showing off. They settled on space whale to save everyone's time and went for an early lunch. So yes. We call it the space whale. Rare beasts indeed. We are lucky. Some whale watchers spend weeks trying to grab a sighting at one of those." The vehicle started to pick up some speed.

"We're in a slipstream of some sort. We have inertial dampeners though, should be ok."

"Has any of these ever crashed? It's just what was a small thing in the distance is quickly becoming a huge coming-straight-for-us looking rock. Not to alarm anyone...," said Brian.

Sam quickly pressed the red button on his beepity boop and the vehicle transitioned into an adjacent space passing right through the giant rock coming back to normality after it passed.

"I may have just had a trouser related accident there Muse," said Famine.

"Wow, Jesus. God on high," Sam thankfully gasped leaning back.

"Ok, I think we hit a dimensional slipstream and the vehicle did not have time to make evasive maneuvers. I'll have to leave a probe there to warn others. I apologize, these things are usually ninety-nine point nine nine nine percent safe. That was an aberration."

"So, who is that guy then?" asked Famine of the group. He was referring to a man, a naked man. A naked man with a smile on his face sitting on the central table. His legs were crossed, and he had his hands on his knees.

"I'm as bemused as you, my friend," he said.

"Why are you in our vehicle? Where did you come from?" Famine was wondering why he was the only one asking these questions.

"Not overly sure, couldn't tell you mate. I fancy an orange. Do you know when you just really crave something? For me, now, it's an orange, it's all I can think about.

"So, you have no idea why you're here, who you are or where you're from?"

"A little bit is coming back. I think my name is Alan. I'm from America. I think I'm in the middle of a DMT trip right now, I recognize the sacred geometry. Why I'm naked though is anyone's guess, I'm just thankful I have a form. I was in a slipstream as a liquid streak of information. And now I'm here. Hey, nice robe mate," he said toward Death.

"Weird thing about this place for me, it is like I have been here before many times, as if my existence started here, not on Earth. And when reality ensues, that seems like the make-believe place. I am more real and complete here than anywhere."

"That was why we sped up toward that bastard of a rock, we rode his slipstream like a wave, not sure that's ever happened before."

"Well, I think I am dissolving a little bit travelers, yep there goes the hand." His fingers were now phasing.

"Nice to meet you, sorry for the random incursion, didn't mean to interrupt, hey there goes my left leg! Takes a while this doesn't it, taking a long time to say goodbye, getting kind of awkward, right! Any second now, I do like that robe..." With that Alan left.

"Usual sort of occurrence that, Sam?" asked Famine.

"No, that is strange even in this place."

"Back on track, the signature is registering that Bastion ahead. No wonder we had initial troubles finding him, this is a gated community. They value their seclusion and privacy; they are somewhat exclusionary and xenophobic. It will not be a warm reception; they view outsiders with suspicion and contempt."

The Bastion was smaller than the one they came from but that was like saying an elephant is small as it was standing next to a beached whale. This Bastion like the others had an immense hole in its dome at the top center with several thousand smaller holes dotted at the sides. A lot of them had been boarded up with crude signs painted on them. Brian saw: *Private property, attack dogs and watch out, I know kung-fu,* or *just saying, my neighbor has more expensive stuff.* They went a kilometer to find an open entrance. They stopped at the perimeter. There was a small booth with an agitated mustached gentlemen in a uniform resembling a traffic warden. It hung well on him and was a great source of pride. He polished his boots every day even though no one ever sees them behind his booth, but he knows and that was enough.

"Permit please," he said authoritatively.

"We don't have a permit but-" The traffic warden like mustached man interrupted Famine.

"Without a permit or proof of an appointment confirmed by a resident here on this clipboard, I refuse you entrance to this Bastion! I know your types, with your robes and such. You War, I saw you on TV fighting, we don't want your sort!"

"My name is Sam Godfrey, these are my associates, Harry Fairfield and Barry Leakey. We are from Beyond and Beyond law enforcement. I have jurisdiction over this and all Bastions. Refusing my entry will end in arrest and prosecution. We are here on business, stand down."

"Well, I never, talking to me like I'm a common loiterer. My job is to protect the privacy of these residents."

"Either let us few in now or I promise hundreds of my like will forcefully enter and that will be a bigger disruption for your residents. While we are here, we will be discreet in our duties and will avoid all unnecessary disturbances to these residents.

"Well, I suppose I don't have a choice now do I? Can I see some identification?" Sam passed the uniformed man a flat metal disc which he inserted into a slot on a panel. It re-emerged and he passed it back to Sam.

"But if I hear any complaints, I'm lodging a formal complaint to your superiors!"

"That is your right sir," said Sam. A small barrier with red and white stripes lifted and Sam turned off the windshield wipers. The ground was around five miles down and the bubble made light work of the journey. Brian was in no rush to leave the bubble, the seats were more comfortable than a Sorrento slate grey plush fabric recliner armchair. War, readying himself to leave drank a mighty gulp of mead from his horn and passed it to the Prophet who happily took a gulp. Brian looked at his cigarette and decided not to indulge, after becoming what he was now, it suddenly seemed to lose its hold on him. He was only going to smoke out of habit, but he realized he didn't care to continue this vice. He placed it back into the packet in case he changed his mind later but was quite sure his addiction was ethereally curbed. The Prophet on the other hand smoked like it was his last, blindfold on and a litany of gunmen, the Prophet by the wall. He was always sure his last words would be a limerick. Muse stretched, Famine coughed, and Pestilence grunted.

"We are very close," said Death.

"I concur," said Sam with the beepity boop. A drone descended and took some candid shots and ran away.

"CCTV?" asked Harry of Barry who shrugged.

"Does not have the same energy, does it? Seems dystopian. We came from a utopia and now we're in a paranoid locked down nation. It feels almost soviet. I'm getting a strange feeling about this place, subdued atmosphere, almost no beings to be found, the reality seems fixed, it's not as fluid, ever-changing and malleable as the last Bastion. It's real and gritty. I don't like it, Muse make it stop," said Famine.

"We are being watched," said Death.

"Please explain?" said Muse.

"Since we have landed there are seven individuals following us in the shadows."

"Are we in danger," asked Muse.

"You may be but we are the law here. It would take an idiot to challenge Bable."

"You used the contraction!"

"Yes Harry, it's growing on me."

They took a left at a closed convenience store with a metal grate pulled down its entrance and a sheet behind a broken window. A moon shone above the hole in the dome, almost perfectly straight above them. The left turn led to a park, a path lit by *The Grange* antique silver cast iron ornate lamp posts, standing three meters tall apiece. The park was quite vast and took ten minutes to traverse.

"I think I can sense me, I'm in the general vicinity of that building in front of us with the blue paneling and yellow door.

"The beepity boop confirms that. Death, you get the same reading?"

Death nodded and they approached the abode.

"I'm surprised he has stayed static; he is by all accounts aware of us by now. If he knows we are coming, why does he not try to escape?" asked Muse.

"Well, he certainly didn't originally manifest here. My guess is he thought his best bet of not being found is to reside in a xenophobic Bastion," said Sam.

"It's what I would have done," said Harry.

"Maybe it's a null game, he knows he has nowhere to run, wherever he goes he will be found."

Sam took charge, slightly nervously he knocked on the door. A pasty sickly-looking gentleman in an open kimono answered the door. Inside smelled like oxtail soup and cannabis. Sam could see a pair of samurai swords hung on the wall atop a habitat for a leopard gecko. White with panic at the sight of Sam's badge he blurted out something nonsensical and tried again.

"It's er medicinal, you know. Eye problems, you know, trouble sleeping that sort of thing. The license is in the mail." He was shaken and paranoid, either from police at his door, too much cannabis or a combination of the two.

"Actually, in most Bastions, it is legal or tolerated. I am not aware of your laws regarding that so let's assume that I am still under the impression of its positive legality. Do you live alone?" The man scratched his arm and stuttered.

"I er, yes I, er, I live alone officer. What is this, you know, regarding?"

"We are tracking down an individual and we have determined that here is his location. It is an omni-God.

"Like Brian! I saw you on TV!" he said noticing Brian. He bowed sincerely and gulped air from an oxygen tank.

"You may be wondering about the oxygen, this being the Beyond and Beyond. You see we believe that our ethereal nature is a hindrance. We believe it detracts from spiritual and social advancement. For the most part, we are stripped of the divine and live corporeally. We grow, we decay, and we die. I chose this existence freely with no regret. I know that my demise means I'll be born again here anyway, my existence will continue but we believe knowing death makes us purer. And holy shit you are Death himself aren't you!?" The man hobbled forward and touched Deaths face with each palm on each cheekbone.

"My bird watching club is never going to believe this! As for a missing deity, you know, being mortal, I can no longer sense such a thing but please come in. My name is Arron." Arron was still visibly shaking.

"Perfect place to hide is it not Death?" asked Famine.

"Oh, cookies! May I?" asked Harry.

"Those are erm... special cookies." Harry understood the insinuation and took one anyway while no one looked. He tried eating it as fast as he could and hoped no one asked him a question. The home was small, compact but well presented. Death was in love with a Persian Qum silk rug.

"Tea? Gentlemen? Miss?" he said nodding at Muse.

"Perhaps shortly, we are going to have a look around Arron. Is there a cellar?"

"We have three bedrooms upstairs, you know, here in the hall, living room and kitchen and yes a cellar. But honestly, you know, I have not noticed anyone, it is just me."

Harry peeled off from the group to search upstairs as Barry headed to the cellar. Sam entered the well-presented living room. There was a large Tylko bespoke black bookcase but no God. Harry and Barry also returned to the hall with no sighting of God.

"What about that?" asked Brian pointing through the window at a large yurt in the back garden.

Chapter 23

Satan and Jeeves sat in one of the many beer gardens. He chose a small circular table that could sit five. Jeeves picked up a coaster advertising the film Space Jam. It had to be 25 years old at least.

"She needs to be bought new stuff," he said to his master.

"What was that Jeeves? You are mumbling again, So help me, straight to the moon!" There was a short awkward silence.

"Who's she?" Satan eventually said.

"Muse. She needs newer things my deplorableness. But still, I can add it to the collection," he said pocketing the coaster.

"I cannot believe it, my son, the heir to the throne of darkness. At his will, he will reign supreme, at his whim all will bow and pledge an undying alliance to his sovereign rule of the iron fist and indiscriminate wrath. That is what he is supposed to be but look at the bastard now, he's cleaning up empty glasses! I saw him smiling at me through the window while aimlessly wiping down the counter. He is doing this on purpose, the whole thing is a charade. It's just a thorn in my paw Jeeves's!"

"Your odiousness, it is not my place to interfere in your family affairs but permission to be candid?"

"It may be the last words you ever speak Jeeves but go ahead. Knowing that never before has anger boiled up inside of me like this, and all those in my vicinity may be indiscriminately placed in the proverbial splash zone!"

"Your son was never cut out for a leadership role, apart from maybe one day being promoted to scoutmaster, he has all the badges."

"Your point Jeeves?!"

"I feel that perhaps this is youthful rebellion, but he is twenty-four years old now and what may have started as a resistance to his imposed conditioning may have now blossomed to an actual personal drive of self-improvement and growth. Much like you intending to patch things up with our absent Omni-God, a few decades ago never would that thought be entertained. Sir," Jeeves tensed up but presented a clam uniformed composure as his good breeding has instilled.

"I need to do something about this. Look! He's giggling with that whore of Babylon! He could find a thousand like her in perdition, what is so fascinating about this harlot? I need to kill something; something has to die!"

"Sir, perhaps a sip of your Frappuccino will put you at ease."

"If your compassion does not include yourself, it is incomplete." Shadow guy was swaying slowly and hypnotically.

"Wrong place at the wrong time shadow thing!" Satan impaled the shadow guy on his trident and absolutely nothing happened. It just passed through him like the trident would pass through air.

"An eye for an eye makes the whole world blind!" the shadow guy said. A small gap of his shadow face disappeared into a smile.

Across the table, one of the Seraphim took note of Satan's actions. Satan was not to know that stabbing the shadow guy with a trident was a pointless exercise in futility and Muse, the beautiful Muse, he thought would be very interesting to learn of this unprovoked sadistic act. Satan's son marched into the garden with a newly found sense of responsibility and purpose. Shadow guy was lagging awkwardly behind him.

"Satan, did you just try and impale shadow guy with a trident?" Shadow guy stretched his two-dimensional torso to show three holes that he placed on himself on purpose. Like in most confrontations, Satan's face only knew how to have a defensive grin. He stood seven feet tall before you even got to the horns. He took a purposeful step toward his son who physically was standing his ground but mentally soiled himself.

"You insubordinate willful little shit! Stand your ground in front of me, Satan!"

"Shadow guy has lodged a formal complaint. He is willing to drop it for a pint of Adnams Southwold bitter. No one was hurt so I think I can overlook this."

"Are you warning me now? Is that what is happening?" the top of Satan's head erupted into fire. Shadow guy used it to light a shadow cigarette. Satan picked his son up by his collar.

"Erm sir?" muttered Jeeves. Satan looked to his left and Jeeves pointed ahead of him. There stood the Seraphim. Satan let go of his son, smiled awkwardly and the Seraphim returned to their seats.

"Look what do you want from me?" asked his son.

"I want you to be what I thought you would be after you escaped from the wretched womb of your mother! We wanted the best for you!"

"But my mother is dead, her last words were 'that horned bastard killed me, escape and run away you are probably next, pass me that orange.'

"Mistakes were made. Look, your station is far beyond that of glass collection! It's unbecoming and you are coming back to hell with me!"

"Bugger hell and bugger you, you're a demented rabble-rouser and that fog by your ankles isn't cool, it's cliché and pretentious! I have found a Shangri La here, a place where I'm wanted, needed and appreciated. You cannot force me and if you attempt it I think the Seraphim would love an excuse for a skirmish. My stint in hell is over now. Buy shadow guy that drink," his son effeminately sauntered back into the bar and Satan worked on his Frappuccino smiling. The fire on his head went out with a wisp of smoke. It smelled faintly of watermelon.

"What do you make of that Jeeves? I'm almost proud, the asshole took some initiative and stood up to me. He didn't run away like a little girl. He stood face to face with me knowing how much I think about his life. How little I cherish it, how small and insignificant it would be for me to end it. Yet he stood! There may be hope for him yet. It's in his genes Jeeves, the blood lust, the deviousness, the sociopathic disdain for all the living and none living, all those positive qualities. It will awaken within him, stir in his depths, it cannot be quaffed! It will manifest inside of him, and he will return! Of that, I am sure!"

"It will take time and space, sir," said Jeeves.

"Or a hypnotist? Try and seek out those qualities, subdue any shred of altruism! Maybe if I place him in an octagon with a humpbacked simpleton, have them duel to the death you know, my Son armed to the rafters, the simpleton a crudely carved club made of Styrofoam. Maybe arrange for a pessimistic self-harming goth girl to illicit any latent despair in him. These are just thoughts, thinking aloud. And where is God? This is taking far too long. Michael has not kept his eye off me since I have sat the self-righteous hall monitor! With his white wings, just an overgrown cherub is what he is. This is a good Frappuccino."

"Sir, besides your son, the mantra dispensing shadow figure, the Seraphim, are you enjoying your excursion from perdition?"

"Wind in my hair, sun shining, fancy coffee, still and serene? I despise everything about it Jeeves..."

Chapter 24

Death was the first to approach the circular yurt dwelling made of a lattice of flexible poles covered in red fabric. "Do you think somebody is in there?" asked Arron "No, it's empty. Nothing to see here," came a voice from inside the yurt. Death saw God meekly lifting his head to the window. As Death looked right at him, he quickly sunk his head. A handful of twenty-pound notes slid under the door.

"Oh look some money!" came the voice again from the yurt.

"It's not mine, must be yours! You must have dropped it just now, well give it to the charity of your choice and I'll let you be on your way!" the voice was muffled. Death knocked on the door patiently.

"I can't come to the door right now, this is not a great time, I'm naked and can't find my towel."

"God please answer the door," said Death calmly.

"The door is broken, damn locksmiths are cowboys, won't be here for quite a while. I guess you will have to come back another time!" Death tried the door and found it open. Sitting in his red polka dot underpants was God. His feet up on a teak root coffee table.

"Ah, guests! Welcome to my home, please come in!" said God.

"I had no idea he was, you know, in here. I'm not complicit in any, you know, crime," said Arron craving his oxygen tank. Muse walked up to Arron who was coughing semi violently into his hand.

"I took this seminar with Sekhmet. I think I can clear that cough and remove the need for your oxygen tank," Arron shook his head.

"No divine intervention Muse. I appreciate it but my beliefs prohibit it, in a sense, we want to die, to know Death. I mean Death is standing right here of course but that's just, you know, muddying the waters."

"I thought Death was not aware of this realm?"

"He is, you know, on an instinctual level, he visits but he, you know, doesn't register that he's been here. A lot of you have higher selves here too, part of a, you know, bigger entity. It's where a lot of you begin."

"Why did you run away?" asked Famine of God with as much empathy as he could muster. God sighed and looked down at his earl grey tea. It was a somber and sobering sigh. Muse placed her hand on top of Gods.

"It was my birthday, not just any birthday but my thirteen point eight billionth birthday and you just did not turn up. I mean I sat by that phone; look, I have become despondent with my work for some time. I have lost that spark. Creation, destruction, life in the most varied and numerous forms. That will has gone. I guess I was just tired. Tired of a life tinkering in my workshop. There are only so many clocks and ventriloquist dummies you can make before your mind wanders to the 'what is the point' state. You guys don't need me, it's all automated now anyway. Since I have gone, I bet no human life has changed for the worse. Maybe a bit of a crappier hangover or a little less patience for the paperboy who seems to deliberately miss the letterbox in favor of the sodden bush. I'm redundant. Outdated and in the way. But here? I have travelled this realm and have been met by zeal and exhilaration. I can't leave, please. This is my kismet. My dream, my salvation, please. Don't take me home."

Sam sighed as seemed to be the shared behavior. He placed a hand on God's shoulder. "It's not as easy as that I'm afraid, you are illegally squatting here, there is red tape, certain protocols and rules to adhere to. You do realize on your departure you tore reality itself? It's not meant to look like that my friend, that is not ok. It can only be fixed when you come back. Now you can apply for entrance but it's a bureaucratic nightmare and there is no guarantee you'll succeed. Emergency visas were distributed to your friends to get you to come home as it was and is of great importance. They love you and want you back."

"How can I go back? How can I leave knowing what I am leaving behind? To willfully leave the oasis to roam the desolate desert. I can't do it, I won't!"

"As fragile as possible, please grow up," started Famine.

"We all go through our patches where we feel like the insignificant cog in the pointless machine. But we don't just run away, it's not healthy. We love and we know loss, we have passions, and they pass but we put on our boots and dickeys if your that kind of person and get on with it. Yesterday, if you asked me about happiness, I would have told you it's an abusive falsehood, unattainable and anyone who professes they have it are liars and charlatans. But in less than a day, it can all change. Now? Me and happiness enjoy kippers! I have found something special and new, love, in Muse. And God? She loves me back. How it can all change in a day. Come back with us and I promise maybe a day, maybe a week you will look at the vast immense indescribable ineffable beautiful world you have created, and you will smile again. Whether that smile comes from your accomplishments or the people around you. We love you, God. Sir."

"But you don't know what it is like to have something so perfect and then have it just taken away!" said God defensively.

"I know exactly what that is like God. I had this RV. It was a coachman chaparral 373MBRB bunkhouse fifth wheel RV. The most beautiful thing in existence it was, had it for a whole afternoon before it committed suicide off the edge of a cliff. Right now, it's safe to say I'm homeless."

"Well, there is my Birmingham loft apartment you are free to stay in?" said Muse.

"See that God, altruism! Compassion, kindness, Muse has made my point! The Earth is still worth your time, and it will make you proud!"

"Perhaps it was a bit hasty and rushed to leave it all behind," God stood up.

"And don't think I have not noticed you, Brian. I have been following your life quite closely."

"Sorry if I have not lived it according to your expectations but to mirror Famine, yesterday I was nobody important, not really. Never impacted the world around me positively or negatively, I didn't hate life, I just kept a healthy distance from it. But now I have been on an amazing journey and met what I consider friends, even in such a short period. I feel cared for loved and appreciated. Tell me yesterday that that would happen, and I would have never have believed you, prosperity and happiness can always be just around the corner."

"And I got to punch Otis!" said War.

"Yeah, and War got to punch Otis! Please come back with us," said Brian.

"You are among friends," said Pestilence politely. "Life can surprise you it's true. Today I found the perfect toilet!"

"That has been a long quest," said God.

"I know! And I'll treasure that memory, always will but I must move on." God knew they were right. If Pestilence can walk away from a perfect toilet, he could walk away from Beyond and Beyond.

"Muse?" asked God of Famine with a smile.

"Believe it, it's true!"

"Jeff the Prophet, never thought I'd see you leave your tree."

"Jeff!! My name is Jeff! Of course!"

"I have checked up on you from time-to-time Jeff, subsisting on the earth's energy alone, was a real accomplishment."

Death investigated his robe.

"I know it's not much but happy birthday." Death passed God an action Jackson Action figure that had belonged to Brian of which he never asked Brian for

"It's a good one as well God, articulated limbs, three catchphrases and comes with a parachute."

God had a tear in his eye.

"Sorry, it's not wrapped."

"It's fantastic! Wow! It's the 1987 version. The patina is gorgeous!"

"We did have some other gifts, but they are in a space dwelling car somewhere far off into the nether. Shadowed by a gas giant or some other celestial body or phenomenon. With my omniscience back I can find them for you."

"We are all regretful that we forgot to pick you up for your birthday. Really. It will not happen again," said Pestilence.

"Will you come back with us?" asked Muse.

"It only takes a day for everything to change. I can set you up with my friend Amphictyonis. She has always thought that you're cute.

"Well, it's about time I should confess something to the group. How to put it delicately. As far as Amphictyonis is concerned, I don't lean in that direction."

"You are telling us you are…?"

"Always have been, no point in hiding it anymore. But although I have tried to hide it, in this realm? I have been on a rampant sexual awakening."

"Well that's just dandy!" said Famine.

"That's really special, congratulations," said Pestilence.

"Each to their own!" bellowed War. The Prophet pointed at Brian.

"So, he is God, does that mean that he is also?" God looked inquisitively toward Brian.

"Very much just run of the mill heterosexual Jeff. Well, a willing one anyway, not a lot of takers."

"Are you kidding? You are an Omni god! I bet you'll clean up! If it were not for Famine," Brian got the insinuation and blushed. They all stood in the garden and Arron came in with some tea. Pestilence offered Brian a cigarette.

"You know Pestilence? I think I'm good. I have no time for that anymore. Have no drive for it." Pestilence shook his shoulders and passed the packet to the Prophet.'

"I do enjoy a cup of tea," said Death carefully placing the cup into his hood.

"I guess I was easy to find, registered you the second you appeared. Heard rumors of a locked-down Bastion and thought it was my safest bet. Sorry for any inconvenience Arron. I have had a great time here I truly have, the best of my existence."

"Think of it as a holiday God. We were on holiday ourselves."

"Yes, Pestilence but our experience was the inverse, God got Utopia, we got a malfunctioning broken down feeling sorry for itself rotten crab infested bastard of a caravan, that liked to find new and novel ways daily to torture and annoy us."

"If this transition to your realm is made any easier. With the right papers and with the protocols adhered to, it is plausible, as a practicing notary, that I may be able to arrange a holiday visa. It's not much, maybe two weeks out of the year. But please never again rip yourself out of your existence."

Sam was genuinely aware of Gods plight.

"And the country club with the cucumber gin and the oiled-up yoga instructor guy?"

"I think I can arrange membership. Despite everything you and Brian and Death especially are famous, stupidly famous. I doubt there is any club, association, organization, institution, body or troupe that would not be thrilled to include you."

"Ok, I am now in a good place! Holidaying here will be better than that time we were all in the Isle of White where War got lost in the corn maze and decided to just walk in one direction right through the corn walls."

"We were just talking about that!" marveled Famine.

"But we now have two Omni gods. What are we to do about that?" asked Muse.

"You know, I might give life a try," Brian was crossing his arms and looking willfully toward the sky.

"Lost me their mate," was War's input.

"Life War, life! Muse has said repeatedly that we are capable of so much good and progress, not to give up on humanity! I want to live up to that expectation. I can live life. I have got to know you all and never have I been included or involved like this with any other person or persons. I have been on a journey of a lifetime and will never forget it. I love you all. But I am going to part with my divinity fudge, go to my apartment, feed my fish, watch some telly and figure out how to make a prosperous life for myself. I may stumble and fail but I will get back up. Get to know my beautiful neighbor, try and find a job I am passionate about, not the grey soul-destroying bin and half-eaten tuna sandwich adjacent desk. I wanted to hide for so long, but a latent drive has formed, and I am unique! I get to know there is a God, well a litany of them. Where those live on faith alone, I get to know you are all here and that is of great comfort."

"He is right," started God.

"Here I am feeling sorry for myself because I feel cheated and Brian is willing to give up divinity and fudge itself, all on the off chance that his mortality might deliver prosperity. If he can do that, I can leave the Beyond and Beyond. I think it should be called Beyond the Beyond…Beyond and Beyond fits the ear wrong."

"That leaves one question," said Death.

"What about us? Me, Famine, Pestilence and War. The divine wager? Brian died an atheist."

"Several times," said Muse.

"Yes, several times."

"For now, humanity can rest peacefully. I do not incline currently to take any action that involves you or the other horsemen fulfilling your duties. Jeff, you win the wager."

"That'll be twenty quid," said Jeff.

"Looks like the Birmingham loft apartment is safe," said Muse.

"Brian if you are serious about living out a mortal life…"

"Which I think, you know, is fantastic," said Arron who had been standing there the whole time, somewhat unnoticed.

"Can we call on you occasionally? I think I have found a friend in you, and it would be a sad state of affairs to lose you."

Brian walked up to Muse and hugged her.

"Nothing would make me happier. Except maybe a nap, it has been a long day."

"And Amphictyonis might be interested if you come to the bar now and again! Here," the Muse pulled out a mobile phone.

"Dimensional phone to keep in touch. I have taken the liberty of adding our contacts in there."

"Right, we ready to vacate?" asked Sam of the group.

"Was, you know, good to meet you all. Death, an honor," said Arron scratching his blue left arm with his three-fingered hand and gills.

"The rug is highly coveted Arron, worth a few pennies as well. Take care."

Arron turned away at the door to sit in a large tub of lemon water. They walked out of the house, the moon still very much above them through the giant hole in the dome. Stars and Bastions lit up that sky. They walked again through the park, being watched from the shadows as they did. Muse took off her shoes.

"Something about grass underfoot. Being rooted to the world, a tactile connection. We spend so much time indoors," Muse was not speaking to anyone.

"Try it Famine…"

"You get wonderful supple grass, guaranteed I get dog shit and thorns. Used needles and ants climbing up my feet." He looked at Muse's pleading face and caved in, removing his shoes.

"Ok, yeah I get it, it is pleasant. I feel more rooted and yes that's dog shit. Anyone got any water I can wash this off with?" A general flurry of negative headshakes happened, and War tried to whistle nonchalantly.

"War, pass me that mead, will you?" asked Famine grabbing his left foot. War was conflicted, sobriety was becoming a possibility and that scared him to his beard. The last time he was sober he stayed up all night doing Famines taxes, not well or legibly. If anything, he revised the taxes, which was nigh on impossible for the average Mensa student at the Massachusetts Institute of Technology. Reluctantly he slowly produced the dregs of mead, and in a sunken fashion he handed it over.

"We have CCTV drones scanning us. What about that bastard, the one with what I think was a pet dog? Hope the bastard gets fined," Death was appreciating the streetlights. It was a beautifully maintained park with lazy creeks, moonlit sky hedges and rotund trees. In the distance was a giant redwood towering over everything else. They were following a gravel path. Finding the bubble was relatively easy as they passed the boarded-up convenience store. Before it was in sight, Sam pressed a button on his beepity boop and a car alarm sound beeped three times in front of them. A small, hooded lady in rags appeared, forming in the corner with a wrapped baby.

"Please? You must help me, take my child with you, he will have a better life with you!"

"Bugger off," said Famine pushing her off to one side.

"What?" he said to the accusing eyes.

"I'm not looking after some brat, the cheek of it, here have this massive responsibility because I can't be bothered. It's like someone passing you a bottle and saying, here, you throw this away. I'm sure there is something akin to child services or a footstep of a church. Putting me in that position, Jesus H whatchamacallit. I was in the right there," Muse nodded.

"You kind of were, as far as impositions go that's right up there with being asked to give someone you don't even know a kidney. A kidney they sort of don't need but keep in storage just in case."

The bubble shone brightly under the halo of the streetlamps, clean and white in stark contrast with the subdued solitude of this Bastion.

"I get motion sickness from these things," said Pestilence. Brian, Muse, Famine, Pestilence, Death, War, the Prophet, God, Sam, Harry and Barry all entered the bubble with a lot of room to spare.

"I hate this bit," said Pestilence again as the bubble hit top speed immediately. War tapped his fingers.

"Nice tea," said Death speaking of Arron's tea.

"Yes, it was!" said the Prophet.

"Would have been better with a digestive biscuit. Maybe a slice of Gers Ogaily cake." The Prophet spent so many years in solitude that the surreal nature of this adventure was euphoric. He could not stop smiling.

"Itching for adventure I am, no antagonist to speak of no one trying to foil our plans like no big bad and whatnot. Little disappointing. I thought the Seraphim would gets involved, maybe Shadow guy was to overhear us discussing gods' departure like relaying that to the Seraphim. The Seraphim being the gits they would use it as an excuse to war over the throne. Heaven and Earth in turmoil and chaos..."

"Quite succinct for you War?"

"But everything kind of just worked out!" bellowed War.

"Why does there have to be an antagonist War?" asked Pestilence.

"I don't know, adventures usually have them! Like a pirate or a hoard of Viking warriors, maybe a vampire or two? Just feels like we could have had some like tension. An adversary we overcome, really round up our story and stuff like. Something to rally against. The worst character we met was that little shit of a campsite shop with a single banana that looked like it was on its way out."

The bubble ascended the five miles to the booth with the traffic warden mustached man.

"You guys again? I hope you are on your way out?"

"Like why else we would be here?" asked Famine confused. The small red and white bar lifted listlessly in a tired fashion. Again, the view of sacred geometry danced for the group, flying to Bastion three. War was tapping on the glass.

"Whale...space whale? Hello?" he tapped the glass again.

"Space whale?"

"Let's just pray for no high nude travelers, was off-putting, did not enjoy that experience," said Famine.

"Naked man?" asked God, feeling he had been left out. It sounded like an experience he would have liked.

"Some nude guy that almost made us crash into a random rock was high on DMT and decided to start his psychedelic jaunt in the middle of this ship. He dissolved in an awkward manner leaving a discernible sweat butt print on the pristine white surface. He smelled like talcum powder and confusion." They passed the tree.

"I spent some time on that tree, see those abodes that look like fly eyes? That one there with the three orange lights? Kebab there is phenomenal!"

"So, you enjoyed your stay?" asked Death who had been quiet and relaxed.

"You know when I have a soul that I escort to the nether, I always ask if they had enjoyed their time in the respective locals."

"Time works differently here Death as you might have guessed. This last day may as well have been months, even years. At the same time, it feels like no time has passed at all." The Bastion was in sight. From the bubble, it looked like the size of a small moon. They approached one of the millions of entrances. Again a giant holographic face appeared.

"Welcome to Bastion three brave travelers! Try our Jupiter berries!"

"They are pushing those Jupiter berries," said Famine.

"Nasty things, taste like jerky that's sat on a fish whose last meal was sprouts and haggis." Sam approached one of the millions of holes. The bubble came to a slow stop with a soft hum. Sam casually turned around on his seat and leaned out of the window that autonomously parted for him. He placed a small disc onto a panel. With a beep, it allowed them in. The craft began to descend to the ground at massive speeds. Pestilence felt sick to his stomach, he was the only one having trouble. Brian on the other hand was still more comfortable than he had ever been. He could fall asleep. War was disappointed that he did not get to see his fishy.

"This vehicle makes light work of this freefall," said Pestilence.

"Any chance of a small bag?" asked Pestilence. Sam opened a panel by his knees. There was a puncture repair kit for a pushbike, three issues of Anglers Mail, an orange and a small paper bag. Sam passed it to Pestilence who threw up. Muse almost gagged herself at the sound of vomiting.

"Very pleasant, thank you for that experience," said Famine to Pestilence.

"It's the free-fall. Don't know why I'm having so much trouble with it. I'm fine on roller coasters and planes, boats are a bit iffy."

The touchdown was satisfying with the assuring sound of pistons. What was now a large group of travelers set foot onto a promenade. Neon signs and glowing tiles converged all their energy to a spectacle for the arrival of the group. A sea shanty about a lost pigeon was sung in the background, whilst a thousand mechanical elves bounced toward the group.

"God and God, which is which? Both are famous, life's a bitch! We love you this much!!" They stretched their arms several miles in each direction. One of the mechanical elves stepped forward with a pen and a pad.

"Can I have your autographs? Maybe a drawing? A short sonnet, a recipe for a low carb meal, directions from Birmingham to Amsterdam? An abstract concept?" The pad was handed through the group. Even the Prophet signed. The mechanical elf let out a giggle and ran away sideways through time.

"This place has been a bastard on my senses," said Brian.

"I kind of want to go at this point."

"Bye!" shouted the sky. The scared geometry turned into a giant thumbs up.

"Alrighty then...again at the twist of this knob next to the red button we will begin our journey back to the ethereal bar. Me, Harry and Barry will stop for a pint and be on our way, we want to make sure you get back safely. Here take these pills, it will help with vertigo."

Sam produced, again one of many handheld devices and one by one scanned the group. "Prophet, you have scurvy mate. Eat a lemon. God, you have carpal tunnel syndrome."

"I was in a seminar, I can fix that God, sir."

"Why did we travel to this Bastion only to use the knob on the device? Could we have not just done that from Arron's Garden?" asked Famine.

"We have better reception here. You are all safe to travel, the scanning was just a precaution. Ready or not, everyone says 'cheese!'"

The group said cheese as the knob was twisted. To an onlooker what they would have seen would have been a group of people turn into black and white static and shot instantaneously into the sky through the great hole, a chem-trail of light perfectly vertical. A small bird was slightly annoyed at the noise.

Still being very much an ephemeral deity, Brian fared much better with the tunnel than previously. The faces were less jarring, the light fantastic clearer and supple. The Prophet, again like a bullet, shot past him shouting 'WEEEE!' The whole time cross-legged. In a few short minutes, he was expelled rather violently out of the tunnel. He turned his head to see it fizzle out of reality. It was not long at all for a tavern to form in front of him. This time he perceived it to a much higher degree. Details, colors dimensions, faces-it was all so haptic. He looked at the bartender and could see who she was, as she is and who she will become. It was true omniscience. He even knew if the next patron was going to win or lose the next game of pool.

"Sorry about my brother," said the cactus.

"He likes to mess with people's heads," it said.

"Might I trouble you for a pint of bitter?"

"Who brought you outside?" asked Muse.

"And stop begging people for drinks, you hopeless alcoholic!"

"Well, it's not like I have arms or legs now, is it? Can't exactly exercise mobility. My only contribution is that I make the place look pretty, should be worth an allowance of some sort so I can buy my own bastard drink!"

"You might have a date with the waste disposal if you're not careful. Crap this can't be good."

Like Brian and Muse, the rest of the group had managed to appear in the garden and Satan had just noticed God. The situation was tense. Satan was highly unpredictable, the grasp on his trident failing to add calm. His defensive grin was still in place, a fire starting on his head. The Seraphim rose and stood behind God. Death brandished his scythe

"Good to see you sir!" said Michael.

"We are with you all the way," said Uriel. Jeeves took two large steps backwards, partially hiding behind a hedge. War was eating popcorn. God waited. He was also nervous. Muse held Famine's hand tightly and Pestilence gulped.

"Boring…" said the Prophet and wandered into the bar. The weather changed; a storm cloud approached with a slow rumble. The sun hid and rain pelted down. A crash of lightning lit up the view of the trees. Satan took one step forward and his face changed. His lip trembled and his eyes watered. He fell to his knees.

"I just want you to love me!" he whimpered.

"Why can't you love me! You are all I have!" God got on one knee with his right hand on his left shoulder.

"There there, come on now! There is no need for that now is there. It's going to be ok buddy."

"Buddy?" asked a broken Satan.

"Yes, buddy! Look a lot of time has passed, water under the bridge, bygones, a new day and all that!"

"I waited so long for just a call or a postcard, I spent so much time resenting you." God helped Satan to his feet. He did not expect reconciliation.

"But I love you! The whole trying to murder you and all your kin…" Satan sobbed and wiped his nose on his sleeve.

"Bygones?"

"Bygones," said God. His son was looking through the door the whole time and smiled to himself with a chuckle.

"Can we talk God? I have a lot to tell you. Come on, meet my son, he is a believer of yours, a good kid to be honest!"

"I would love nothing more Lucifer. Hey Muse, Brian, Death and other assorted friends, I am going to spend some time with my friend here."

God threw his left arm over Satan's shoulder standing significantly shorter and jokingly punched him in the stomach with his other hand.

"Before you go, God, I was wondering if now with your newfound erm, friend, I can open up the divine realms again in the bar. I don't suppose it needs guarding anymore?" God gave a thumbs up and he and Satan left for a booth in the corner.

"No one knows where God lives. He values his privacy. The only way to get to his complex is through that door, well I heard some salvage hunters once accidentally stumbled across it. Happens from time to time but to open the divine realms, going to get a lot more traffic in this bar. May need some help. Prophet, I'm sure we could find something for you here if that thought has crossed your mind?"

"I make a mean Ramos gin Fizz? My Tom Collins was coveted many decades ago in the jazz hut. I can cook and clean. I'm looking forward to being able to ask a patron 'the usual?' whilst aimlessly cleaning a glass with a rag. I can also test the pickled eggs. I can do that thing with the Guinness, you know, the cloverleaf. I can tell bar jokes, Death walked into a bar and said, 'hi I'm Death.' and the barkeeper shouts "WHAT DO YOU FANCY!" see? Off the top of my head. I would love a job if one were going is what I suppose is what I am trying to say..." War got up

"Fill my horn with mead, wench!" Said War to the waitress. She snatched the horn angrily and filled it.

"Wench yourself you beard covered ox!" War smiled and walked back to the group.

"Think she fancies me!" he said finally quenching his sobriety.

"I don't think I even paid for that. Hey, look!" War pointed to a tear on space.

"Muse has you any binoculars, I think I sees something..."

Sam who was standing at the bar getting himself Harry and Barry a drink walked to War. The Muse passed War some binoculars from under the bar. Peering through them, War saw a couple of dozen human shapes in yellow hazmat suits and backpacks. They were holding long tubes that ejected a milky white foam on the tear in space.

"I thought the union were not working on that until Tuesday?" asked a random Seraphim who shrugged and sauntered off.

"I must admit that was a fast first response. They must have come ahead."

Muse motioned for the group to converge. War did not see straight away as he was fixated on the waitress.

"No matter how hard the past, you can always begin again," said Shadow guy passing the group.

"That guy needs more depth, figuratively and literally, you know, being two dimensional and everything."

"Ahem, right. Well, I think the day is over. We sought answers to the tear in space explained by the Beyond and Beyond which is, as we speak, being repaired. We found God's key in Deaths horse' pummel bag and used that, the beepity boop, Brian and Death to locate and bring home God. As promised, we got answers for Brian. Rescued a Prophet from his solitude, got God and Satan to reconciliation and traversed a higher dimension. Drank far too much, made new friends and came back safe and unscathed. A full day, tell me if I am forgetting anything...oh and War punched Otis, throw that on the pile. Before we go our separate ways one last drink?"

"I could abide by that, but I'm short or currency," said the Prophet.

"Don't offend me, it's top-shelf stuff for us, I'll write it off as a business expense. Now that Satan is no longer angered, the weather outside is quite nice. Table and chairs? Can't go wrong."

They sat down in the lazy sun, exhausted but content. Muse raised her hand to get the attention of a waitress. She made a gesture for a drink and with her finger made a large circle referring to the group. The waitress pointed at the taps and Muse shook her head. She pointed at the house liquor and again Muse shook her head. The waitress pointed at the top shelf and Muse nodded. The waitress blew a decade of dust off them and poured the drinks.

"What have you enjoyed most of all today, Brian?" asked Death sleepily.

"I think the part where you said you were not going to kill me, that's high up on the list."

"Fair enough. For me it was the architecture and furnishings of Gods complex," Death let out a rarefied chuckle.

"For me it was Muse," Famine squished his face in affection to Muse.

"For the love of God that's disconcerting. Some things should not be shared with friends, that face will haunt me. For me, the toilet." The drinks arrived.

"For me it was sharing my treasure, to not have any treasure? No beast of a man should live like that."

"First cigarette after my tree stint." the Prophet maneuvered his tongue over one of his few teeth.

"For me it was getting Brian to an answer about his being. Famine, you're a close second," Muse tapped on the table and drank. Sam, Harry and Barry were still in the bar a couple of tables away from Satan and God. Satan's son had joined them.

"Well, me and War have been talking and we are going on a voyage."

"Voyage you say?" Famine was a little shocked.

"Yeah, we are going on a treasure hunt! War thinks he remembers where most of it is. I'm promised pirates adventures and scantily clad maidens. Can't be bad."

"If the offer still stands, I'll take residence here?" asked the Prophet.

"We can find somewhere for you." Muse said thinking about the collection of broken toys that passed as those she took in.

"Famine I take it you're coming back to mine?" Famine had actual color to his cheeks.

"Erm, ahem! Er yes, yes I am... going home with Muse. In Muses apartment," he grabbed a handkerchief and blotted his sweat-covered forehead. "Damn it's in my eyes, I'm blind here guys," Muse let out a guttural laugh at Famines unease.

"For me, I have a cottage in the Cotswold's. It's not much but has everything I need. A book and an earl grey tea," Death sounded content.

"For me, it's back to the apartment. Day one of the whatever is to come and I'm hoping for a tax rebate. Maybe a second fish. Not another theological escapade through reality itself," Brian drank his undefined liquor.

"Well, I'm off then," said Death. "I'll see you all at Christmas. Happy hunting Pestilence and War. Brian, it has been an experience, it really has. Muse and famine, congratulations on your recent entanglement. Prophet I'm sure I'll see you soon. I will try and pop in more."

"We are off too, were taking an elevator to Tanzania. Maybe hire a donkey. Gentlemen! See you at Christmas."

"I'll hang here a while with Muse," said Famine.

"I need to say goodbye to God as well as the rest of you. Muse I have the phone, keep in touch." Muse blew a kiss and Brian placed a hand on Famine's shoulder.

"You helped me get through all of this, thank you Famine. And eat a burger," Brian mumbled thanks and sought out God. When he found them, Satan was very much still a little bit on fire, so he didn't get too close.

"God? Me? I am off home, any last bits of advice?"

"Always keep receipts for your toasters."

"Thanks, very special, I'll treasure that wisdom," Brian said as God laughed.

"Look I don't know… it's easy. Don't try to save the world. You cannot help everybody. The negative will always be present, just try to leave the world a little better than you found it, whether that is in hard work or the love and friendships of others. A small act of kindness is still an act of kindness and can reverberate in many unexpected ways. Faith is good but love is better. I don't have all the answers to a perfect world, the ability was, is and will always be with you."

"That is actually of great comfort. And on principal, all my receipts are in an old shoebox on top of my wardrobe."

"So this is the guy?" asked Satan of God. God nodded.

"Hello, sir. I hear you are to become mortal again. Want any advice from me?"

"Sure, why the hell not."

"So, the best way to poison an enemy, shag his mom and steel his sheep…"

"You know what, sorry to cut you off, I need to be going. I'll see you guys another time."

"Christmas!" shouted God to a receding Brian.

"Again, I'm off," said Brian to Famine and Muse. "I'll take the elevator."

Famine and the Muse held up their hands and waved. *So, this is it,* thought Brian. *The longest day of my life at an end. One night's sleep and I'll believe this has all been a dream.* He smiled and walked toward Igor. From the window, he saw Jeeves coming out from behind a hedge. He felt something like a washcloth touch his shoulder.

"Oh hey, shadow guy." Shadow guy moved his hands to cast a shadow on the wall. It was a crocodile. Brian waited for an explanation and after fifteen seconds the shadow guy walked away.

"Well, that was pointless," he said under his breath.

"Brian!" said Igor as he stepped into the elevator.

"I think I parked at an equestrians Not overly sure exactly where Igor." Igor pressed on the mindbogglingly complicated elevator interface. He threw up some pictures.

"This the one? With that guy outside swatting at that wasp?" Brian muttered under his breath and shook his head.

"This one? That looks like a creepy shadow in the top window doing jazz hands in the haunted stable. I guess ghouls are not that into the macabre anymore. Look he's breaking out into a little dance. I can see by your expression that that too is not where you want to be. How about this one?"

"Yes, that's it! That's where my car is!"

"Would you like a loyalty card? You can use the elevator miles in all good ineffable plane shops and services. With this card, one free elevator trip can also be yours."

"I will take the loyalty card but only for this trip to be free. I do not see myself using these services any time soon as I am to be in mortal realms again very shortly."

"Did you ever find out what you were? Why you emanated divinity?"

"Yes Igor, turns out I'm God."

"Takes all sorts!" Igor pressed a hexagonal cog and twisted it exactly 13 degrees to the left.

"So a god-like me or?" Igor trailed off.

"Omni god. As in the prime mover, the catalyst of creation, the first thought. Alpha and omega, all that ghost jazz."

"Suppose I should call you sir. The trip may take twenty minutes. So Omni god, complex gig. A lot of people asking you for things I guess, make me a little taller, why does my sweat smell like eggs, fix it now!"

"Not yet no. You see when I get home, I'm suppressing divinity, thought I'd give life ago. Any headphones in here?" *Erm, headphones* thought Igor knowing he had some somewhere. They should be right there on top of the water cooler.

"Check that slot behind you."

Lo and behold were the headphones. He reached in his pocket to retrieve the dimensional phone.

"Got to be some music on this," he thought aloud.

"Muses chill playlist. I have never heard of any of these bands. Am I that old and out of touch?"

"What bands are they?" inquired Igor.

"I don't know, Glass Gods, Our Dystopia, Everlinn?"

"Yeah, you won't find those bands on Earth. More of a higher realm thing, give Everlinn a listen, I used to date the hot chick on drums."

Brian spent the next twenty minutes listening to the Muses playlist. This was the way to travel. Not being picked apart into your constituent bits and shot through tunnels in the form of information. It was comfortable, with no sense of movement and the music was as it described itself, chill. Before Brian knew it the doors opened. He gave Igor the headphones back.

"Safe travels God, and Godspeed!"

The elevator shot up vertically and arced to the left out of the atmosphere. The ground underneath where the elevator was let out a wisp of smoke that smelled like freshly cut grass. Brian walked to his car that had several parking tickets under his windshield wipers and he smiled. He was back in reality. That was a clear sign. He sat, hands on the wheel and eyes closed. He made time stop. No wind, light from windows frozen in beams. Not a sound to be heard and he reached into himself with a singular thought. To place away in his darkest depths his divinity. A single bright spark behind a curtain.

"Move your piece of crap car!" shouted someone behind him as they swerved around him. Brian looked at his hand and it was just a hand. He smiled. It was not as it was as it is and as it will be, it was just a slightly bigger than usual hand with a freckle on it and a small scar from a protractor on the end of his index finger. He could no longer count atoms. He giggled at how naked he felt. He did not know what was to come. He laughed louder, ecstatic at his mediocrity. Sure, he felt smaller, but he carried with him from his experiences a sense of drive, purpose, passion and elation.

It was a short time later that leaving his car parked on his communal drive he climbed the three flights of stairs to his apartment. He let himself in throwing his keys, wallet, phone and Jafari's foreign bent cigarettes into a bowl on the table by the front door. He fed his fish which, for the first time in its life seemed to pay attention to Brian. *What now?* he thought. *I guess I just must see if anything can happen, after all, it can all change in a day. Prosperity could be just moments away.* There was a knock on his door. He opened it to his beautiful long-haired neighbor, who wore a towel wrapped around her, soaked to the bone. "Hi, sorry, Claire. I think we have met once or twice. We have been neighbors for years, have never really spoken. My shower has just broken and the hot tap on my bath is on the fritz. Can I shower here? I promise I won't be too long. What was your name again?"

"It's Brian, Brian Aldiss. Would you like a cup of tea?" Claire laughed.

"A bit old fashioned but sure, what do you have?" Brian investigated the tea box he bought against his will.

"We have Yogi, jade leaf, matcha, Harney and Sons and Twinings. Oh, and some PG Tips."

"PG tips can't go wrong. So what do you do then Brian?" said Claire walking into the bathroom.

"It's a good question Claire, I guess anything I want to..."

It was Christmas for three more minutes. Three minutes until the bastard bird would chirp happily from the clock as if everything was just fine and dandy. God hated that bird. He hated it as a gift. He bought his son a villa In Tuscany and in return he got an obnoxious cuckoo clock. Always happy, always chirping. He sat on a table made for ten alone and with a small Christmas paper crown he got from a Christmas cracker. The food was cold and even his help was on leave for holidays with the family. His phone had been in front of him the whole time. Every time he called; he got the answerphone. A small patch of paint had come away at the table where he had tapped it willing the phone to ring. He truly had given up an hour ago, but depression clung him to his chair. On cue, the bird came out of his house and God finally left his chair. On the twelfth ring of

the clock, God grabbed the bird by its neck, ripped it out of the house and threw it to the ground. He sighed and sat next to his destroyed clock.
"They forgot me again..."

Printed in Great Britain
by Amazon